100 MILES FROM NOWHERE:
murder remembered

By

Lila Conover Bishop

This book is a work of fiction. Places, events, and situations in this story are purely fictional. Any resemblance to actual persons, living or dead, is coincidental.

© 2003 by Lila Conover Bishop. All rights reserved.

No part of this book may be reproduced, stored in a retrieval system, or transmitted by any means, electronic, mechanical, photocopying, recording, or otherwise, without written permission from the author.

ISBN: 1-4107-4222-9 (e-book)
ISBN: 1-4107-4221-0 (Paperback)

Library of Congress Control Number: 2003092827

This book is printed on acid free paper.

Printed in the United States of America
Bloomington, IN

1stBooks - rev. 05/21/03

DEDICATION PAGE

To my husband, Chuck, who is the
love of my life, and has always encouraged me
to reach for the stars!

7/28/03
Dear Mother,
I hope you enjoy this book, without you none of it would have been possible! I love you.
Lila
Proverbs 3:5+6

CHAPTER ONE

In the summer of 1991 a small group of people gathered at a long deserted homestead southwest of Yuma, Colorado, to watch the County Coroner, Sam Davison, carefully lift some human bones out of an old cistern. The group consisted of a couple in their early fifties, Lisa and Dick Cavanaugh, Lisa's younger sister, Becca Hollander, a much older couple, Bertha and Fred Johnson, and the County Sheriff, John Ruger. Lisa, and Becca had come to Colorado to research their Grandfather Hollander's homestead, and had found more than they bargained for. Buried beneath a haystack in the old barn, was David Johnson's car...and David was the only sibling of Fred Johnson, their mother's childhood friend and life long resident of Yuma County. David had been missing for some 43 years, and now they stood watching as the Coroner lifted his bones out of the old cistern.

Sam worked methodically. After carefully placing the bones on the sheet covered stretcher, he carefully probed the soil beneath where the body had lain, lifting one small shovel full after another onto an old screen door for sifting, stopping suddenly as his shovel hit something solid.

"Must be a rock..." he mused, reaching down to brush the soil away. But it wasn't a rock. "Uh, oh! What have we here?" he muttered to himself, turning the object over in his hands. Puzzled, he looked up at the sheriff. "It's another skull, John! Were we expecting another skull...another skeleton...down here?"

John stood there in stunned silence, looking first at Fred, then at Lisa. "I don't know. Were we?" Lisa looked on in horror, not saying anything. "I'll ask you one more time, Miss...were we?"

Lisa nodded, "Yes," she whispered, weakly. "I...I was." She struggled hard to maintain her composure. "Maybe...two...m..,more."

John looked at her in stunned disbelief, blinking as if trying to clear his mind of irrelevant information. "What did you say?"

"I said," Lisa struggled with the words that were barely audible. "I said...there may be two more bodies ...uh, skeletons...down there." Totally drained, she looked for a place to sit down, but now the stunned sheriff had regained his composure, hitting her with a barrage of questions, without giving her time to answer any of them. She looked about ready to bolt when Bertha intervened.

"Here, Lisa girl, you come over here and sit down by me," she said. "This has been a terrible thing for you to have to go through." As soon as Lisa sat down by Bertha the older woman pulled her head down onto her ample lap. "Now, You jist rest here a bit," she crooned, rocking back and forth. "You jist rest...an' Bertha'll take care'a you." She shot a look of disdain at the sheriff. "Now, John, questions kin wait. This girl's been through too much!" She rocked back and forth. "An' it's not like she hasn't been tryin' ta cooperate. Why...she's the one that brought us out here! Have ya fergotten that?" She paused, briefly, then added, "Yep, I think any more questions kin jist wait. Ain't that right, Poppy?"

"Oh, yes...I agree completely." Fred answered. "You jist git on with findin' them skeletons down there..." He motioned for John to get back down into the cistern with the coroner. "An' the questions kin wait till later. We'll personally vouch fer Lisa. She'll answer all yer questions. Later!"

Just then someone yelled, "Two! They got two skulls up there on that stretcher!" And Lisa, her eyes closed, was aware of people running, crowding around them. "Who's the other stiff, Sheriff?" someone called out from behind Bertha. "There are two skulls there on that stretcher...so, who's the other one?"

Well...we knew we couldn't hold 'em off forever," John said to Sam, giving him a hand up out of the hole. "So, we might as well go face the music." Then, turning to face the reporters, he called out, "Keep back of the ribbon, folks! Or you can just go on back to your cars. I still set the rules...and the boundaries...here!"

(ABILENE, TEXAS, ONE MONTH EARLIER)

Lisa Hollander-Cavanaugh was not one to seek help. She was more apt to be giving it. So, she felt almost silly sitting in this cozy room across from a therapist. "I'm sure you've heard this a thousand times..." she started, "but, I don't quite know...why I'm here...exactly. My Dr. thought it might be a good idea for me see you."

"And that was because...?

"Well," she started, self-consciously, "I've been having these terrible headaches...lately. But he didn't feel that they had any organic basis, you see. Which means...the only way to treat them is with pain medication, which I detest taking. So, we decided that this might be the best way to go. Quite frankly, Della, I feel like a silly school-girl! And, being a therapist, myself, I know that I shouldn't feel embarrassed...but I do. Anyway...here I am! So, let's see if you can help me get to the root of these awful headaches." She grinned, awkwardly. "If you can, I will be forever in your debt." Now, having gotten started, she sighed a great sigh of relief, at which they both smiled.

"O.K. We'll give it our best shot, Lisa." Della looked thoughtful, then said, "And, if you were dealing with a client of your own...you'd probably ask..."

Lisa laughed and joined her with, "And just how long has this been going on?" She thought about it a moment. "I've tried to pinpoint just when they started. I guess it's been about a year. I was having them after I came home...from my mother's funeral." She shifted in her chair. "But, come to think of it, I can't really say that, either. Actually, they started before that, but they just got more...more intense, more demanding...after Mother's death."

"So then...how long before your mother's death did they actually start?"

"You know...I can't really say. It's strange, but I think they've actually been...I've actually been...having them for some time. Like a number of years."

"But...they just became so bad after your mother's death?"

"Well...gosh, this is hard!" Lisa shifted, uneasily. "They were always bad...when I'd have them...but, they weren't so demanding. They...didn't rule my life. I mean, I worked. I had a life. Of course you would have thought I owned stock in Excedrin! I'm sure you've heard the slogan, 'I've got a headache this big'..." she chuckled, gesturing with outstretched arms, "and it's got Excedrin written all over it'? Well, I used to joke that they wrote that one just for me!"

"OK. So, actually, your headaches go back quite a long time, but since your mother's death they have increased in intensity...and frequency, right?"

Lisa nodded, and, squinting into space with furrowed brow, she barely whispered. "It's...as if they...it...has a life of it's own. It's no longer headaches, plural. Now it's this one huge ache. Pushing! Demanding! Never letting up." She looked directly at Della and grinned, wryly. "And believe you me...Excedrin doesn't begin to touch it anymore!"

"Pushing? Demanding? Sounds like it's trying to get your attention," Della mused. "And just what do you suppose it wants you to see, Lisa?"

Lost in introspection, Lisa took a moment, then shuddering, she lifted her gaze to her therapist, who sat patiently waiting. "Haven't got a clue. I just have this horrible feeling that if I don't get some relief soon...the top of my head is going to blow right off..." Then, in a voice barely audible, and blinking furiously to stay the tears, she added, "And when it does...I'll never be able...I *might* never be able to get the lid back on!"

They sat in silence for a few seconds as Lisa composed herself. Then walking to the window, she leaned into the pane, watching a fledgling blue jay take its solo flight from the branches of a nearby spruce. "Poor little guy. Where's your mama?" she asked softly...partly to the jay, but mostly to herself. "She shouldn't have gone off and left you all alone...to have to figure things out all by yourself. Poor little guy." Dropping into the chair nearest the window, Lisa sat quietly rubbing her temples.

"Poor Lisa. Your mama left you all alone...to figure things out by yourself, didn't she?"

Lisa winced, now rubbing the back of her neck, "Well...I guess. I guess she did. It's sure exasperating, though...to have to figure out *what exactly* it is that I'm supposed to be figuring out!"

Della nodded, "I'm sure it is...would *have to be*...exasperating." She went to the window to adjust the blind, slightly darkening the room. "Of course, with you being a therapist, I don't have to tell you that your mind already has all the information it needs...to take you where you need to go." Lisa nodded assent. "Now, Lisa, I want you to allow yourself to just rest here a moment," Della said quietly. "Just close your eyes and try to see yourself lifted, easily, floating freely in a quiet calm place." She paused briefly, then continued, "Your mother is also there, in that quiet place. Do you see her?" Lisa sighed, nodding, a smile playing at the corners of her mouth. "And...she has something to give you. Go to her and accept whatever it is that she wants to give you." Again Della paused, "Now, Lisa, release your mother...knowing you can call her back anytime you need her...just let her go. Everything's fine now. And you feel good. You feel relaxed...comfortable...and able to share with me what your mother gave you. All right?" Lisa nodded. "Good. Now open your eyes and, when you feel comfortable, tell me what her gift was."

"Grandfather's farm. She told me to find Grandfather Hollander's homestead. How strange. And something else...she said to take Becca with me! Becca's my little sister. Rebecca, actually."

"And that's all? Just find the homestead?"

"Yes," Lisa nodded with relief and puzzlement. "Well, I'll be! Here I was all set for some deep, dark, horrific something-or-other and it's just...*genealogy*! I guess she wants me to finish what she was working on. Can it really be that simple?" she asked, with a laugh. "Incredible! All that pain...can it really be so simple?"

"I'm sure I don't know. Can it?" Della queried, toying with a pencil on her desk. "Do you think you can locate your grandfather's homestead? What all would that entail?"

"Well...I'd have to go to Colorado. That's where he took his family when my father was seven. Seven, or perhaps eight. They moved in a covered wagon...from Kansas…in the early nineteen hundreds." She paused, "I guess I *could* do it. In fact three years ago when we were all together for Daddy's funeral we talked about it. But nobody seemed really interested...except me...so, I just let it go. I guess I told myself…maybe, someday."

"Maybe *this is* your someday."

"Possibly. But why now?" Lisa puzzled. "What's the old place got to do with anything, anyway? It's not like it really has anything to do with our genealogy."

Della smiled. "Well...I'm not sure this is about genealogy, Lisa. Correct me if I'm wrong, but, it seems to me that you took a flying leap, here. You went from 'find Grandfather's homestead' to 'find Grandfather's ancestors'. And...that's not what Mama said, my Dear. Remember?" she paused to give Lisa time for that to register. "No...I'm more inclined to think the significance is in the place. How about you?"

A grin tugged at the corners of Lisa's mouth. "What I think is, you're right, of course. Isn't it amazing.? Our brains know exactly where we need to go...but, given the opportunity, will resist with the tenacity of a mule!" Lisa rose and stretched. "Well, since we now know where we need to go, I guess all that remains is for me to go home and figure out the how and when...and convince Miss Becca that she needs to come with me."

"And will that be a problem?"

"Actually, yes...I think it might be. Like I said, she wasn't interested before. And since Mama's gone, well, personally, I just don't think she'll want to be gone from the boyfriend for that long. Oh, well..." Lisa rose from her seat, "you never know unless you ask...right?"

Della smiled, nodding. "Well...you can always tell her...'Mama said'..." To which they both laughed.

"Oh yeah, right!" Lisa shrugged, heading for the door. "But...you never know. Maybe..." she chuckled. "Maybe...that'll do it."

CHAPTER TWO

Wednesday Lisa had a light caseload at the office so she took her sack lunch over to her husband's office where a sign painter was just putting the final flourishes on the door. Cavanaugh, Cavanaugh and Sloan it read, Attorneys at Law. Black lettering with gold trim.

"Very smart" she nodded to the painter as she entered. "I like the gold touches. Truly elegant!" Her husband, Dick, was the second Cavanaugh in Cavanaugh, Cavanaugh and Sloan...the first being his grandfather, Henry...and they had just expanded their practice to include Dick and Lisa's daughter, Amy Cavanaugh-Sloan, who had just passed her bar exam, necessitating the move to a much larger suite. Fortunately they had found this suite in the same building, an old art deco renovation in downtown Abilene that had managed to survive years of neglect until a restoration committee saved it from ruin in 1976, and, wonder of wonders, the new suite was on the same floor, just down the hall and to the left. It made moving a lot easier.

."I'm so glad you were able to get this suite...so you could stay in this building..." Lisa told Anne, the secretary, as she did a quick two-step shuffle through the reception room and on into Dick's office. "I love all of this art deco stuff...can't get enough...Oh, I see Dick's not here. Will he be back soon?"

"He just went back down the hall for another load. Here let me get this chair for you..." Anne began displacing books from the chair to the floor. "I see you brought your lunch...there's fresh coffee through that door...if you want any. I just made it, so I know it's fresh!"

"Thanks, Anne. You know you don't have to move that stuff for me...here let me do it." But by that time Anne had finished moving the books. "Well, then, I'll get the coffee." Lisa said, disappearing into the kitchen. "Do you take cream and sugar...or just cream? I forget."

"Neither," laughed Anne. "I just like it black and hot...that was the 'other secretary' ...remember? The one that got away...before the move! I still think it was pretty rotten of her to take her vacation now… but she kept saying her airline tickets were non refundable! Man I wish I'd thought of that one before she did!"

"Oh, yes...I remember Dick mentioning that she was going back east. Family reunion, right?" Anne nodded as she dug her lunch sack out of the back of a drawer and pushed some things aside to make room on her desk. Just then Dick and Amy came struggling through the door with a dolly loaded with boxes from the other office.

"Oh...Hi Mom! I didn't know you were joining us for lunch," Amy groaned, trying to get the front of the dolly across the raised threshold. "But after this load I'm sure ready for a break." She straightened up, turning to face her Dad, "That is, if this slave driver here says it's OK to break now...I think this is our fifth load this morning. What'd ya say old man...ready for a break?"

Dick mopped his brow and neck with his already too wet handkerchief. "Boy, I hope no damsel in distress needs to borrow this one...I could almost wring water out of it! And what's with this 'slave driver' and 'old man' bit?" He snapped Amy with the wet handkerchief. "Show some respect, girl! After all, we're doing this so *you* won't have to work out of your car!" They all laughed at that, and Anne went to get coffee for Dick and Amy.

"Dad tells me you are going up to Colorado...wish I could drop everything and go along." Amy said, settling herself on a large stack of boxed books. "Well, I guess this will make a good enough place for a picnic. Dad, grab that chair in the corner...dump the books and pull it over here..."

"Listen to her...been on the job less than a month and you'd think she was the president of the company...barking out orders right and left." Dick settled into the chair and reached for his coffee. "Whoa, now *that's* hot coffee!" He blew into the cup. "So, Lisa, did you get ahold of Becca?"

"Actually, I did...first thing this morning. You know, if you don't catch her before breakfast, you might not get another chance to before bedtime!"

"Yep, that's Aunt Becca...always on the go. You know, teaching is really the perfect job for her. It gives her plenty of time in the summer to run and play, or whatever..." Amy said between bites. "Mom, this meatloaf is great! I love cold meatloaf sandwiches, and with just a hint of mayo...mmm mmm perfecto! So glad you thought of it."

Her mother beamed. "Well, here...pass this one over to your father...and we'll *all* enjoy the cold meatloaf. By the way I brought one for Grandpa, too. Where is he?"

"This moving's too much mess for him...He took an early lunch with a 'client'...said not to look for him back this afternoon." Dick laughed. "Personally, I suspect the 'client' is Grandma."

"I'm sure of it," Anne interjected. "He had me make reservations at the Country Club, and said it was an awfully nice day for a long drive."

"Speaking of reservations," Lisa said, "I invited Becca to meet us at Longacres for supper. I thought you two could help me persuade her to go with me to Colorado." She looked directly at Amy, "You, can tell her how you'd *like* to go...but can't take the time off...and you *don't want me* to drive it by myself, right?" Then, looking at Dick, "And *you* can inflict on her the wonderful dramatic argument you gave me...about how the roads 'just aren't safe for a woman alone...nowadays...and so far from home!' I figure with the two best lawyers in Abilene arguing the case...well, I won't have to say a word. She'll surrender before we get halfway through our main course. And then we can just sit back and enjoy our coffee." Lisa rose, picking up her lunch things, "What time will you be done here? I told her to meet us at seven, but...it looks like you've still got an awful lot to do."

Dick finished his cup of coffee, then cleared his throat, "Yes, we do have an awful lot to do...but we cleared our agendas for the rest of the week. There's no way we can get it all done, today...or tomorrow, for that matter...but, come Monday we ought to be in pretty good shape. So, since you told Becca seven...we'll meet you, at *Longacres* at seven." He went to the door and held it open for her, giving her an affectionate peck on the lips. "By the way...have you decided when you want to leave?"

"Well, since I just finished up a couple of *majorly heavy* cases, I figure other people can handle the lighter ones and I ought to be able to tidy up by the week end. I've got a lot of time coming to me, and nobody at the office is on vacation right now, so... it looks good. Maybe, Monday. Of course everything depends on Becca at this point, doesn't it? I really don't want to go alone..."

"And I don't want you driving across country alone!" Dick interrupted, walking her to the elevator and pushing the down button. "Amy and I will be very persuasive. She'll go."

As it turned out, it wasn't as hard as Lisa thought it would be. In fact, Becca was actually excited about it. She was getting a little bored and thinking of going somewhere for a little vacation, just hadn't decided where to go. Only she had one condition, that they take some time to go to the mountains while they were there.

"Absolutely...it would be obscene to be that close to heaven and not partake," laughed Lisa. "Boy did I have you figured wrong. I just thought you wouldn't want to get that far away from Mr. Wonderful. So what's up...are you two still..."

Becca stopped her cold, "Well, 'Mr. Wonderful' is wearing a little thin. Oh, you can be sure he won't want me to go...even if it was just up to Amarillo...for only a day! He's just getting too controlling, and I've about had it. I guess this will be a good test of how right we are...or aren't...for each other. So, yes, my dear sister, I would love to accompany you to Colorado. And we'll have a blast."

CHAPTER THREE

By five o'clock Sunday evening Lisa was packed and had her luggage in the car so that she and Dick could just have a quiet evening together. They went out for supper at a favorite place and had just gotten back to the house when Dick said he'd forgotten something and would be right back. He soon returned from Wal-Mart, where he'd purchased an assortment of snacks, tissues, paper towels and Windex. "...Because I know how you hate a *dirty* windshield," he said, unloading the stuff onto the kitchen counter. He had *already* fitted out the trunk with all sorts of things one might need in case of an emergency, so Lisa kidded him about "overkill".

They had just settled into their cozy evening at home when Amy showed up with a grocery bag full of goodies for the trip. "Sorry...Ray couldn't come. He's helping a buddy fix something-or-other...and it just *had to be done tonight!* Oh, well...he sends his love, and says for you to be careful on your trip...as he'd hate to have to break in another mother-in-law!" Lisa laughed, putting her bag on the table. "I brought an assortment of fruit...apples, raisins, peaches, pineapple...because I wasn't sure which Aunt Becca would like. And here are three different kinds of crackers," she said, unloading the bag. "Oh, and Mom, I put in some hard candy, and...just in case you didn't think of it...I brought some paper towels and Windex. I know how you *hate* a dirty windshield!"

"Your Dad remembered that, too!" Lisa laughed, and giving Amy a kiss and hug, she turned her around to face Dick's contribution.

"Yoo-hoo," Becca called. "Can somebody get the door?" Amy rushed to her aid. "I just got to thinking we ought to have some stuff in the car to nibble on...just in case..." She put her bags of goodies on the table with Amy's. "Oh, I see somebody else thought of this..."

"Two somebodys!" Lisa corrected. "And...might I ask...did you, by any chance, *happen* to think to get paper towels and Windex?"

"Uh-huh." Becca answered, pulling them out of a bag. "Sure did! I seemed to remember that you just *hate* dirty windshields!"

Laughing, Lisa showed her the other two bottles of Windex. "Now...you all come with me for a minute," she said, herding them out to her car, where in a small box behind the driver's seat was a roll of paper towels and a bottle of Windex. "Do you think by chance that we will have enough?" she teased. "After all, it's a well known fact...I *really do* hate a dirty windshield!"

A neighbor broke into their fun, calling out from her front porch swing, "Lisa, I do hope you'll have a good trip! And, you might want to do what I do. I *always* carry some window cleaner and paper towels in my car, (at this Amy had to turn her face away to control her laughter)...because you never know if that water they have at the filling stations will be clean." (Now Becca and Dick were laughing outright) "And there's nothing worse than trying to see through a haze of dead bugs..." She stopped, puzzled. "Did I miss something...?"

"Oh, Susan...it's not you. Come on over here," Lisa motioned. "Come on...you'll see."

"Well...talk about overkill!" she stammered, seeing the four bottles. "And here I was going to offer you some of mine," she laughed, "...if you hadn't already thought of it!"

They all settled comfortably around the kitchen table while Lisa showed them a map of the route she and Becca would be taking, and Dick brewed some coffee. "I figure we might as well sample some of these goodies...since there does seem to be more than enough for the trip," he laughed, opening a package of Oreo's and pouring five mugs of coffee.

"Amy...I believe Susan is the only one here who uses creamer. Would you please..." She was already at the cupboard reaching for it before he finished.

"Can one more crash this party? I think my wife's here...without an escort..." came a voice from the kitchen door?"

"Hey, George...of course, come on in. We've just been talking about Lisa and Becca's trip." Dick reached for another mug, talking as he poured. "We were all anticipating what they would need..." he said, handing George the coffee, and gesturing to all the 'stuff' on the table and counter, added, "Think we've got enough '*stuff*' here?"

George laughed, taking it all in. "Well, you might could use some Windex..." he drawled. "Do you think three bottles is enough?"

"Oh...it's not three, George...it's four!" Amy exclaimed. "Mom already has one in the car...and would you believe, Susan was..."

"Yes, George...I was going to offer her another," Susan said, interrupting Amy. They all sat around talking and laughing until they had finished off the Oreo's and coffee, shared their assorted travel stories, and discussed all possible routes to Colorado at least half a dozen times.

Finally Amy broke the spell, getting to her feet with a stretch and a yawn, "Good grief...it's after eleven and I have to work tomorrow...whether the rest of you do or not!" She hugged and kissed Lisa and Becca wishing them a good trip and was out the door. The rest soon followed.

"So much for our quiet evening together..." Lisa wound her arms around Dick. "Guess we'd better turn in...since I told Becca I'd pick her up at six."

"You go on up...I'll be right along," He teased. "I want to clear up these mugs...since I know you '*hate'* to get up to a mess in the kitchen..."

"Oh, yes, I do hate a messy kitchen...almost as much as a dirty windshield..." Lisa laughed, punching him on the arm. "But not quite! Come on, mister," she said, turning off the kitchen light. "I'll race you!"

The next morning Lisa was just getting ready to walk out the door when the phone rang. It was Becca. "You won't believe this, but my alarm didn't go off...so...I'm not *quite* ready. Just give me another half hour. O.K.?" Actually, Lisa was glad for a few extra minutes with Dick. They spent it snuggling in their porch swing, watching some birds get their morning started. Then it was time to go.

CHAPTER FOUR

They headed North out of Abilene on Interstate 83, ticking off the towns; Hamlin, Aspermont, Guthrie, Paducah, Childress. They were making good time. At Shamrock, where they stopped for coffee, Becca took the wheel and drove to Liberal, Kansas. They reminisced about their childhoods, told jokes, and sang every pop melody they could remember from the days of their youth, then started in on the Gospel songs.

"Wow! I'd forgotten just how well we harmonize!" Becca exclaimed, as they gassed up at Garden City "We sound sooo good...I tell you we ought to get ourselves a manager and go into show biz! What do you think, sister of mine?"

"Oh, yeah...really." Lisa laughed. "I could just see you with a manager! Remember you're the sister that never lets anybody tell her what to do...or when to do it. He'd book us into Nashville...and you'd say 'Just who do you think you are...telling us we have to be in Nashville on the 12th...I have plans of my own, thank you!' And you'd say it with just the right touch of haughtiness...your chin lifted ever so slightly. Oh, yes...I can see it all!"

"Well...I guess I can get pretty testy at times," Becca retorted. "But, you have to admit...nobody pushes me around," she finished with a chuckle. They paid for their gas and headed North. Lisa drove, lost in thought, while Becca tried to find a 'golden oldies' station on the radio. "Why haven't we ever done this before?" she asked.

"Well, I don't know. Usually when I come up...everybody's busy with their own lives," Lisa mused.

"I don't recall your ever asking me, before...did you?"

"Well, to be quite honest...I'm not sure if I ever did, or not. You know, you're so much younger than I am. And...I think I just assumed you wouldn't want to go up there. With me, I mean. Frankly, I was surprised when you said you would come!"

Becca looked puzzled. "Why, were you surprised? You know how I love an adventure. This trip sounded like an adventure to me. I was excited! I've been very curious, you know, because...well...I don't remember anything about the place. I know we lived there when I was small..." Not finding what she wanted on the radio, Becca turned it off, then continued, "but, try as I might, I simply can't remember it. Mama used to tell me things...but they're not *my* memories...and when you said we were going to locate Grandpa's homestead I thought it would be really neat to... well...to just *be* there. I can't imagine why you thought I wouldn't want to go!"

"Well, to be honest, the rest of the family, Barb, and Bill and Scott...they never want to talk about our lives before we moved to Abilene...when the folks divorced...when you were little. I've tried to get them...separately...one on one...to go with me, but they're just not interested. They say that's all in the past, and they want to leave it that way. I guess I never thought to ask you, thinking that, since you're the youngest, you would be the least interested. I'm sorry. I didn't give you the chance to say no...on your own."

"Or yes, either."

"Right. Or yes, either."

"Well, if everybody else is so adamantly opposed to going back...why are *you* so interested?"

"I...don't know, exactly. I've always thought of it as a sort of wander lust in me...that I just like to go, for the sake of going. It doesn't matter where, so long as it's 'on the road again'. But, I don't think that's it all together." She was thoughtful, then added, "No...it's like there is a part of me that's lost there...that I *really need* to find. I don't know what finding Grandpa's homestead will do for that...but, it seems, I must find it. So, here we are...on our way."

Becca was quiet for a few minutes, then began to sing again. Lisa joining in with the harmony. At a break in the song, she said, "You are right...we do sound good together! Do you ever sing specials...at your church...or anything?" Becca, laughing, was shaking her head. "Well, you really should, you know...you have such a strong, clear soprano. Great to harmonize with!"

"Now, Lisa...you know I really don't go to church that much. I'm sure if I were to ask them if I could sing..." she giggled, "they would expect me to come to their services!"

"Well, duh...I'd rather think they would!" Lisa laughed. "So, are you still attending that little church out west of town?" She glanced over at Becca. "I *know*...you said you don't go much...but when you *do* go."

"I guess you could say that. Though I haven't been in several months. We had a change of Pastors, and...I guess he...the new one...is O.K. But...it's just that *I liked the other one*. It's not the same."

"Have you tried talking to him? The new one, I mean."

"No. What would I say? Hey, I don't have anything against you...but I wish we still had our old Pastor! No. It's not his problem, really, it's mine. And I know I should deal with it...but I just don't. You know?" Lisa nodded, her eyes on the road ahead. "Well, big sister, what would you do? No, don't tell me. I know you'd handle it...better...or differently, anyway." She was quiet a moment. "Like I said, I just need to deal with it. Get over it."

"Have you tried going somewhere else?"

"Well...no, not really," Becca worked at suppressing a grin, "It's just easier to stay home and be disgruntled!" Then, looking sheepish, "*I know* what the Lord wants me to do. I just...I just haven't done it." After a moment's silence, she added, "Maybe... it's like you said earlier...I don't want anybody telling me what to do...or when to do it." She stole a glance at her sister, who was keeping her eyes focused on the road, "But, the Lord isn't just anybody. I should *want* to please Him. I should, really want to." Lisa's silence was consensual, not judgmental. They were both quiet for a time, then Becca cried out in alarm, "Oooo, would you look at that sky!"

Lisa grimaced, "I have been watching it...for some time. It's getting nastier by the minute. See if you can get a weather report." She had been fooling with the radio, getting mostly static, and was glad to let Becca mess with it. "I hate static..." she laughed, "almost as much as a dirty kitchen...or windshield. And, speaking of dirty wind-shields, this one definitely needs cleaned." She wheeled into a station on the outskirts of Colby. "It looks like we're heading right into it..." They had picked up I-70 at Oakley and were now heading due west. "...and I like to make sure my tank is full when I have to do battle with the weather." She tried to clean the windshield with the solution prepared by the station, but it just made things worse, so out came the Windex and paper towels.

Becca laughed, "Now you've gone and done it! A clean windshield guarantees we'll get a storm! I'm for seeing what that cafe over there is offering...how about you?"

"Yeah, go on over if you want. I'll pay for this gas and pull the car on around there..." She headed into the station, then turned back and hollered, "Go ahead and order me some coffee...if it's good and fresh, OK?" Becca waved her acknowledgment, then ducking her head against a gust of wind, vanished inside the restaurant..

The waitress was a cute little 'Chatty Cathy', about Amy's age, with red hair and very blue eyes. When Becca asked if the coffee was fresh, she said "It is now!" and hurried off to make a new pot. By the time Lisa got to the restaurant the rain had started to pour. She parked close to the door, but still caught the full force of it, and the air conditioning in the building made her shiver in her wet clothes, so she cupped the hot coffee in her hands close to her body to soak up the warmth of the brew.

"Whew...I didn't know how badly I needed this coffee. Glad you thought of taking a break. Anything looking particularly good on their menu?

"Well, I overheard some truckers at the cash register saying if they're anywhere near this place they wait to eat until they get here. Seems the chicken fried steak is unbelievable, better than Grandma's!"

The little red haired waitress was back, pen poised to take their orders. "Yeah, and we sell a lot of liver and onions...if you like that sort of thing. People drive over from Oakley, just to get our liver and onions. But, I've never tasted it myself...the idea of eating organs, well, you know!" She shuddered. "I'd sure go for the chicken fried, if it were me!"

"Well, you look like you know what's good for you, so that suits me." Becca declared.

"Me too." Lisa nodded, then asked. "Is that a salad bar over there?".

The waitress nodded, "It's all you can eat...just use a fresh plate each time you go back, OK? The plates are on the end of the line." She pointed to where the buffet disappeared into the adjoining room. "I'm glad you decided against the liver and onions...I don't even like to have to serve it." She shuddered, then added, "The *smell* you know..." as she left to turn their order in.

At the salad bar, Becca exclaimed, "Just you look at this."

"I wish I had...before I ordered! They didn't leave anything out, did they? Look, there's poached fish, and both fried and broiled chicken. I would have been just fine...without ordering anything else."

"Yeah, me too. And look...over there...real deserts! And I'm not talkin' just soft serve ice cream! Oh, I really do wish we had checked this out first."

Lila Conover Bishop

"Well, even though I *am* hungry, I don't want to overdo it...and get sleepy at the wheel." Just then their waitress walked by and Lisa stopped her. "Have they already started on our order? We were just thinking...with all this..."

The waitress interrupted, "I'll check. If they haven't...you want to cancel it?"

Lisa nodded, sheepishly, "If that would be all right?"

"Sure! I'll go see." She was back in a minute. "Caught 'em just in time!"

"Thank you ever so much. You're worth your weight in gold!" Lisa exuded. "And...we'll be sure to remember this place the next time we come through." Then, to herself, she added, "And you, my dear, have earned yourself a nice tip."

The rain had stopped just long enough to let them get back into the car without getting wet, but they ran into it again at Goodland, and it was a real battle to stay on the road. It just kept coming at them, onslaught after onslaught, each one getting a little more fierce. They didn't even see the sign telling them they had crossed into Colorado. They just kept slogging it out, with Lisa wishing they had just stayed at Goodland. She tried valiantly to keep up a decent speed, but the big trucks went around them like they were standing still. "This is really making me nervous...Becca, say something...talk to me...get my mind off of the road."

Becca started to tell her about some people that had been killed...in a storm like this one...a while back...just east of Abilene.

"For crying out loud, Becca! I said talk to me...not scare me to death!" Lisa laughed. "I'll bet you're a great one at calming all those little crumb crunchers you teach. What do you do? Tell them if they don't behave themselves...you'll just have to let the nice policeman take them off to jail?"

"Sorry!" she grimaced. "Maybe we should just sing."

"Yeah," Lisa nodded, "Just not 'Nearer My God To Thee', OK? I'm prepared...you understand, but...not ready to go anytime soon!" she chuckled. "Oh, look, we're coming into Burlington. I didn't even know we had crossed the line." She was quiet for a minute. "You know, since we haven't been able to get a weather report, I think I'll pull into that station up there, and see what they can tell me about this storm." Getting as close as possible to the door, she made a mad dash into the station. Returning, she said, "It's just as I thought, *not good*! And I was planning to go North from here to Wray...which is only about an hour away...but they said this storm is supposed to last till midnight...with really strong wind gusts. If you don't mind, I think we should just hole up here 'til morning. I don't relish driving in this stuff...especially at night..."

Becca nodded, "Yeah, I know...it ranks up there with static, dirty kitchens and..."

Lisa joined in, "Dirty windshields!" They laughed as Lisa pulled into a fairly new and clean looking motel. She was glad for the carport, so she could go in without getting soaked again. "Well, we really lucked out on this one...they only had one room left and it's a non-smoking one," she said, opening the trunk and getting a bag out. "What all do you need, Becca? Let's get it out here...in the dry...before I park the car. We have to enter from the front, anyway. Here, you can go on up if you want," she said, handing her sister the key. "Second floor, first door on the right."

CHAPTER FIVE

Lisa had turned on the weather channel when they hit the sack, to see what was being forecast, and the next thing she knew it was morning. They had both slept through what remained of the storm, and awoke to a new world, sparkling fresh, washed clean by the wind and rain. Water puddles in the parking lot made a great playground for some house sparrows, and nearby they heard the joyous song of a meadowlark as they loaded the car.

"What an absolutely gorgeous morning!" Becca exclaimed.

"Yes, it is," agreed Lisa, turning the key in the ignition. "And...as gorgeous as it is...I'm so glad we're heading North, instead of into the sun. The brilliance hurts my eyes this morning." Digging a pair of sunglasses out of her purse she exclaimed, "Oh, that's much better!" Then, turning onto highway 385, she added, "Next stop, Wray, Colorado!"

"So...what's at Wray?" Becca queried.

"Well, it's the County Seat, for Yuma County...so the records we want will most likely be there at the courthouse."

"Sounds like you know what you're doing." Becca, grinned. "Have you gone digging around in courthouses before?"

"Actually, yes, I have. Researched Dick's family line back to when his family came to the states. I was making a family tree to pass on to Amy. And...I did get Momma interested in gathering information on *her* side of the family. She couldn't help much with Daddy's. Mostly didn't want to, I think, rather than couldn't...but I don't blame her. Whenever I'd ask questions about his side of the family, she'd sort of clench her teeth and shrug her shoulders. Usually change the subject entirely. It took awhile...since I'm like a bulldog when I go after something...but, I finally got the message and left it alone." She chuckled, "I guess I should say I left *her* alone, about it...but I never did stop gnawing on that bone!"

"So...have you looked for *it* before? The homestead, I mean?"

"Years ago I wrote to a distant cousin of Daddy's...in Oregon. He told me that Daddy had always told him that the homestead was North of Yuma...close to the Phillips County line somewhere...but that he had never seen it. I also corresponded with one of Grandpa's sisters, about that same time. All she knew about the homestead was that Grandpa Eric and his wife Patty left Kansas...because his folk didn't want them to marry. So they went off on their own and settled in the sand hills of Colorado. She said she never could understand why, when they had lived in 'Utopia', that they would go and trade that for a 'sand pile'. She said her papa used to say, 'Sands good for little kids to play in...but it don't grow much in the way of cash crops!'"

"So, you haven't actually *looked* for it..."

"Not beyond writing letters to relatives, no."

"But, you've been back here before?"

"Yeah. I've been back a few times...mostly when Dick and I were going to the Mountains. It wasn't too far off the beaten path, so we came. The last time we were here we went out to the cemetery where Daddy and his folk are buried at Yuma, and drove around the town. Looked up the house we lived in, and the grade school, and the church we attended. Usually had lunch at a nice little café...that *hadn't been* there when we were. We talked to people that had lived there all their lives...but didn't remember us at all. Now, *that* really felt weird...to have lived there...and not be remembered. I left feeling a little sad, like I was supposed to do something...like I had some unfinished business to take care of...but without a clue as to *what* that unfinished business was." She pulled into a parking place behind the Courthouse.

"So, you think maybe finding the homestead will satisfy that need?"

"I don't know. Maybe it will." She shrugged, "Maybe it won't. At least we'll give it the old college try! Right?"

"Right." Becca laughed, opening the door to the Courthouse. "But remember, I'm just with you...I don't have the foggiest notion of how to go about doing this research stuff."

"Well, believe you me, it's not hard," Lisa grinned, "or *this* 'simple sister' wouldn't be doing it!"

They found their way to the Recorder's office, where she directed them to a back room full of old record books. The room was not too brightly lit and had a faintly musty smell of book bindings mingled with ink and paper dust. "If you need help, come and get me...otherwise you're on your own, Ladies." She started to leave, then turned back, waving her hand to indicate where thy should begin. "You might want to start with the wills. Do you know when your Grandfather died? If he had a will, it would list the property coordinates. If he still owned the property at time of death, that is. Like I said, come get me if you need help." Then she left them alone with all those books.

"O.K." Lisa murmured, "So, we'll start with the year he died." But, to their dismay, there wasn't a will to be found. "Well, if he didn't have a will...maybe he sold the land before he died, so let's go across the room, there, to the Deed Books."

"Sooo, which one should we start with?" Becca asked.

"Well, We know they married in 1902...and evidently that's when they left Kansas, so...

I'll start with 02 and you do 03." It took quite a long time to carefully scrutinize each page.

26

"Will ya look at this handwriting," Becca exclaimed. "It's absolutely beautiful!"

"Mine isn't...it's barely legible! So, I would say the recorder for 02 was not the same for 03."

"Definitely not!' Becca answered, looking over her sister's shoulder. "I've finished this one, so I'll start on 04," she mumbled absently, shoving the big book aside.

"Watch out!" Lisa yelled, jumping off her stool and darting past Becca in time to catch 1903 just in the nick of time. "Be careful. These old books have seen better days, and I wouldn't want us to be the cause of their demise.

Becca winced. "Oops. Sorry about that. I thought there was more room..."

"It's OK. No harm done." Lisa re-shelved both 02 and 03, then took down 1905. "Bingo...here it is!" she exclaimed a few minutes later.

They had the recorder show them on a large county map exactly where the property was situated. "Would you like for me to run off a copy of the plat for you? It has all the owners names on the property around your Grandfather's...also the public lands. Here, this one was made in 1922," she said, getting out another book and looking up the coordinates. "By this, I see that your Grandfather had already disposed of the property by 1922, so his name won't be on the plat, but, here..." She lightly colored in the area that had been his, in red pencil. "This way you know exactly what he owned," she finished.

CHAPTER SIX

"Yuma, here we come!" Lisa exclaimed, as she eased her car onto I-34, heading west.

"Now...*that* was fun," Becca said. "Looking through all that legal stuff, and *actually* coming across our Grandparents' names. Like they were real people...who were really alive, and owned property. Not just names in the family Bible." They were silent for a time, each absorbed in her own thoughts. Then Becca asked, "So, Lisa, do you have any vivid memories of our Grandparents? Or, like me, do you just remember things people told you about them?

"Well, Grandma died when our Dad was 14. So, of course I never knew her. But Grandpa actually lived with us for quite awhile before he died. Mother used to say that, after Grandma died, he just never got over her death. Took his family...there were seven kids...back to Kansas to live with his mother, while he just bounced from pillar to post, mostly doing farm labor for friends or relatives. According to her, most of the kinfolk thought he was shiftless...just plain lazy. But she said that he couldn't do a lot of physically hard work because he had injured his back...in some kind of farming accident. Personally, what I remember about him, is that he was a kind old man, who sat around under a shade tree in our backyard...and whittled neat things out of scrap wood." A smile tugged at the corners of her mouth. "I still have one of those carvings...that he made me. It's a little bird inside a cage...carved just that way, so the bird could never escape."

"Wow, I'd like to see that sometime..."

"Sure. When we get back I'll have to get it out for you." Lisa was quiet a moment, then added, "I used to love to sit and watch him make things, partly because he'd give them to me, and partly because he sang to me while he worked. He knew the neatest songs...had a wonderful voice. Deep and rich. Daddy once told me that Grandpa sang professionally when he was a young man. Had, in fact, been offered the chance to tour Europe. But...he got married instead...and ended up homesteading in Colorado."

Becca smiled. "Ah...so *that's* where we get our musical talent. I knew we didn't get it from Mother's side of the family!" she said, laughing. "Mama always said *she* couldn't carry a tune in a bushel basket!"

"Oh, yeah. But everyone in Daddy's family sang! Played instruments too. I remember one time there were a bunch of them at our house. They got so caught up in their music making...that Mother had a hard time getting them to quit long enough to eat. She finally yelled at them, 'It takes *strength* to make music...so come and eat!' then seeing they hadn't budged an inch, she added, 'Or I'm just gonna throw the whole mess out!' And, *that...*" Lisa laughed, "finally got them to the table." They drove on in silence a few minutes, Becca carefully taking in the countryside. Finally they passed the Yuma city limits sign.

"Well, here we are," Lisa proclaimed, "in the huge metropolis of Yuma, Colorado!" They first got a motel room, then some lunch, and then Lisa showed Becca around town. The house that they had once lived in now housed another family with kids, as evidenced by the toys strewn about the front yard. "And, the old library just up the street...has been replaced with a new modern one...behind it" Lisa said, wistfully. "There it is. I spent a lot of my free time in that old library." They made quick work of their tour, driving past the old schools that the children had attended. "And...this apartment building is standing on the lot where we once attended Church," Lisa said, sadly. "It doesn't seem right, for the Church not to be here." Pulling into a service station, she gassed up and cleaned the windshield. Twice. First with the cleaner the station offered, which didn't do too good a job, then with her own trusty bottle of Windex. Finishing that, she announced with baited breath, that it was time to find Grand-father's old place, and eased the car out of the service station.

At the light she turned south on state highway 59. Passing the airport, she felt a shiver of excitement. "You know," she said, "when we discovered the coordinates at the Courthouse this morning, I thought there must have been some mistake...because Daddy's cousin had told me it was north, you remember? But...seeing the airport there ...well, this just *feels* right. I don't know why, but it does." She glanced at her odometer, marking the miles so she would know when to turn west. "Becca, would you get the camera out of the glove compartment, please. I don't want to forget to take pictures."

Becca nearly dropped the camera, getting it out, because her attention was on something else. Suddenly she grabbed Lisa's arm and yelled, "Eesie, stop the car! Oh, please...*please*, stop the car!"

"OK...OK! I'm looking for a place to pull over. What's the matter? Are you sick or something?" Lisa pulled off onto a road going into a cornfield.

"No...I'm not sick...or anything. I...we...just have to go back! It's that house, back there. The one we just passed. I have to see it, Eesie!"

Lisa, grinned at the use of the old nickname Becca had given her as a toddler, because she couldn't say Lisa. "Well, OK...Becca. But, we'll be coming back by after we see Grand..."

Becca interrupted, "I know we'll be coming back by, but...*please*...I really need to see it *now*. Can't you turn around and go back?" She was so distressed, that Lisa nodded and turned the car back, slowly approaching the large gothic house they had just passed. "There...there's a driveway...pull into it...*please*!"

Lisa turned into the drive and stopped. "It's not much of a driveway, Becca. I don't know if I should attempt going up it very far. It's pretty sandy, too. I sure don't want to get bogged down in *that*," she said. But, when Becca opened her door to get out, Lisa grabbed her arm, "No...no, Becca, don't get out! Not *here*. There are probably rattlesnakes. It looks like this place has been deserted for years."

"But...I have to see it!" Becca exclaimed, trying to shrug off Lisa's grip.

"OK, then...but stay in the car! And...I'll try to drive up a little further. But, girl, you'd better pray we don't get stuck!" She tried to straddle the old rutted trail, keeping a wheel on the center so she wouldn't hurt the undercarriage of her car, all the while praying that the tumbleweeds and nettles weren't making hash of her paint job. It took several minutes, with Becca saying over and over, "Closer, Eesie, closer...it's *the* house." Finally they came to a barbed wire fence, and could see that the house just ahead was surrounded by white-faced Herefords.

"Well...*now* we have to stop," Becca said, getting out of the car. "But at least now we can see where to step. The cattle are doing a pretty good job of keeping the weeds down here." By the time Lisa had grabbed the camera, and caught up with her sister, Becca was trying to figure out how she was going to get over the barbed wire. So, Lisa held the top strand up and put her foot on the lower one letting her go through. Then Becca held the wires for Lisa, and the two women gingerly made their way up to the house, frightening some cattle off of the front stoop. "Wow...it's *the* house, all right!" Becca was awestruck. "I can hardly believe my eyes. I've just gotta see inside."

"Watch your step, then, Becca," Lisa said, snapping pictures right and left. "That stoop doesn't look any too secure!"

"Hey...if it held *those cows*...it'll surely hold us!" Becca said, disappearing into the dark doorway. Lisa followed, taking even more pictures inside. Suddenly Becca cried out, "Oh, my...I've gotta get out of here!" And she didn't slow down until she got to the fence.

That's where Lisa caught up with her. "Here, let me hold that wire for you, Becca. My goodness, girl! What's your hurry? You look like you saw a ghost?"

Becca shivered, "I think maybe I *felt* one! Let's get out of here." Lisa slowly got the car turned around and then gingerly made her way back down the long driveway. As they were about to turn south on 59, Becca grabbed Lisa's arm once again. "Uh, Lisa...I feel really awful! Would you mind terribly...if we just went on back to town?"

Lisa shook her head, "No. Of course I wouldn't mind. There's no hurry," she said, noting that Becca had started to cry. "There's no hurry at all."

Just then a dark blue Ford pick-up truck with a camper on the back, pulled in beside them. A young man, in his early thirties, leaned out the driver's side window. "Could I help you ladies with something? I saw you from the house over there." He waved his arm to a nice looking farm across the road and south about a quarter of a mile.

"No, we...we're just tourists," Lisa offered. "And wanted to get some pictures of that old vacant house. I'm sorry if we were trespassing...I didn't see any signs posted to keep us out."

"No. You weren't trespassin'. Houses' been vacant for years...and I just run some cattle there. But I wanna...caution you. It's just not safe."

"Oh...we were *extremely* careful. My sister thought it reminded her of a house she'd seen before... and...well, we just couldn't resist the temptation. But, thank you for your concern."

He touched the brim of his baseball cap, nodding to them. "Like I said, you wanna be careful...those old places...sometimes they're plumb rotten inside. An' then, too…there are rattlesnakes *everywhere*." With that, he backed out onto the highway and roared away toward town.

"Look," whispered Becca, pointing to the ditch on her side of the road. "He's right! It's a rattlesnake!"

Lisa caught just a glimmer of the tail going into the weeds. "Well! I, for one, am glad we're in our car...*and it's out there*!" Lisa exclaimed, pulling out onto the road. "And we're out of here!" They made it a quick trip back to their motel.

CHAPTER SEVEN

They went straight to their motel so that Becca could lie down for awhile. Lisa got her a cold compress and drew the drapes to darken the room, then she went downstairs and did several laps around the parking lot and visited with the owners of the motel who were working on the flower beds out in front. When she went back upstairs Becca was sound asleep. She took out paper and pen and wrote, first to Dick, then to Amy, and took the letters down to catch the afternoon mail pickup. By the time she got back, Becca was up and raring to go.

"Let's go get something to eat, Lisa. I'm hungry."

Lisa looked at her watch. "But, it's only ten minutes after four...too late for lunch and a bit early for supper, don't you think?" she teased.

"Hey! Have you forgotten...that we haven't had a bite of anything since breakfast? Come on, girl. If I had known you were going to try to starve me...well, I might not have come with you!"

"O.K. You win. We'll go eat." Lisa picked up her purse and car keys and headed to the door. "But, I've got an idea. Let's take some of our stash, over there," she waved her arm at the box of goodies that so many well intentioned friends and relatives had contributed to, "and go have a picnic."

"What a great idea!" Becca unloaded a few things, then picked up the box, "Wish I'd thought of that."

"What difference does it make...who thought of it?" Lisa laughed.

"Well...it just seems to me...that I never have any clever ideas. Everybody else comes up with the really good ones. Will you please throw my purse into this box, since I have my hands full? Thanks."

As they headed east from the Motel, Lisa suddenly turned in at a grocery store. "I just had a brainstorm! Let's get some cold watermelon."

"Now see, there you go again...with the good ideas. Why couldn't I have thought of cold watermelon? You see what I mean? It doesn't take a genius to think of watermelon," she joked, as they entered the store. "So, why didn't I think of it?" Lisa just shook her head, laughing.

"Oh, yes! Here it is. And this piece looks about right for the two of us, don't you think?"

Becca nodded. "Do you ever get yellow meat?" Lisa shook her head, making a face. "Me neither. Somehow it just doesn't *look like* watermelon." She found a package of plastic eating utensils, plastic cups and some heavy duty paper plates, declaring how she hated those flimsy ones, and they made their way through the much too crowded aisles to the check out. "Oh...I just thought of something...be right back..." Becca called over her shoulder, as she darted off in the direction of the dairy products. Re-emerging a few minutes later with some containers of yogurt, she dropped them onto the counter. "I couldn't decide which...so I got several different ones," she said, breathlessly. "This way, you can take your pick."

Lisa feigned a look of disgust, "Now...why couldn't I have thought of that? Some people...get all the good ideas!" at which they both laughed.

"Yeah, but you have to remember," Becca laughed, "Mama always said, 'even a blind hog will stumble over an acorn once in a while!'..."

"Private joke?" the checker wanted to know. Becca tried to explain what they were laughing at, ending with the 'blind hog' analogy, but the checker just looked at them strangely.

"I think you would have had to have been there...for it to have been funny." Lisa offered, lamely. The woman just shrugged and wished them a good day.

At the park they settled on a table near the water, with a tree nearby to block the afternoon sun. "Look, Becca...there's a squirrel eyeing us!" Lisa pointed toward the tree. Her motion made him scurry back to the safety of his tree. Running up one side, then crossing over behind it, he started down the other side, stopping midway, tail switching back and forth as he assessed the situation.

"Darn...my camera's in the car!" Lisa murmured, as she tossed some cheese crackers near the base of the tree."

"Keep him busy...and I'll get it," Becca offered, getting up. When she moved the squirrel darted up the tree and onto a branch, where he sat motionlessly watching them. He was still there when she got back with the camera. "If we just ignore him, he'll probably come back down."

"Right. Well, I'm ready for some of this melon..." Lisa paused, "and guess what we *didn't* think to bring? A butcher knife...to divide it," she answered herself. "So, I guess you can eat at that end and I'll take this one," she said digging in with a plastic fork, which promptly broke. "Oh, great..." She tried another, which also broke. Then she dug in with a plastic knife, cutting out small pieces that could then be forked. "You see, there's more that one way to skin a cat!" she exclaimed.

"There's only one thing missing," Becca mused, digging away at her end of the melon. "Salt. Now why didn't *either of us* think of salt?"

"Well actually...there *is* some...in my glove compartment…" Lisa said, tossing a chunk of melon over to where the squirrel, having come back down from his perch, sat contentedly eating the crackers. He ran around behind the tree and peeked out at them, as Lisa went to the car for the salt. But by the time she got back he was back too...and eating the melon. "Now that's a good, boy..." she said, tossing another piece. Only this time she dropped it closer to them, making him venture even closer. Another squirrel cautiously approached, only to be chased off by the first one.

"Feisty little bugger, aren't you?" Lisa laughed, holding out a cracker to him. Becca grabbed the camera and shot it just as the squirrel took the cracker. "Now, Becca...hand me the camera...and you try feeding him." Lisa said. Then, as Becca sat coaxing the squirrel, she asked, "So are you going to tell me what happened out there...today? At that house."

"Uh, well...there's nothing really to tell..." Becca started.

"Whoa there, little sister! Remember...*I was there*." She sat back and waited.

As the squirrel had taken Becca's last offering back to the tree to hoard it, she turned back to her sister across the table. "Well...it sounds too crazy...and...I really don't know where to start."

"You might start with why you thought that house was familiar to you." Lisa prodded.

"It's the house in my dreams...*exactly like it*," Becca began. "I've been having these dreams all my life...about a house in the country. And, Lisa, it's *that house*. I know it is!" She paused, collecting her thoughts. "And...that makes me wonder..." she searched her mind for the right words.

"If...it really was *just a dream* that you've been having all these years?" Lisa probed. When Becca nodded she continued. "And now you're wondering...if it might be a memory?"

Becca just sat there, looking very perplexed. "I don't know what to think. How can I tell the difference?"

"Well, we could try exploring the dream a bit...and...just see where it takes us?" Lisa offered. "What do you say, want to give it a try?"

Becca shuddered. "It's pretty scary...the dream I mean."

"And you have it...frequently?"

"I'd say so...at least once a month, sometimes more."

"And it's always the same?" Becca nodded. "OK, then, I want you to tell me the dream." Lisa reached across the table and took Becca's hand. "Just relax...and close your eyes if you wish...and just tell me the dream. Try to remember it *exactly* as it is." She waited a moment, then asked, "Are you into it?" Becca nodded. "And, is there anybody else there with you?" Again she nodded. "OK...so, can you tell me *who* is there in the dream...with you? Do you know these people?" Becca looked frightened as she shook her head, no.

"All right. So you're with people you don't know," Lisa proceeded, cautiously. "And what is happening? What are you doing?"

Becca looked up, "We're riding in a car. I don't know where we are, but we ride for what seems like a long time, and then we come to the house...*that house*! Up a very long driveway...to *that house*. And that's the dream...over and over, the same thing, night after night."

"All right, Becca. Now, I want you to take some slow deep breaths. Breathe in...hold it...now let it all out. That's right. Now, do it again. Breathe in, deeply. Now, blow it out slowly...like you're blowing a feather, slow and easy. Now...this time, breathe in, and when you let it out I want you to feel your body relax. Just let go of all the tension. You feel rested and very safe. You are *totally* relaxed. Now, Becca, I'm going to ask you some questions, and you are going to answer me...because you are totally comfortable and safe. Just keep breathing in and out very slowly...comfortably." Lisa felt Becca's hand relax in hers. "Now, Becca, close your eyes and go back to the time just before you went in the car...and tell me where you are." She waited for Becca to respond.

"At Mardred's house."

"And who is Mardred?"

"Mardred...nice lady...her taking tare ob me."

"And what are you doing?"

"Took a nap, but I waked up. Mardred dunno I waked up. I berry twiet."

"What is she doing?"

"Tooking supper...for John. He her husban'. He nice too."

"So...she doesn't know you are up from your nap?"

Becca was shaking her head. "No bodder Mardred. She tooking supper. Smell good. She singing."

"A song that you like?" Becca nodded her head, smiling. "What do you do now, so that you won't bother Mardred?"

"Doe outside...sit on steps...an' sing," She began to hum, I Must Tell Jesus. "Sun feel dood. I don't hab a toat...but I not toad."

"Is that the song Mardred was singing?" Lisa asked. Becca nodded slowly, smiling to herself. Then Lisa continued, "So you went outside...and are sitting on the steps. Are you watching for John?"

"Uh Huh. Tar tumming. But it not John. Dey wabe at me...doeing berry slow." Becca leaned for-ward as if trying to see where the car went. "Roun' torner. Tant see it no more. All don." She shrugged, resuming her humming. Then a moment later, "Tar tame back!" she exclaimed with delight. "Stop at Mardred's house. People det out." She suddenly became very agitated. "Say I hab to doe wif dem. I say no...no...no! I stay wif Mardred!" Becca began to cry, her voice rising. "Dey pick me up...put me in tar! I tall Mardred, but...she no hear me. Man put his hand on my mouf...so Mardred no hear me! Den we doe berry far in tuntry." Becca was now so agitated that Lisa went around the table and held her.

"It's O.K., Becca. You're safe, here. Now, I'm going to count to three, and I want you to open your eyes. When you open your eyes you will remember everything you told me...and you won't be afraid. O.K.?" Becca nodded, shuddering, as Lisa counted, "One...two...three...O.K. Becca, open your eyes." With a huge shudder, Becca opened her eyes. Lisa asked, "Are you all right?" Her sister nodded, slowly, sadly. "Do you remember what you told me?"

"Yes," Becca began, "But...that's incredible. Who were those people? They hurt me! When they took me off of Margaret's steps..." she shuddered again, "I was struggling, and they bumped my head on the concrete. I...my head was bleeding! Oh, Dear God..." she glanced heavenward, "what does this all mean?" Then, turning to Lisa, asked, "So...big sister...what do *you* think it all means? Is it just a dream? Or...a memory?"

"Oh...I'd call it...a memory, Becca. In my opinion, it's *not* just a dream. But...as to *exactly* what it means," she shrugged, "I'm sure I don't have a clue." She paused for a moment, then asked, "So, how old do you think you were...when this happened?"

"Uh...I felt very little...probably about three...two-and-a-half...to three. Somewhere in there."

"Well, that would definitely fit the language skills you were exhibiting." Lisa sat quietly thinking, but was brought back by a soft nudge on her fingers. The squirrel was sitting squarely in front of them on the table. "Oh, so...Mr. Squirrel...you just *can't stand* to be ignored...can you? Well, here..." She handed him a cheese cracker, and he was content to stay right there and eat it. Becca gave him the next one, then Lisa got up, "Whew...this concrete seat is getting to me. I've got to move around...or my legs aren't going to work too good. Let's take a walk by the pond."

Becca nodded, taking a few crackers out and leaving them on the table, then getting to her feet, she joined Lisa. "That will probably be more than he can handle."

"Don't count on it...what he doesn't eat, he'll store for tomorrow." They walked for about twenty minutes, then headed for the car.

"Boy, I'm tired! Like...*completely* wrung out," Becca sighed, getting into the car. "I think I just need a shower and my bed."

"Now *that* sounds like a winner to me!" Lisa said. "And...I hope you never again let me hear you say that you never get any good ideas!" Becca laughed, trying to keep up the banter, but it was the laugh of one going through the motions. She was too drained to produce anything else. And back at the motel, both women were asleep as soon as their heads hit their pillows.

CHAPTER EIGHT

Wednesday they were surprised to awake to a leaden sky. The weather forecast had called for rain, but not until late afternoon. So they grabbed a quick breakfast and headed south on 59. As they neared the old house from yesterday Becca sighed, "I just keep wondering why they took me to that house?"

Lisa slowed the car as they passed, "I'm sure I don't know. Have you, by any chance, remembered anything else?" She paused a moment, then continued. "Like...do you remember going *inside* the house? It seemed to touch a nerve yesterday when we went inside."

Becca sat quietly watching the house, turning in her seat until she could no longer see it. Finally she spoke. "As I was waking up this morning...I actually did remember some more of it. I could see us going up that long driveway. He pulled the car up in front of the house and they...*he*...carried me in. He took me into a room...on the left...and put me down on a couch. It was very rough, like...stiff. You know...like that old nylon frieze' stuff?" Lisa nodded. "He told me to lie down and go to sleep, and he would come and get me...*later*. I was crying and he told me that I had to be quiet...and go to sleep. I don't know whether he said he would spank me...but I know I was afraid that he would hurt me. I must have slept...because the next thing I remember is waking up and the room was pretty dark. There was light shining in a window, so I could see." She grew quiet, watching the road ahead, trying to remember more.

Lisa interrupted her reverie, "Well, according to our map, here's where we turn west." She handed Becca the plat that they had brought from the courthouse, saying, "Here, Becca...help me watch. This is all unfamiliar territory to me, but see, it looks to be about seven miles. It's the last section there...next to the Washington County line...where we need to turn left." After what Lisa thought was the right distance she turned left and drove quite a way, without seeing anything but empty fields. "I wonder...if we're even on the right road." She mused, as she swung into a field where an elderly man was tinkering with his tractor, "Think I'll just ask this farmer."

He came over to the car, wiping his hands on a grease rag. When Lisa showed him the plat he told her she needed to go back to the main road, turn left and go down another mile...and that would be the road they needed. That would put them right on the Washington County line.

"Well, that wasn't *too* bad...we only missed it by a mile!" She laughed, thanking the man. And he retorted with something about his old man saying if you're only off a mile, it might as well be two thousand. "I guess that's right," Lisa laughed. Thanking him she backed slowly out onto the road. He called after them to watch out for the rattlesnakes, as they pulled away. "We will," Lisa shouted back, "And thank you!" He nodded and touched the brim of his hat, watching them a moment or two before he turned back to his tractor..

The next road was, indeed, the right one, and as they started down it, Lisa felt absolutely giddy. They were almost there! Then she saw the snake in the road and her elation turned to dread. "Talk about omens!" she shuddered. "And I don't even believe in omens!" She stopped the car and looked back at the snake. Then she slowly backed up, making sure her tires ran over it. Then she went forward until she could see the snake in her rearview mirror. "He's still alive," she said, reversing the car once more. "Now...this time...I know he has to be dead!" she declared, lowering her window and sticking her head out to see, as she slowly drove up beside the snake.

Becca screamed, "Get your head back in here...he'll jump up and bite you!"

Lisa laughed, "Nah...he won't be *biting* anybody. He looks very dead." She felt very smug driving away. At the crest of the next hill she exclaimed, "Oh, Becca...look at that. Just look at it! It may be in the sand...but it's beautiful! How could he...Grandpa...have just let it go?"

Below them lay a calendar scene, with several old trees surrounding a small two story house and some outbuildings. "This is it! We're actually here! And who would have guessed that all these trees and buildings were tucked away back here? From the main road it all looks so...so *flat*!" She drove on down to the house, watching for any sign of life. There didn't appear to be anyone at home, so they just sat there in the car for a bit, wondering what they should do next. "Well...I don't know about you, Becca, but I just have to get out...have my feet on the ground where our grandparents walked," Lisa exclaimed, getting out of the car, and watching carefully for any sign of snakes. She walked up to the house, and rang the doorbell. Then, getting no response, she tapped on the door.

Becca had followed and, stepping up to the door, she banged on it with her fist. "Now that's how you knock on a door, Lisa! You want someone inside to actually hear it!" she declared, smugly. Still there wasn't any response. "Nobody's here," she said. "I wonder if the house is vacant?"

Lisa squinted into a nearby window, "The place *is* deserted...not a stick of furniture." She came back to the door and tried it again. It wasn't locked, just stuck, so she backed off. "Maybe there's a back door..." she mused, gingerly making her way around the corner. Suddenly, what had started out as just a gray day, got much darker, startling Lisa. She looked up at the sky, and calling for Becca to join her, scurried back to the car. They made it just in time. First there was a bright flash of lightening, then a huge clap of thunder and it began to pour. It was a regular deluge. "Boy, that was a close call," Lisa said, starting the engine. "And, since we have no idea how long it's going to last, I think we should go." She turned the car around and headed up the driveway. "Besides, I don't want to get stuck out here...in all this sand..."

"And snakes..." Becca added, shivering.

"Right, and snakes!" They noted that the snake they had run over was still lying there in the road. "Now, see...I told you he was dead." Lisa said, feeling quite powerful. "And there he lies...*very dead*. And that feels pretty darned good! I actually *killed* a rattlesnake!"

"Well, if you're so brave...why don't you get out and cut the rattles off...to show Dick and Amy what you did?" Becca taunted.

"In this rain? You've gotta be kidding." She was silent a moment, then added, with a chuckle, "Besides, I can be pretty brave with this car around me...for protection...but I'm not sure what I'd do if I was staring one in the face!"

"Oooh, yuk," Becca shuddered. "I know exactly what I'd do. I'd run the other way! And, I really hope we don't see any more snakes!. That's one yesterday...and one today. Now, dear God," she added, prayerfully, "I think we've met our quota! Please, let somebody else have a turn, thank you."

"Oh...Becca!" Lisa exclaimed, in disappointment. "And...just which one of us *didn't* have the bright idea to bring the camera with us today? I intended to get pictures of the house. And... I could have at least taken a picture of our snake!"

"Not *our* snake, thank you! Your snake," Becca retorted. "I'm not claiming *any* snake...dead or alive!" They laughed. "Besides we'll be back. And I wanted to stop at *that house*...again," she said as they passed it. "But not in this deluge." So, they went straight back to town. And, since it was still raining too hard to actually do any sightseeing, they went back to the motel, and watched a replay of *To Kill A Mockingbird* on the TV. Before it was over, they were both snoozing, and when they woke up the rain had stopped, and it was time for supper.

CHAPTER NINE

They ate supper at the local greasy spoon, then drove back over to the park, where they walked awhile. Suddenly Becca exclaimed, "Lisa, I need to go back to that house! It's...I think I'm remembering something!" She headed for the car.

"Wait, Becca...it's almost dark..." Lisa, said, following. "We can't possibly..." But, as her words were falling on deaf ears, she hurried to catch up to her sister.

"It'll still be light for at least another hour, and that's plenty enough time...for what I need," Becca said, getting into the car.

"O.K. Whatever you say." Lisa drove them back to the old house, where once again they pulled up to the barbed wire fence, cautiously making their way through, and shooing the cattle from the stoop.

As they walked into the dimly lit interior Becca said, "Something isn't quite right...and I can't put my finger on it." She ventured in a little further, but upon hearing a distinctive whirring sound backed right out. "Snakes! There are snakes in there..." she squealed, visibly shaken. "Let's go!"

"Did you see them?" Lisa asked, following Becca in hasty retreat.

"No...but I definitely heard them! It made my skin crawl!"

Back in the safety of their car Lisa asked, "Well, did you figure out what wasn't right?"

"Huh uh," Becca said, shaking her head. "But...I know something's wrong."

"Well...give it some time," Lisa said. "It'll come to you." Back in town, Lisa stopped at Alco for some writing paper before returning to their motel for the night. The store was trying to close, but let her come in since she just wanted a tablet. And then they also let her purchase a liter of Coke...since she was already there anyway.

When they were ready for bed Lisa said, "Becca, I got this paper to try something. I want you to draw what you saw...when those people took you to that house. First, draw what the outside of the house looked like...when you drove up to it. Then...I want you to make me a map of the interior. I want...I *need*...to see what you saw inside that house. Think you can do that?"

"Yeah...I guess. I can at least try," Becca said, nervously, taking the writing tablet her sister offered. She closed her eyes for a few moments to refresh her visual memory, then began to draw. After she had drawn the basic house, she added some outbuildings and trees, finishing with the driveway. Laying the pencil down, she smiled, "Well...I think this is pretty accurate."

Lisa nodded. "I'm sure it is...but remember you can *always* add to it...if you should remember some other detail that you might have forgotten." Becca nodded. Then Lisa continued, "Now, on this fresh sheet of paper...try to draw the inside of the house."

Once again Becca started to draw, then stopped abruptly. "Uh...I told you...something was wrong out there. And now...I feel like...really awful...doing this!" She tossed the tablet down, then the pencil, and buried her face in her hands.

Lisa retrieved the paper and pencil, and putting her arm around Becca, gently probed, "What's wrong, Becca? What *exactly* is making you feel so bad?" Becca shrugged Lisa's arm off, then jumping up, began to pace, agitatedly, so Lisa said, "I think I'll go get some ice...and...fix us a coke, OK?" Becca continued pacing, but when Lisa returned, handing her the coke, she took it and sat down in a chair by the window.

100 MILES FROM NOWHERE: murder remembered

Lisa pulled another chair over close by and settled in. "Becca, remember...what we did the other day when we worked on your memory?" She nodded, absently. "Well, I want us to do that again...OK?" Again Becca nodded so Lisa went on. "OK, then...once again I want you to relax, and take some deep breaths. Just like before." Becca took in some slow deep breaths, blowing them out, softly. "That's right. Now, let yourself drift. Just drift away on a beautiful cloud...knowing that what you remember can't hurt you...that I'll be right here to help you...that you are completely safe." In a matter of seconds, Becca's countenance went from highly agitated to totally relaxed. "That's good," Lisa continued. "That's very good. Now, I'm going to count to three...and when I say three, you are going to take me inside the house with you...and tell me what happened there." She counted. "Now, Becca, what happened? What happened to you...when you got up from your nap?"

"It dart-time. But light tum in window, so I tan see."

"And what do you see?" Lisa coaxed.

"See table and shares," Becca said, slowly, searching her mind, "See bid fing...wif drawers. See window. Light! Tar light in window! Daddy and Mama tumming to det me!" She looked excited. "See ...Daddy's tar in window...I doe see him...but...tan't det door open." She appeared to be struggling. "Now...it open. Oh! See Daddy tum in house." She suddenly pulled back. "He berry mad...at Becca! Hide by share..." She scrunched down in her seat as if trying to hide. "Oh, no, no! Man...he mad at my Daddy! He...he hab a dun! Watch out Daddy! Oh...no! Daddy...fight wif him. Bid noise. I tared...hide by share!" She was quiet, as though trying to see what happened next. "I peek at Daddy...see him...by man. Man not moob. Daddy say...'Oh, Dod...he dead'!" She looked relieved, "Daddy not dead...udder man dead."

Lisa sat transfixed. "Then...what happened?" she whispered. "How do you know he's dead?"

"Daddy yell...'Hank! Tum help me! Den udder man tum...frum tares, obber dare," waves an arm. "He say...'What happen?' Daddy say, 'He went trazy! Dun doe off. He dead. You hab to help me.' Man say 'No'." She shook her head. "Daddy say, 'Yes'...an he drab him. So...man say 'Otay'. Den...dey tarry dead man out...to tar." Becca squinted, trying to see what happened next. "Put him in tar an' doe away!" She looked puzzled. "I trying, don't doe way, Daddy." Now Becca was so distressed that Lisa put her arms around her and rocked her back and forth. "Daddy...doe way and leab me...in house," Becca whimpered, "I *berry tared*."

Lisa said softly, "I'm going to count to three, Becca, then you're going to open your eyes...and you're going to remember what you told me...but...you're not going to be afraid, OK?" Becca nodded, solemnly, as Lisa counted.

Becca gasped for air like a drowning person, then looked incredulously at her sister. "I...I can't believe it! Could that really have...happened? Lisa...what kind of a man was our father? I saw him. I saw him...kill that man... then take him away. And...he just left me...there." She looked dazed. "Oh, my! That's just...too bizarre!" Burying her face in her hands, she wept, while Lisa sat silent, gently rubbing her back. "Tell me...that this couldn't be real, Lisa," Becca cried. "Tell me I just imagined it all. Tell me..."

Lisa whispered, "I can't tell you that you imagined it. It was *too* real. But, I truly do not understand what it's all about." Continuing to rub Becca's back and shoulders, she searched her own mind for something that would ease her sister's distress. Then she said, "Becca, I want you to think hard...and tell me *what* the men were fighting about."

After a few moments Becca shivered, "Well, it's weird, Lisa, but...I think...I get the distinct impression that...they were fighting about...me. It had something to do with *me*."

Lisa probed further, "And what *exactly*...did they say...that makes you think it was about you? Did they use your name?"

"No...I don't think so. Not...my name. But...I was watching at the window...when Daddy jumped out of the car and ran up to the door. He was really mad. And...he came through the door yelling, 'I told you no! The deals off, you son-of-a-____! You shouldn't have gone ahead!' And then he just plowed right into the guy. They were both yelling and cursing...fighting...all over the room. Then...there was this terrible noise! Lisa...the gun! It...the gun went off. I heard a shot!" She was on her feet, pacing, back and forth, rubbing her temples, "No! No, actually...there were *two* shots. And one of them hit the window behind me...went right over my head! Glass...little bits of glass...sprinkled down around me, so...I moved. I had to move over. In fact," she squinted as if trying to see into a dark room, "I seem to remember...climbing up...into the chair. Yes, that's it! I climbed up...into the chair... that I had been hiding behind!"

Lisa picked up the drawings that Becca had done earlier, and showing her the one with the floor plan, said, "OK, Becca, sit down here beside me, and just take me through it, step by step. Beginning with where you were, when the fireworks started."

"Here," Becca said, "I was in this room on the left, when I saw the car lights...and I got down from the sofa and went to the window and looked out." She pointed to the living room window, where she first saw the car. "Then...I went into the entryway. It had a table at the back, here...and a single light bulb hanging in the middle of the room. Uh, I seem to recall there was a round braided rug on the floor, here...between the front door and the table." She drew a large circle to represent the rug, then put two large x'es on the circle to represent the men. "After they moved him...I...saw...there was blood on the rug. And...there was a window...here...to the left of the front door. And a big chair...here...in front of the window. That's the chair I hid behind...and climbed up into." She paused to sip on her coke. "When they went out, I got down, and watched them from that window...watched the red tail lights go down the driveway. Then...I just remember climbing back up into the chair. I was so afraid!" She sighed, staring into space for a time. Finally she got to her feet and stretched. "Well, I'm completely drained. What do you say we call it a night?"

"Good idea," Lisa agreed. She was getting a monster of a headache and was ready to take some Excedrin and go to bed, herself. It was the first headache she had had since they arrived.

CHAPTER TEN

Lisa was running, but she wasn't getting anywhere. She was running in deep sand, and someone was chasing her. "Oh, God, no...don't let him catch me!" Then she was flailing her arms and kicking, "Let me go...let me go!" And suddenly she was aware of someone standing over her, shaking her.

"Wake up, Lisa! It's only a dream. You're OK." It was Becca, standing over her, shaking her. "Hey, Sis...you were having a bad dream. But it's OK. Nobody's gonna get you! Come on, now, wake up."

"What? Oh, Becca...it's you." She struggled to sit up, catching her breath as if she had been running a race. "Oh, my...that was some dream! I was running from someone...and couldn't get away. Too much sand...I kept bogging down! Well...that was *too real*!" She struggled groggily to her feet and headed for the bathroom. "What time is it anyway?"

Becca looked at her watch in disbelief, "It's only four-twenty-three! Sorry to wake you...but you've been kicking the tar out of me all night. I finally decided if you were going to kick me it might as well be for something I had done...like waking you up!" She was sitting cross-legged on the bed when Lisa came back into the room. "So, who had you running like a scared rabbit?"

Lisa shuddered at the analogy, shaking her head, "Beats me. I just know I was giving it all I had...scared silly! My hearts still pounding. Here feel this." She put Becca's hand over her heart.

"Well, my word...you really were scared." She looked at Lisa, thoughtfully. "So...does this happen often?" Lisa shook her head. Then Becca teased, "Maybe Dick should have warned me about the dangers of sleeping with his wife...I could have at least taken out more liability insurance..."

"Oh yeah...?" Lisa hit her with a pillow, "Payable to who, Miss Independence?" she laughed.

"That's 'payable to whom' if you don't mind...and you don't need to make it sound like I don't have anybody in my life...that would miss me...if anything were to happen to me..." She tossed the pillow back. "Now...if you don't mind...could we phuleeze get some shut eye? Remember, you're the one that's been sleeping...not me." Pulling the sheet up under her chin, she flounced over, turning her back to her sister. With an exaggerated sigh, she chuckled, "And you'd better believe me when I say sleep deprivation does not wear well on this particular Hollander." Then, with a final "Good-night", she turned out the light.

About thirty-five minutes later, she sat up and turned the light back on. "Now, I'll give you three guesses who can't get back to sleep? And the first two don't count," she murmured to her sister, who was finally sleeping soundly. She rummaged around for a book from her satchel, and read until she was finally sleepy. Then she got up and turned off the alarm on Lisa's bedside table and, climbing back into bed with a smile, she purred, "This is one morning that we are sleeping in, dear sister...after all, we are *on va-ca-tion*!"

Much later, over her burned bacon and dried out scrambled eggs, Lisa mused, "I must have forgotten to set the alarm last night. Dick's never going to believe this." She pushed her over-browned hash-browns around the plate with her fork. "Even when I try to sleep in...when we're on vacation...I never can." She took a sip of her coffee. "Ahh...Thank God...at least the coffee's good!" She took another sip. "Can you believe...it's already ten-o'clock? I can just hear our Mama say *'the day's half over, and you're just now havin' breakfast?'*" She chuckled into her cup.

Becca kept her eyes averted to her own over-done plate of food "Well, something I remember Mama saying, was, 'if you sleep late...it's because...'" she paused for effect, "you must've *really* needed it." She grinned sheepishly at Lisa. "So, I guess...*we* really needed it!"

"Well," Lisa drawled with amusement, "That's what seven years difference in our ages will do for you. Mama surely had mellowed by the time you got to be a teen-ager!" She sipped her coffee.

"I guess she probably had," chuckled Becca.

"No probably about it, girl! She had definitely mellowed." Lisa sat quietly enjoying her coffee, then putting her empty cup down she asked, playfully, "O.K., so, given her new philosophy on sleeping in, I guess I needed it...because...I had those weird dreams that kept me running all night. You see, I worked too hard..." She ran her index finger around the rim of her empty cup, then asked, coyly, "So? My dear sister, what's your excuse?"

Becca just shrugged her shoulders and reached for the check, "Oh, I dunno...but, it is kinda hard...to sleep with a kicking mule...even in a king size bed!" She laughed, heading for the register, "I'll get this. You get the tip."

Back in the car Lisa asked, "So...what was that? About the kicking mule, I mean? I suppose you're going to tell me...that I...kept *you*...up."

"You did...but I forgive you." Becca said, condescendingly. "And, by the way, did you ever find out who was chasing you all night?"

Lisa didn't exactly answer; just 'sort of' shook her head, no, squinting into the morning brightness. They were heading south, nearing the airport when she suddenly hit the steering wheel with the palm of her hand, "Oh, darn! I can't believe I did it again!" She quickly pulled off at the airport and, swinging the car around, headed back to town.

"What? What did you do again?" Becca asked, picking up all the 'stuff' that had tumbled out of her purse when it slid off of her lap at the sudden turnaround.

"We...I...came off without the camera! That's what. And would you just look..." Lisa gestured with a flourish of her hand, "It's an absolutely gorgeous day out there. Perfect for pictures! So...we'll just have to go back, and get the darned camera."

Arriving back at their motel, Becca admonished with a laugh, "You know, it might just pay us to keep the 'darned camera' in the car!"

"Oh, I thought of that," Lisa answered, unlocking the door to their room, "But, the 'darned thing' just happens to belong to Amy. And Amy says it's very expensive. I practically had to take a blood oath to get her to loan it to me. So...I'd rather not tempt fate...or anyone else, for that matter...and have it be the reason someone decides to put a rock through our car window while you and I are fast asleep."

Inside, while Lisa rummaged through her bag for more rolls of film, Becca picked up the much discussed camera and let out a low whistle, "I see what you mean about expensive! And you're right...people have been known to break into cars for less than this expensive." She started out the door, then darted back into the room and retrieved a brown paper grocery bag from their waste basket. "This will be a good disguise..." she said, popping the camera into the bag, "for when we're not in the car...and the camera is!"

"Great idea!" Lisa exclaimed, laughing. "Whoever said that you..." and Becca jumped in so that they finished in unison, "...never get any great ideas?"

CHAPTER ELEVEN

This time there were no hitches; no rain, no forgotten cameras...and no rattlesnakes in the road. And, the girls were having a wonderful time traipsing around their grandparents homestead. They managed to get the front door unstuck, and wandered from room to room like they had discovered the magic kingdom, with Lisa frenetically snapping pictures right and left, at every turn, as if she were trying to capture something intangible. Something more than just empty sunbeams streaking through dirty casement windows, and their Nike' footprints that imparted new life to long undisturbed and forgotten dusty hard wood floors. It was like she was trying to peer into the dark unknown, to reclaim the more than half a century of time since her people had filled those rooms. They held her captive, spellbound, listening for their voices, half expecting at any moment to find them still there...just as if they had never left at all. She was transfixed.

Becca broke the spell. "Come on, Lisa. Let's go see what's outside."

Lisa yelled, "Hold it!" but snapped the picture one second too late. Instead of Becca framed in the door-way, she only managed to capture a sense of movement in the disturbed dust of the room, something ethereal, not quite there. Something she would never have captured without that *very expensive camera* of Amy's. She was still standing there breathlessly watching the door, a pilgrim on hallowed ground, when Becca re-appeared in the doorway.

"Come on..." she called, impatiently. "There's more to see...you can't stay in here all day!"

"OK." Lisa slowly let out the breath she had been holding. "I'm right behind you!" She stepped out of the house into the bright light of day, and immediately threw her arm up to shield her eyes. "Oooh, I...need to get my sunglasses, Becca. This light is sooo bright." She slipped into her car and got her sunglasses, but when she got back out the light still hurt her eyes. Stepping into the shadow of the house, she exclaimed, "Well...let's do it. But, I need to stay in the shadows until my eyes adjust...OK.?"

Becca nodded, leading the way into the old barn. "Oh, my...will you look at all this stuff! Lisa, look at all the antique farming equipment...and these tools. Wow...I wonder when they were last used?"

Lisa was astonished. "Oh my gosh! Becca look at this neat old John Deere tractor!" She stepped up onto it's platform, ignoring the years of accumulated dust. "Oh, wow! This is really something!"

Becca was walking around with her mouth open. "This is sooo amazing!" She was quiet for several moments, trying to take it all in. Then she asked, "Lisa...how would we go about finding out who owns all of this stuff now?"

"We'd just have to go back to the courthouse," came the dazed reply.

"Well...we probably don't have time to make it to the courthouse today...right?"

Lisa looked at her watch and shook her head. "Huh uh...not today. It's almost four, and I don't have any idea how long it would take to do the search. Or...how difficult it might be. Some are real buggers. I guess, for starters, we might check on who is currently paying the taxes." She got down off of the tractor, brushing the dirt off of herself. "But, you know, Becca, that is a *great idea*..." Then with raised eyebrows added, "Oh, yes...you did have another one! And, *I'd* also like to know who owns all this." Stepping out of the barn into the bright light, Lisa winced...even with the sunglasses. "Oh, darn," she cried. "Looks like I'm getting another migraine! I can hardly stand this light. I guess I'd better go back to the car and get some Excedrin. Maybe head it off! Feel free to poke around as much as you want. There's no hurry." Cutting across the yard to the car, there were places where she was almost ankle deep in sand. "Boy this stuff is hard to walk in..." she muttered to herself. "It sure would slow you down if you ever had to run in it."

After taking the Excedrin, Lisa sat in the car with the door open, her head resting on her hands on the steering wheel. She closed her eyes, and felt herself drifting off into nowhere. Peacefully drifting. But then it wasn't peaceful anymore. She was running, her feet making a strange noise. It was not the good familiar sound of feet hitting the solid earth, but rather the strange sound of shoes scrunching into sand, being quickly sucked downward, making it almost impossible to go forward, to pull free. It was the sound of dragging, slow motion, so that she, who was the fastest girl in her class, could go nowhere in this God forsaken sand. And then other noises began to drown out the sound of shoes in swallowing sand. The ragged inhale, exhale, synchronized with the harsh pounding of her own heart filling up her ears and head till she thought it would burst, drowning her in the noise of her fear. And then there was one more sound...that started low and was in perfect time with the others, but soon began to overcome them all. It was the sound of her own voice screaming "Nno! Nno! Nnno!"

She was snapped back roughly by Becca shaking her and calling, "Lisa! Wake up! Wake up! You're dreaming again!"

"Ohh...and what a horrible dream! That sand kept pulling me back..." She sat up and shook herself. "Oh, my...head." She dug her keys out of her bag and dropped them into Becca's hand. "I think we'd better head back... and you'd better do the driving." She got out and let Becca help her around to the passenger side.

Back at their room Lisa climbed into bed and Becca went to Alco to purchase an ice pack for her head. The ice, coupled with her prescription pain medication put Lisa out for the night, and Becca went down to the lobby to read, as she waited to intercept Dick's every-other-night call. He was alarmed that Lisa's headaches had started back up and told Becca to assure her that he'd call her back the next night.

The next morning Lisa woke with no headache, but she felt really wrung out, so at the breakfast table she announced. "I need the mountains! Let's go to the mountains, and give ourselves a break from...from all this stuff!"

Becca thought it was an absolutely marvelous idea, and "chalked another one up for Lisa!" To which they both laughed."

CHAPTER TWELVE

By two o'clock Lisa and Becca were eating lunch in a little canyon just west of Boulder. It was a place that Lisa had remembered from her childhood, and where she had brought Dick on their honeymoon. There was a beautiful waterfall back off of the road on the right hand side several miles up the canyon. You couldn't see the waterfall from the road, but there was a pull off and a huge rock with a hole in it by the side of the road marking the place, so that you couldn't miss it. To get back in to where the falls were, you had to leave your car and hike down a long rocky path to the bottom of the gorge at the base of the waterfall. That's where they ate, sharing their leftover crumbs with a friendly nuthatch.

When they were finished eating, Lisa said, "Follow me...I'm going to take you to the beginning of the world!" She led Becca up the mountain beside the waterfall, then behind rock formations that took them to a spot above the waterfall. "Now...isn't this something?" Lisa panted, breathlessly, when they reached the top.

"Oh...It's like being in another world!" Becca exclaimed, stretching out on a boulder in the sun. "This is magnificent! How did you *know* about this place?"

Lisa stretched out beside Becca in the sun, her hand shielding her eyes. "Well, once when I was still pretty young...like first or second grade, I imagine...Daddy brought us here. On a vacation, I think. We stayed in a cabin...somewhere...not too far away, and came here for a picnic. We loved the 'donut rock'. Daddy took our picture...with Bill and Scotty on the top and Barbie and me sticking our heads through the hole." She was quiet for a minute, her brow furrowed in puzzlement, "I was just trying to figure out where Mama was...because I don't remember her being here with us. And now that I think of it...she isn't in any of the pictures that I have from that trip. Hmmm, I'll just have to give that some thought. But, come on..." she pulled Becca to her feet, "Let's hike upstream a bit."

A few minutes later, they stopped in a place so quiet that all they could hear was the gurgling of the stream. Lisa whispered, so as not to violate the silence, "You see? It's like Daddy said, 'the beginning of the world...with us the only two inhabitants!' It's so far removed from everything." She sat down on a rock and took her shoes and socks off, dipping her toes into the icy water. "Oh, Becca!" she squealed with delight. "It's so cold!"

Becca joined her sister on the rock, and dipped her toes into the icy foam, but quickly pulled them back onto the warm rock. "That's *too* cold for me, thank you!" She eyed Lisa, candidly, then asked, "So...what kind of a man was our father, anyway?"

Lisa was quiet. First she repositioned herself, so that the sun wasn't in her eyes. "I wish I hadn't left my sunglasses in the car," she murmured, pulling her knees up and wrapping her arms around her legs. Resting her chin on her knees, she sighed, "I don't know what to tell you, Becca. I think he wasn't...a very good man." Her voice trailed off, sadly. "What can I tell you?"

"Well...for starters, you can tell me...what *I was doing in that house*?" Becca almost shouted. The sound and tone of her voice startled them both. She blinked, trying to regain her equilibrium. "And...you can tell me what he...*Daddy*...was doing there? And *who* those other people were? And...tell me about the man they carried out...who he was?" Her voice had been steadily rising, now it plummeted like a deflated balloon, "Oh, Lisa...I feel like I'm going crazy!" She sat staring at the water bubbling over the rocks, then quietly, her composure restored, she said, "I know...*you* really can't tell me all of that! But, Lisa, you *can* tell me…about *me*. You're so much older…surely you know *some…thing*…about me, I mean. Just…tell me about me."

Lisa sighed, a great heavy sigh, "Oh, Becca. I wish I could help you with all of this. I've been racking my brain, Honey…trying to remember. I figure I was probably ten…if you were about three." Lisa looked earnestly at her sister and shrugged. "And…so…what I remember about being ten you could probably put in a thimble. I don't know why, but…there's just not much there." She studied the mountain on the other side of the stream, then began again. "When I was nine…we moved from Boulder…to Yuma. I had a hard time fitting in, we had moved around so much…three times when I was in the second grade, and twice in the fourth…from Longmont to Boulder…then to Yuma. It was really tough." She paused, sighing. "But…you, Becca…you were *my* baby doll." She smiled at her little sister.

"So…you actually do remember *me*…as a baby, I mean?"

Lisa smiled nostalgically, "Oh, yes. Of course I remember you. I loved everything about you! I bathed you…dressed you…hauled you around in our red flyer wagon. Like I said, *you* were my baby doll."

Becca was crying, "Then *why* was I at Margaret and John's house…and why did those people snatch me off of their steps?"

"So far…I haven't remembered anything connected with that, Becca. I'm sorry, Honey." Lisa stroked her sisters arm. "Maybe…we can work on that memory some more…if you feel like it…" Becca nodded. "If you could just give me something more to go on, it might help *me*…to remember something that connects…OK.?" Becca nodded again. Just then a cloud covered the sun. Startled, Lisa jumped up. "Uh oh…that looks like rain! We'd better get moving…first things first. We don't want to be trying to make our way down that mountain by the falls in a rainstorm." Becca agreed, wiping her eyes on her sleeve.

They worked their way back as quickly as they could, trying to beat the gathering storm. But by the time they got to the head of the falls, it had started to sprinkle, and Lisa prayed that they could make it to the bottom before it began to rain hard. They did, just. Then it poured.

Lisa laughed, shouting so Becca could hear her above the roar of the falls coupled with the sound of the storm. "I don't care if we get a little wet...just so we're down off that mountain! The hike back to the car is a piece of cake!" But they weren't just a little wet, they were soaked through and through by the time they reached the car. As they stepped out onto the pavement by the 'donut rock' the rain stopped and the sun broke through...just that fast. Lisa wanted to take a picture of Becca with her head poking through the donut hole...but Becca declined, offering to take hers, instead. Laughing,, they both decided to forgo any pictures in their *drowned rat* status, and spent some time moseying around the rocks near the car so the sun could dry them out a bit before they got in and headed back down the canyon.

They checked into a room in Boulder, thankful that they had followed their instincts and brought along overnight bags and a change of clothes. After they cleaned up and had a bite to eat, Lisa called Dick, hoping to catch him before he called Yuma. She did, and he was glad that her headache had subsided and that they had had such a good day in the mountains...in *their* special place at the 'beginning of the world'. He was just sorry that he hadn't been able to be there to share it with her. They both agreed that they needed to go back there together, and wondered why they had waited so long.

Lisa and Becca sat out by the pool in the balmy evening, sipping cokes and talking about their day. There was nobody in the pool, and they jokingly regretted that neither of them had had the 'bright idea' to bring along their swim suits. Then Becca said, "I want to do some work on that memory...it's never going to let me alone until I get it figured out. But, Lisa, I'm also scared."

"And what are you afraid of?" Lisa asked.

"I'm afraid...that I'll find out something...terrible. Something I really don't want to know."

Lisa leaned over and took Becca's hand, "Your mind...already has all the answers...to all the questions you have about the past. It's just up to us to find the right key...the right word...to unlock the door. And if it will make you feel any...less afraid...remember that you are here. And you are perfectly safe...so, whatever else that memory is about...no matter how bad it might be...it's also about survival. Your survival."

Becca had had her head down while Lisa was speaking, but now she looked up with a spark in her eye, "Yes! That's right! It is about my survival, isn't it? I *am* here. So...whatever else happened...I survived! I *am* here!" She smiled, bravely, "Well, let's get started, then."

Lisa smiled at her, "O.K then, let's get started. Take in some deep, deep breaths and let them out slowly...relaxing. You are feeling no tension, just pure relaxation...like being at the beginning of the world...before anything could ever go wrong...just relax." Lisa felt the tension slowly ebbing out of Becca's hand. "That's right, now...close your eyes. Now, Becca, I want you to go back...back to the night you were in that house." Becca nodded, serenely, her eyes closed. "Now, you are watching the men. And Daddy calls for Hank to come and help him...and then they carry the man out. Do you see them take him out?" Becca nodded, slowly, sighing. "Now where are you and what do you see?"

"At da window. See dem put him in tar." Becca's countenance changed to one of terror. "I tared! Daddy...don't leeb me!" she cried.

"It's OK, Becca" Lisa patted her hand. "Now, tell me...where does the car go? Can you see it going away?" Becca nodded. "OK. When it gets to the road...can you still see it?"

Becca strained forward in her seat, trying to follow the car, "Uh huh. Me see it."

"Which way does it turn, Becca?"

"Dat way...tar go dat way," she said, pointing to the right.

"Oh, they didn't go back to town, then," Lisa mused. "OK, Becca, what happened then?"

Becca shrugged her shoulders, sadly, on the verge of tears. "I dunno."

"Think, Becca...what happened next?"

"She...tame down tares. Dot water. Wash floor."

"Who? Who came and washed the floor, Becca?

"Da lady dat smell bad. She say she always dot to tlean up dare messes. She berry mad."

"And...did she take care of you?"

Becca shook her head, "Oh, no...she doe back up tares. Leeb me. I try." She clouded up like she was about to burst into tears.

"Don't cry, Becca. I'm right here. You're safe, remember?" Becca nodded, her lower lip quivering. "Now honey...did anybody else come?" Becca shrugged her shoulders. "Think. Think back, we aren't in any hurry. Did you go to bed...in that house?" Becca shook her head, sadly. "No? Well...what did happen after that? Did anybody come...and talk to you...anybody at all?"

Suddenly Becca sat up straight, excited, "Tar tumming! Oh, Daddy tumming! I be dood, Daddy! I doe home now!" She smoothed her hair with her hands and wiped her eyes. "Hear Daddy tumming!" Then her eyes clouded over in shock and dismay, "It not...my Daddy."

"Who...who is it, Becca? Who came in the car?"

Becca sniffed and rubbed her nose. "Dunno. I dunno. Man an lady tum. I dunno dem."

"What do they do?"

"Dey say, 'Well...what are you doin' here?' Put me in tar...an doe way. I tared! I trying. Daddy not fine me! I tared! I *berry* tared." She started to cry.

"All right now, Becca, I want you to wake up when I count to three. And when I count to three you are going to remember everything you have told me...even where those people took you when they left the house...and you won't be afraid. You'll feel very well, and not be afraid at all. OK?" Becca nodded, and her sister counted; one, two, three.

They sat there in silence for a few minutes, then Becca shook her head. This gets weirder by the minute! What do you think?" She leaned toward her sister, "Can this really be...*real*?"

Lisa nodded. "Oh, yes, I think it's real, Becca. Much *too real*!" She sat quietly thinking, then said, "Tell me about those people, the man and woman who came and got you."

"Well, they were both very well dressed...in suits. The lady even had a perky little hat on! They looked like they had just come from some...uh, something...like maybe a banquet or something. Oh...and they were both tall and slender. Well, at least they seemed tall to me, but since I was so little...anyone would have seemed tall. Right?" she laughed.

"I suppose so," Lisa agreed. "Can you recall anything else about them...like maybe their names? And... did they speak with the other woman when they came in?"

Becca was shaking her head, "No...that's the funny thing, you know. They came right over to me when they came in...like they already knew I was there. And...they didn't speak to anyone else. Just took me and put me in their car...between them, in the front seat. The man didn't say much...but he seemed ...well, at least not scary, you know? And the lady...Beverly...that's what he called her...was very nice. She kept telling me that everything was going to be OK. And she put her arm around me...and..." Becca closed her eyes a moment, straining hard to remember, "she kissed me. She kissed me...on the top of my head, and patted me. She also smelled good...not like that other one. So...who were they?"

"You said her name was Beverly...did she call him anything?"

"Uh...I don't think so. No, wait. Yes...she did. When he started to put me in the back seat...she stopped him," Becca searched her mind for the exact words, "and she said, 'No, Bob! Put her up here...with us.' That's right. She called him *Bob*!"

"All right! Now...where did you go...when you left the house with Beverly and Bob?"

"I'm not sure..."

"OK. Which way did their car turn, when you left the driveway?"

Becca smiled, "Uh...that way!" She pointed to the left. "We turned left! Back...toward town. They had the car radio on...and she was humming something that was playing on it. Actually, they seemed very nice." She was quiet for some time.

Finally Lisa asked, "Anything else?" Becca shook her head and sighed. "Well...that's OK, then. We've certainly done enough probing for one night!" Lisa said, patting Becca on the shoulder. "Let's give it a rest for now."

"Yeah...lets. Boy am I dead dog tired tonight! That bed's gonna feel really good." Up in their room, Becca was in bed and Lisa was brushing her teeth, when suddenly Becca sat bolt upright. "So... where do you suppose they took him?"

Lisa motioned that she couldn't hear while brushing her teeth, so Becca sat there cross-legged on the bed until she finished. Then she asked again, "So...where *do* you think they took him?"

"Took who?" Lisa asked, sleepily, climbing into bed.

"Who do you think, silly? The *dead guy*!" To Lisa's blank look, she added, "Daddy...and the other man, Hank...or whatever his name was. I just can't help but wonder where they took him. You know...in all that vast emptiness out there...with nothing but miles and miles of sand and sagebrush ....they could have dumped him most anywhere. And no one would have been the wiser." She was really getting into it, now. "Well...just think about it, Lisa. They could have even dumped him on our Grandpa's back forty, for that matter."

"Yeah...or down an old cistern somewhere," Lisa mumbled, absently. "Good night. Becca...sleep well."

"Good night..." Becca lay there thinking about that for a few moments, then rolled toward her sister. "Uh...Lisa? I know I should know this, but...what's a cistern?"

"Oh...you know. One of those...things..." Her groggy voice was barely audible, trailing off into nothingness, "that you store water...in."

"But...don't you store water in a well?" Becca waited, but there was no answer. Lisa was out like a light, so she rolled over and turned off her light. "Good night," she said softly. She did not get, nor expect to get, a reply.

CHAPTER THIRTEEN

They woke early the next morning and decided to go further up into the mountains; make a day of it. Heading north out of Boulder they picked up highway 7 between Longmont and Lyons. Lisa wanted to take Becca to Ward and Nederland, places their mother had lived when she was a girl. Her father had worked for a time in the gold and silver mines around there, but never had a claim of his own. He eventually ended up in the coal mines, where he got black lung., dying in his fifties. Their mother remembered their life there as a meager existence at best.

Her father's father had worked in mines at Central City and Cripple Creek, until he and a partner had staked a claim of their own. They had actually done pretty well for awhile, until the claim they shared in life became their shared tomb in death. And, according to their mother, the family was so devastated by his death, that they could not bring themselves to reopen the claim, and, over time, had even lost track of where it had been. All Lisa could tell Becca was that it was somewhere between Cripple Creek and Victor.

While lunching at Nederland they decided to go on to Central City, and they spent several hours nosing around there before heading on down to Denver and back out to Yuma. It was very late when they arrived at the Motel, but there was a message for Lisa to call home when she got in...no matter what time it was.

A very sleepy Dick answered on the seventh ring, "Yes...who is it? Lisa...Oh, yeah, Lisa...are you OK?"

"I'm so sorry to be calling you in the middle of the night like this, but the message said to call...no matter what time I got in...so, I thought there might be something wrong. Is everything all right?"

"Yeah...oh, yeah. I was just worried...when I couldn't get you. Are you OK?"

"Yes, I'm fine...and Becca's fine. We just spent more time in the mountains than we had originally planned when I talked to you last night...so it took longer to get back out here. We had a great day. I just wish you could have been here with us. Now, you'd better go back to sleep, since you have to be in court in the morning. I'm so sorry...about waking you."

"It's OK...I'd have been worried if you hadn't. Glad you're having fun...with Becca. See you in the morning."

Lisa laughed, "I don't think so...not in the morning..." But, she could tell he didn't get it. He was way too tired. "I love you. Now you go back to sleep. I'll talk to you tomorrow night."

"Love you, too!" he echoed. "Talk to you...later," and the line went dead.

Lisa sat smiling to herself for a moment before hanging up. Becca called out from the shower to see if everything was all right. "Yes...Everything's just fine. He was worried about us." She sat there thinking about how nice it was to have someone to worry about you, when Becca came out of the bathroom.

"I couldn't hear you...in there. Was everything all right?" She asked again.

Lisa smiled, "Yes...everything's all right. And I was just thinking...how nice it is to have someone...care… that much, that you can wake them up in the middle of the night...out of a sound sleep, when they have a full plate tomorrow and need every bit of sleep they can get...just to tell them you're OK."

Becca feigned disgust, "Well...you don't need to gloat! Some folks...maybe...would just rather not be smothered to death!"

Lisa laughed, "You're absolutely green with envy, girl. And don't try to deny it. It won't do you any good!"

"You're right about that," Becca sighed. "I really *do* envy you. Now, why can't I find someone as nice as Dick? Sometimes I think the good ones...the really, *really* good ones..." She made a casting motion, then pretended to reel her line back in, "have all been *catched!*"

"Oh, now, Becca...there are other fish in the sea. I'm sure of it..."

Becca interrupted, "Yeah...there may be other fish in the sea. But...I'd rather have a man, thank you! I can get fish at any good restaurant!" she laughed. Then in a very dramatic tone, sang, "But, where oh where...has my little man gone? Oh where, oh where could he be...?" Laughing, Lisa joined her, "With his ears cut short, and his tail cut long...Oh where, oh where...could he be?" They dissolved in giggles.

Then Lisa, mocking seriousness, sat up and said, "Well, maybe...*that's* the problem! You've been treating them like stray dogs for so long...you just can't keep one around!"

And giggling, Becca replied..."No...you see, dogs actually get pretty good treatment at my house...I feed 'em...I pet 'em..." then rolling in laughter she added, "...then I make 'em stay outside. Now, I ask you, who could ask for anything more?"

At breakfast the next morning they decided that before they went back out to their Grandfather's place they should go on down to Wray and find out who currently owned it. Their waitress, Dena, told them that she *thought* a friend of her boyfriend was running some cattle out there...if it was the place she had in mind...but she didn't think he owned it. It seemed, he ran cattle in several different locations...anywhere there was some land just standing idle. If someone objected...well, he'd just move his herd to another location. No harm done.

100 MILES FROM NOWHERE: murder remembered

Lisa asked, "I don't suppose this fella...has a name?" Dena just stood there chewing her gum, like she wasn't sure she should volunteer any more information...but at the same time wasn't sure that there should be any reason not to either...when Lisa asked another question. "Well, I'm...just wondering...if *this fella* happens to drive a dark blue Ford pickup...with a camper attached?"

Dena grinned, "Yep...that's him. Name's Rob. Robert." She grinned. "Like I said...I don't think he owns the place. Just has some of his herd on it."

"We understand." Becca chimed in. "So...how would we get in touch with this Rob?"

"Oh, I...well, he comes in here, pretty regular. I could have him get in touch with you...at the motel. *If* he should come in...anytime soon." She took Lisa's money, making change for her.

"Well, that would be very nice. Thank you. He could just leave a message at the desk, if we're not in." Dena nodded, telling them to come in again, and pocketing their tip, she headed over to clear their table.

Becca waited for Lisa to unlocked the car, then climbing in she chuckled, "Friend of her boy-friend, my eye! What'cha wanna bet, he *is* the boyfriend? And...first thing tomorrow morning every head of beef will be off'a that place."

"Yep...I think you sized it up pretty good, Sherlock..." then, looking at her gas gage, Lisa whistled. "And...first thing *this morning*...we've gotta round up some gas...or you and I will be hitching a ride to Wray!" While Lisa pumped the gas, Becca cleaned the windshield, and then they were on their way.

It took several hours to do a title search. And in the end they were surprised to learn that the last owners had defaulted on their bank note...which had left the bank holding the paper on their Grandparents homestead. They were having a piece of pie in a restaurant in Wray, when it suddenly dawned on Lisa that she could actually buy the property from the bank. Leaving their pie, they headed straight for the bank.

Lisa was absolutely giddy. Sitting there at the banker's desk she put in a call to Dick, "I want it!" she ex-claimed, after telling him all the particulars. I have that small inheritance from Mama, you know...and I...I'm just going to buy it. No...no, I don't know exactly what I'll do with it. Maybe rent it out for pasture. There seems to be a need for pasture land here. I don't know all the in's and out's...all the particulars…but it feels right...for me to buy it! And," she continued, "after checking with some local realtors...I think this is a pretty good price. In fact, it looks to me like we're getting a bargain."

Lisa had Dick work out the transfer of funds with the banker, while she and Becca went back to the courthouse to clear up a little matter of outstanding back taxes. Then they hurried back to the bank, where the paperwork awaited Lisa's signature. And a short time later, they were on their way back to Yuma.

Lisa had been driving in stunned silence for a few minutes, when suddenly she pulled over to the side of the road, put the car in park and, turning to Becca, exclaimed, "I did it! Becca, I did it! Can you believe...what I just did?"

Becca squealed, "Yes...I do believe...you did it!" They sat there exulting at the turn of events, both talking at the same time, laughing. A Highway Patrol car pulled up beside them, and they were both so giddy that the officer wasn't sure that they hadn't been drinking. He had Lisa get out and do a sobriety test, just to be sure, but she was able to convince him that they were just excited. That they would have gotten out of their car and danced a jig... except that they didn't want to take a chance on some snake joining them! Chuckling, the officer told them that it probably was a good thing that they had pulled over...since they were so obviously *high* on their good fortune. Then he congratulated them for getting the property back, sharing how his family had been on their land continuously for ninety some years, and, with a wave and a touch to the brim of his hat, he was gone.

Even though it was late in the day when they got back to Yuma, they drove out to the property anyway. It was dusk, so they didn't get out of the car. They just sat there in front of the house talking and sharing their jumbled thoughts and feelings. Then, when it was finally quite dark, Lisa turned the key in the ignition and they drove back to town.

CHAPTER FOURTEEN

The next morning Lisa and Becca were still giddy from the previous day's exploits and decided to celebrate at breakfast with Belgium waffles topped with strawberries and whipped cream, with a slab of Virginia sugar cured ham and lots of hot black coffee...standard celebration fare at Lisa and Dick's house.

"I wish Dick could be here to celebrate with us," Lisa said, pushing back her plate with at least a fourth of the waffle and a pretty fair sized piece of the ham left on it. "And...to help me finish this off! I'm so stuffed... can't eat another bite." Seeing that Becca was also about done, she beckoned for Dena, who was chatting with a customer at the bar.

Becca looked up and grinned. "Guess who's playing patty-cake with our waitress?" She didn't wait for an answer, but continued with just a hint of a pause, "Yep...you're absolutely right...Rob...of the blue Ford pick-up! And don't look now, but they're *both* coming to bring us our check!"

"Well...hello Ladies!" Rob said, sliding into the booth with Becca. "I thought you two had run off to the mountains to play!"

"I told him you were asking about...*that property*...south of town, you know?" Dena said, replacing her gum with a fresh piece. "It's like I said...he don't own..."

Rob, interrupted, grinning, "Na...I don't own it. Been gonna make 'em an offer...but never quite got around to it. Just been runnin'a few of my herd out there. Dena, Honey, why don't you get me a fresh cuppa coffee." He smacked her on the rear as she hurried off to fetch and carry.

"Well, Rob..." Lisa started, "That old place was our grandparent's homestead. If we're talking about the same place."

"Oh, I reckon it's the same place. Lotta trees 'round it. Old ones...been there nearly a hunnert years er so. Gotta lotta old stuff in the barn. That sound like the same place you're talkin' about?"

"Lisa smiled. "Well, yes...it does *sound* like the same place."

He took a swig of his coffee. "Now...this is good'n hot, Sweetheart. Thanks a lot! He motioned for Dena to sit down on his knee, which she was only too happy to do, then added, "Well, I just wanted you Ladies to know that I'm a'goin' down to Wray this morning, to tie up the loose ends. So I can take possession of the old place..." He chuckled, "Legally, that is! And I want you to know...that I'll take right good care of the place."

Becca and Lisa shared a glance that said, "Yeah, right! With your cattle running loose in the house!" But Lisa merely said, "You're too late, Rob. I bought the note from the bank, yesterday." She gave that a moment to sink in, then added, "Actually...we were absolutely thrilled when we found out that we could buy it. But...you know...before we leave...I was thinking that maybe we could work out something with you..."

The news clearly took the wind out of Rob's sails. His eyes narrowed and he put down his cup. "Like what?" He asked, soberly. "Just what did you have in mind?"

"O...I don't know for sure...since I just now thought of it. But...there ought to be something. Like maybe a care taker...in exchange for grazing rights." She stood up to go, picking up their check. "Let's both give it some thought. See if we can work something out, OK?" She smiled, shaking his hand. "It would be good to know there is someone looking out for the place...keeping the buildings repaired...and free from animals."

"And snakes..." Becca added, as Rob stood up to let her out of the booth.

"Right...and snakes." Lisa said. After paying for their breakfast, Lisa turned and waved at Rob, who was too dumbfounded to do anything but stand there with his mouth open. "You will give it some thought...I hope," she called out, stepping through the door. He nodded, tipping his hat.

"How come you look like you just took a pie in the face?" Dena asked, as Rob stepped up to the cash register to pay for his coffee.

"How come you ask such dumb questions?" He grumbled back, stacking the exact amount of change for his coffee on the counter, and heading for the door.

"Hey! Where's my tip?" Dena called after him.

"See *you* later," he grinned good naturedly, flipping her a quarter.

"Gee...thanks!" She laughed.

Rob climbed into his pick-up, but before leaving, he put in a call on his cell phone to the Farmer's State Bank in Wray...confirming for himself that Lisa had, indeed, bought the property. Swearing softly under his breath, he asked, "Well...why didn't you at least call me...and...well, so I could have made a counter offer? You knew I wanted that place!"

"No...what I knew was...that you were content to *use* the place...free. You remember? I called you when we took over the note. That was three years ago, Rob. You could've had it then...or anytime since then. If you wanted it so bad...why haven't you been in to see me? Well...it matters little now. It's gone...and I'm glad that those women...were able to get it back. It seemed to mean a lot to them to have it back in their family. I'm happy for them. They're nice people."

"Yeah...they're nice people, all right...but," he swore again, "I sure wanted that land!"

"Well...obviously...not enough. And, Rob...I'd appreciate it if you didn't swear."

"Oh...yeah. Sorry. Bad habit." Hanging up, Rob pealed out of the parking lot, leaving rubber in his wake. "Man!" He swore again, striking the steering wheel with his open palm. "You could've called me!" He headed toward the auction barn to keep an appointment with a man who had a prized bull for sale. "You *should've* called me!"

Meanwhile, Lisa and Becca were heading south toward what they had started calling the 'old home place'.

This time Lisa wanted to take a good inventory of the property. She had brought a notebook and the camera along to document everything.

CHAPTER FIFTEEN

It was fifteen minutes until ten when they pulled into the driveway, and the day was beautifully clear. There wasn't a cloud in the sky, although the forecast was calling for rain late in the afternoon. They sat in the car a few moments, taking it all in.

Finally Lisa broke the silence. "Well, let's go see what I bought," she said, getting out of the car. Then, chuckling, she added, "Reminds me of the one Jesus invited to his feast, who asked to be excused because he had bought some property...and needed to go see it." She struggled to get the door open, then continued, "People usually *do* see the property *before* writing the check! Of course, one could argue, I had actually seen it, first...but just barely!"

Becca laughed, "Right! I wouldn't have called our first look comprehensive!"

"Let's start with the upstairs," Lisa said, leading the way, camera slung around her neck, and notebook and pencil firmly in hand. "You know, I don't think I even made it up this far...that other time."

"You didn't...but I did," Becca said, breathlessly. "You were too busy taking pictures, downstairs..."

Lisa interrupted, "Yeah...and then you called for me to come outside with you...and we never got back." She stopped and whistled, "Not bad!" she said, moving from room to room. "Not a stained ceiling anywhere. Which means we've got a pretty good roof up there." There was an old badly stained mattress on the floor of one room. "Seems...we've had an occupant," she mused, wandering into the next room. "I started to say 'at least they cleaned up after themselves, but I guess that was too good to be true." The room before her was completely strewn with refuse, including empty food tins. "Well...I'd say...it's been awhile." She picked up a newspaper dated in the 1980's. "I'll be surprised if there aren't mice..."

"Or rats!" screamed Becca, jumping back from a closet door she had just opened. "Will you look at the size of that critter!"

"Becca...shut that door! Don't let that mouse in here!"

Becca laughed, "As if it needed an invitation!" slamming the door. "I don't think anything...like a closed door...will stand in it's way," she shuddered. "I'm ready to go down stairs...any time you're ready."

"Yeah..." Lisa grinned. "Don't tell me you're scared of a little mouse...at least it wasn't a snake!"

"Well, let's just say I'm not overly fond of anything that spends the better part of it's life crawling around in the dirt." She shuddered again. "Gives me the heebie-geebies!" She went to the head of the stairs, "You 'bout ready to go down?"

"I guess." They checked out the rest of the house, making notes and taking pictures of each room, assessing damages as they went. But for all the minor repairs the place needed, Lisa determined that it was pretty sound, structurally. The rooms were fairly large with high ceilings...and old. Looking at the old lighting fixtures, Lisa exclaimed, "Just look at those lights! And I'd bet anything that's the original wiring! Of course *it* will need to be replaced, but I really like those old fixtures." She leaned into the kitchen doorway. "Well, there has been some attempt to bring the kitchen into the twenty-first century...but that old sink will have to go. It's not antique...just old and worn out! Just think, Becca...this is where our Grandma spent most of her waking hours."

Becca nodded, "Oh, yeah...slaving over a coal stove, cooking three meals a day. I'm so glad I was born when I was!" she said, wryly.

There was a full basement under the house with a large coal furnace, and a bin under one window that still held a remnant of coal. "Look...that window is where they dumped the coal into the bin. I wonder if the furnace still works." Lisa said, mostly to herself. The outside entry was blocked by an old chest of drawers piled high with odds and ends. Together they pulled the chest out and tried the door. It was hard to open, but finally did so revealing an inner curtain of dense cobwebs, which Lisa knocked down with an old broom she found in a corner. The entry way smelled musty, it's cement steps layered with the accumulated dirt and leaves of many years. And when Lisa pushed on the sloping outer doors that covered the entrance they wouldn't budge. "Probably locked from the outside," she mused. Closing the door, they moved the old chest back into place. "It's worked pretty well, so far...might as well stick to what works," she said. "Let's go see what that entry way looks like from outside."

Just as she suspected the outer doors were padlocked. "Well...I guess we'll have to have that cut off...so we can put a new lock on. One that has a key…"

Becca interrupted, "Look how the sand has blown and shifted up to that door. No wonder it was so musty...any run off goes right down the cellar steps. But, you know…we could take care of that, ourselves, with a shovel..."

"Yeah...we could. There's one in the shed...there..." Lisa waved her hand, "at the corner of the barn."

Becca looked surprised. "There is?"

At her question Lisa looked up, "Yeah…there's one there in the little shed..." She stopped herself.

"How do *you* know there's one in the shed?" Becca asked. "We haven't checked out the shed...yet?"

Lisa looked bewildered, then stammered, "Uh...well...the other day...when we were here..."

Becca was shaking her head. "We didn't go into the shed. Remember? You had a headache in the barn...then we left. Lisa...we never made it to the shed."

"Well...I don't know...how I know." Lisa looked confused, shaking her head. "Uh...Daddy..."

"Daddy what?" Becca asked.

"Daddy..." Lisa was still a moment, then she continued, "Daddy...uh...I don't *know* what. Now, that's weird. I don't have the foggiest notion of what I started to say about Daddy." She started to walk toward the shed. "Well...shouldn't we go and see...if there really is a shovel in that shed?"

"I guess so," Becca answered, catching up to her sister. The shed was padlocked, like the outer cellar door. "Well...at least we know you haven't been prowling around in the shed in your sleep," Becca chuckled. She walked around to the side of the building where there was a small window, plastered with years of muck. Taking a wad of tissues out of her pocket, she rubbed a clear spot in the window and peeked in. The first light in many years shone through that little spot, illuminating the contents within, and Becca stepped back in disbelief. Coming back to Lisa she nervously queried, "All right, Miss Psychic, what kind of shovel...did you just happen to think...*might be* in the shed?"

Lisa laughed. "Well, let's see." She closed her eyes with her hand on her forehead, pretending to be a Psychic. "I see...I see...just your standard, run of the mill, pointed shovel...with blue paint almost worn off of the handle. But...wait a minute. I see...oh, my gosh...not just one shovel...but two. There are two shovels in the shed! And one is...or was...blue at one time." Lisa shivered, opening her eyes. She looked as if she had seen a ghost.

An ashen faced Becca took her hand, and pulling her along, said., "Look. Look in there, Lisa...and tell me what you see.

Staring through the clearing Becca had made in the window, Lisa's hand flew up to cover her mouth, as she exclaimed, "Oh...my...Dear Lord!" She could clearly see the sole contents of the shed. There was a wheelbarrow, a ladder, and two shovels. And one shovel had just a hint of blue paint left on it.

In shock, Lisa backed up, her mouth open. "I...I need to get out of here!" she blurted out. And turning around, she started walking quickly back across the yard to the house. Her heart hammering, she suddenly had the crazy urge to run. Then she *was* running...running in that sand that kept trying to hold on to her, not letting her get away! "No...no...no!" She heard herself screaming. "No...I have to get out of here!" Then she was at the corner of the house, breathlessly leaning against it for support.

And then Becca was beside her, rubbing her back, asking, "What is it? Lisa...what happened back there?"

Lisa was shaking. "I have to sit down," she said, making her way around to the front stoop of the house. "Becca, my head is splitting. Will you please get me some Excedrin...my purse...in the car. And bring my water bottle." She was holding her head, rocking back and forth, when Becca returned.

"Tell me what's happening." Becca said, opening the Excedrin and pouring the tablets into her sister's hand.

"What do you mean...what's happening? Nothing's happening." Lisa swallowed the pills, hard, almost choking on them. "Nothing...is happening!" she said emphatically.

"Well...I'm no therapist...but even I can connect the dots, sometimes. You get a headache every time we come out here. And...now this stuff about the shovels...and running in sand crying *'no, no, no'*... So? What is *that* all about?"

Lisa shook her head and blinked, "Oh...I don't know...Becca. I really don't know what's going on!"

"Well,...in the words of this not too famous therapist I know...your mind does. Remember?"

"Oh...so...you're saying...that I'm having memories? Flashbacks?" Lisa grinned weakly.

"If it walks like a duck, and talks like a duck...It probably is a duck. Isn't that how the old saying goes?"

"Hun uh. No...I don't think so." Lisa protested, weakly, getting to her feet and heading toward the car. "Maybe we should just call it a day...and..."

"And run away...like a scared little rabbit," Becca said, walking toward her sister. The words jolted Lisa, bouncing around in her head like a ping pong ball. "*Scared little rabbit, scared little rabbit, scared little rabbit*!"

"No...no...stop! Stop it...I say!" Lisa covered her ears to block out the sound of that voice, repeating, "*Scared little rabbit! Scared little rabbit*!" Only suddenly it wasn't her sister's voice. "Stop it! Stop it, Daddy! Please! Please, stop it!" she wept.

Then Becca was holding her, "OK...OK. What was it I said, Lisa? What do you want me to stop?"

Lisa looked at Becca, blinking in confusion, then, lifting her eyes heavenward, she whispered, "Oh, Dear God,...what is this all about?" Suddenly drained, she went back to the front stoop of the house and sat down. Becca joined her, and they sat quietly, watching the clouds gather, but without seeing them. Finally Lisa spoke.

"OK. Supposing this is some sort of memory...trying to surface. I'd just as soon get it over with. So, what do we actually have? We have this place...that I just bought...but, supposedly, had never laid eyes on until this trip. And...I seem to be running...in the sand. And I'm obviously terrified. So...what else is there?" She sat quietly for a few moments, then, turning to Becca, said, "Ask me. Ask me questions. And let's see if I have the answers."

"But...I don't know what to ask." Becca blustered. "What...what should I ask?"

"Anything. Just...whatever. Whatever comes to your mind. Go ahead."

"OK. Well...OK. So...how old are you...when you're running?"

Lisa sat, quietly searching for the answer. Finally she said, "I'm ten. I was ten on my last birthday...in January."

"And...where are you?"

Again Lisa took her time, speaking only when she was sure of the answer. "I'm...a hunnert miles from nowhere."

"How do you know, where you are?"

"Daddy said. A hunnert miles from nowhere."

"Do you recognize this place...does anybody live here?"

Lisa shrugged, "Huh uh. I've never been here before. Don't know who lives here."

Becca, hesitated, then asked, "OK...so....what are you doing here?"

Lisa looked frightened. "Can't tell." She jumped up and went around the corner of the house. Becca followed. "I can't talk to you. Daddy said. Can't talk to anybody!" She hurried away, up the slope behind the house.

Becca called, "Wait, Lisa. Wait for me." She hurried to catch up, joining Lisa at the top of the ridge. Together, they turned and looked down on the house and yard. "Sure looks different from up here," Becca panted.

Suddenly the light dawned in Lisa's eyes. "Becca...I *have* been here before. And you're right, it looks very different from up here. We...came into the yard *this way*...that's why it seemed so unfamiliar. We...came in this way. Look, you can still see the faint car ruts. *This* is where the driveway used to be." Dazed, she turned around and took a few steps back up the newly discovered old road.

"Lisa! Don't go there! There might be snakes!" Becca called. "Come back here!"

The word *snake* snapped Lisa out of her daze. "Oh...right...snakes. Well, I'd just as soon not meet any snakes today!" she exclaimed. Then pointing at the clouds, she added, "Look, Becca...it's about to rain. I guess that's our cue to quit for today." They hurried back down to the house, and then just made it to their car when the first big drops splatted on the windshield.

CHAPTER SIXTEEN

It was a hard rain, blowing in from the southwest and dropping the temperature several degrees in just a matter of minutes. Lisa had her windshield wipers going as fast as they would go, and she was still having a hard time seeing. They went straight to the restaurant when they reached town, but the rain was still coming down so hard that they just sat there in the parking lot for a few minutes waiting for it to let up enough for them to make a run for the door. Then it was over, just as quickly as it had begun, and the sun broke through in dazzling brightness. Going in, they sat by a window overlooking the steaming parking lot.

"I'm always amazed at how quickly storms come and go in Colorado," Becca said, picking up her menu. "They just blow in, and blow right back out!"

"Yeah. I was trying to remember that thing Mama used to say...about Colorado storms," Lisa mused. "It went something like...*it's as if God's in a gosh awful hurry to get someplace...and He*..." she rubbed her temples, trying to remember the rest.

Becca grinned, "Oh, I remember that. *And He doesn't have time to wait...around...*"

"Oh, yeah...that's it," Lisa interrupted. "*...And He doesn't have time to wait around...on the likes of us!*" They finished together, laughing. Just then Dena arrived to wait on them.

"Well, you two seem to be enjoying life," Dena said, whipping out her pad. "So...what can I get you that will make your life even more enjoyable?"

"Well, Dena...I didn't expect to see you. Figured you'd gone home hours ago," Lisa said.

"Relief called in sick. So, guess who gets to pull a double?" She lowered her voice and added, "She's no sicker'n I am. Just wanted a night off. Heck, I had plans of my own! As if that really matters to anybody around here." She directed a scathing glance at her boss sitting behind the cash register. "So... what can I bring you to drink...while you're decidin' on what you wanta eat?"

They both wanted iced tea, and when Dena got back Lisa ordered the trout, and Becca had settled on pork chops. After they finished eating, they decided to go back over to the park to feed the squirrels. But, first, they stopped at the grocery store to get some unshelled peanuts.

It was a pleasant evening. The girls walked all the way around the lake, scattering peanuts as they walked along. The squirrels literally appeared out of the woodwork, chasing each other away from each choice morsel, but there was one squirrel, in particular, that stayed with them all the way. It was the little fella that they had fed on their first evening in the park, and when the girls finally sat down at a table, he quickly scampered up to sit between them on the table top, begging from first one, then the other.

"My goodness...but you are the trusting one," Becca said, holding out a peanut for him to take from her hand. "So very...trusting..." The word just sort of hung out there in the open, looking for, but not finding, a place to rest. Finally Lisa picked it up.

"He, evidently, has found his world to be a good one," she mused. "And safe. He thinks he has nothing to fear from us...that we'll always be good to him."

"And *stuff him* with goodies..." Becca muttered, half under her breath. "But, my little friend...you shouldn't trust so...so easily." A cloud passed over her face, then she added, "You should be more like me." She was quiet for a time, then looking up at Lisa, asked, "So...how trusting are *you*, sister dear?" Then, not waiting for an answer, she continued, "I find it *very hard* to trust people." Then laughing wryly, added, "Maybe that's why I'm not married."

"May be. But, tell me, what do you mean when you say you don't trust people? In what way, don't you trust them?" Lisa queried, cautiously.

"Uh...well...that's a tough one. I guess, I'd have to say..." Becca struggled to find the right words, "motive. I don't trust their motives." She looked squarely at her sister. "Like, someone says they love me. Now, I don't know whether that's true or not. How *do* you know?" Again, not waiting for an answer, she rushed on, "Heck, I never even knew whether my own Mother loved me..." Suddenly her eyes were swimming, and she had to blink several times, to keep them from spilling over. "Lisa...I just don't seem to get it! I tried so hard...always taking her things, checking on her, making sure she didn't need anything… but, you know what? Even though she often told me that she loved me...she died...without me *really knowing* if she did." Tears were coarsing their way down Becca's cheeks, pooling in the wrinkles and laugh lines on her face. She swiped at them, haphazardly, with her hand, like a little child would.

"Oh, Honey..." Lisa went around the table so that she could hold her sister, gently rocking her back and forth, whispering, "I'm so sorry. So very sorry."

Becca wiped her face on her shirttail. Then catching her breath, she sobbed, "So, Lisa...how do you *know?* And...if you don't ever know that people love you...how do you know that God does?"

Lisa was weeping now, too, and praying, "Oh, Dear God...I don't know how to answer her. Please help me find the right words. Please." What she said was, "Becca...I don't have the right words to help you...right now...But, I asked God to help me. And I know He will." She pushed the hair back off of Becca's face. "And, Honey, I know that our Mama loved you...but I feel so sad that you didn't ever really know it. And, somehow...I think it's all connected to what happened to you...here...all those years ago."

Becca dug a tissue out of her pocket and blew her nose, "What do you mean...you think it's connected?"

"Well...in everything you have said...about those people taking you to that house...and all that... well, Mama seems to be missing from the picture. Think about it. You said that Daddy came...but when you heard the car and went to look...you had thought it was going to be *both of them*..." Becca was nodding, silently. "But," Lisa continued, "it was only Daddy. Then he left...and other people came and took you back to town. But, *where* was our Mama?" Lisa paused, then asked, "Do you want to work on that memory some more...and see if we can figure that out?"

Becca nodded, slowly. "Yeah...we could do that. Maybe it will help." She closed her eyes, and took several slow deep breaths. This time Lisa took her back to the house where Margaret and John lived, before she was snatched off of the front porch.

"Becca...do you see Margaret there?" Becca nodded. "OK...then I want you to tell me what happened when she put you down for your nap."

Becca was quiet, searching her mind for that time, then she smiled. "Mardred sing to me. Read me book. I like Mardred. Her berry nice lady."

"Who brought you to her house?" Lisa probed, gently.

Becca's face scrunched up, like she was trying awfully hard to see something that she just couldn't quite make out. "Dunno." She shook her head.

"Then maybe you can tell me, when you came there. Was it daytime...or nighttime?" Becca shrugged, she didn't know that either. Lisa puzzled on it a moment, then took a new direction. "Well, OK. So...when you were with Margaret...did she talk to you about your Mama and Daddy"

"She say...Mama love me...and Jesus love me...and Mardred love me..." Becca smiled.

"OK. Did she say anything else about Mama?"

"She say...Mama hurt." Then Becca added soberly, "She take tare ob me. Mama doe way... tause she hurt." She was quiet a moment, then added. "I try. Want to doe wif Mama. Mardred hoed me on her lap. Say Mama in hos-pit-al, tause she hurt. Becca tant doe. Stay wif Mardred."

When Lisa brought Becca back to the present, as she had done before, they sat looking at each other in amazement. Finally Becca spoke. "So...our Mama was in the hospital." Then she added, "I wonder where. What hospital?"

Lisa was clearly puzzled. "Why...don't I remember Mama being in the hospital...being hurt...and in the hospital? I was ten. So, why don't I remember that?"

"Well...remember, Lisa, you once told me...that you could remember very little...from when you were ten." Becca offered.

"Yeah...that's true. But, you'd think...I'd remember something like that. That would have affected all of us...not just you." Then, thoughtfully, she added, "But, that does explain why you were staying with other people. All of the rest of us kids would have been in school...and Daddy would have been at work...so there wouldn't have been anyone at home to care for you."

Becca nodded. "Makes sense...at least that part of it. But...I'd still like to know what all that other stuff was about!"

"I just thought of something..." Lisa said excitedly, "Mama...always wore long sleeves, because she..."

Becca interrupted, "...had injured her arm in an accident...leaving that old ugly scar!"

"Right! And she never would talk about how it happened. Maybe...that's when...she was hurt. And you stayed with Margaret." Lisa sat mulling it over. "And...if it was an accident...maybe...just maybe...there's some *record* of it...somewhere."

"Like in the local newspaper!" Becca added, excitedly. "Let's go check out the Library, and see if it has the old newspapers stored here...or if we'd have to go somewhere else to find them."

"Good idea!" Lisa grinned, making a 'chock one up' sign with her index finger.

"Yeah...*it was*, wasn't it!" Becca laughed, proudly. "Let's go."

However when they arrived at the library, it was closing for the evening, and they were admonished to "come back in the morning," by a very nice librarian, who would be "more than happy to assist them...*tomorrow"*.

"Well, that's OK." Lisa said, looking at her watch. "I really wanted to go call Dick before it got much later, anyway."

CHAPTER SEVENTEEN

After breakfast the next morning Lisa and Becca made a beeline for the Library, where they discovered all of the old newspapers preserved on micro-film. Since they didn't know exactly what they were looking for, Lisa decided to work forward from Becca's second birthday in October, 1947. It was long, tedious work and by late afternoon they were both questioning whether this was such a good idea, when suddenly Lisa cried out.

"Bingo! This might just be it, Becca. Listen to this front page article for May 18th.

Five Dead, Local Woman, Critical'

Early Sunday morning police were called to the scene of an accident northwest of Yuma, where a car driven by Katherine Hollander...Oh, yes!" Lisa exclaimed. "Yes! This *is* it. A car driven by Katherine Hollander of Yuma, ran into another car, killing it's occupants, instantly. Katherine Hollander was taken by ambulance to Denver where she is listed in critical condition. Joseph Hollander, husband of the driver, was dazed and disoriented, and was transported to the Yuma hospital, where he was held for observation and then released. A passenger in the Hollander car, Edward Bennett, was uninjured. Dead at the scene were Irene and Matthew Scarzetti of Holyoke, and their three children; Robert, 10, Daniel, 7, and Lee Anne, 5..." Lisa quickly scanned the rest of that edition. "That's it, that's all there is!"

Becca quickly loaded the next roll of micro-film on her scanner. "Maybe there's a follow up...you know...like several days later."

"Yeah...there might be. Of course, it goes without saying that we know she didn't die, but I wonder how *'critical'* she actually was. And...how long she was in the hospital." Lisa got up. "I'm going to have this article printed off." While at the front desk, she asked the Librarian if she knew anyone who would have been around at the time of the accident. She didn't. Said she, herself, would have been about five at the time and didn't remember anything about it. But, she did suggest they review some other papers, like Sterling, Holyoke, and Wray, and especially the Denver Post. She could get any of them on inter-library loan, but it might take a few days. Lisa told her to go ahead and send for them, then she went back to see if Becca had found anything more.

"Look, here, Lisa...this paper is dated June first, that's about two weeks after the accident. There's a notice that a special fund has been set up at the bank, by Reverend Bayless, to raise money for the Hollander family. It says Mrs. Hollander, who was critically injured in the May 18th car accident North of town, is still on life support at Denver General Hospital and the family is in need of both prayer and financial support." Looking up from the article Becca added, "Sooo...since she was still in the hospital at that time..." They were interrupted by the Librarian, who came to let them know she had sent for the other papers, and that she would be locking up in ten minutes.

About an hour later, as they sat lost in thought over their pot roast, an elderly couple came into the restaurant, and after speaking to the waitress, came directly over to their table.

"You those Hollander girls everbody's stirrin' about?" The woman asking was almost as wide as she was short. She drug up a chair from another table and sat herself down. "Hope you don't mind us bargin' in like this...but Fred and me have been curious...to see what all the stir's about. So...are you Kate and Joe's kids?"

Lisa nodded, "I'm Lisa, and this is my younger sister Becca. And, yes, we're Kate and Joe's kids...the two youngest ones." She paused, then asked, "So...what is it you've been hearing about *us*?"

Fred, who was a very neat little man with merry eyes, had now seated himself, and extending his hand to each of them, said, "We're yer kin. Well...sort of. I'm a cousin of yer Mama's cousin, Mary Jo Cooper. Course her maiden name was Bradly, like yer Mama's...married Cooper."

"Really!" Becca exclaimed. "That's wonderful! We hadn't expected to meet any kinfolk."

"Well...My name's Bertha. Thought you girls might like to come up ta our place ta visit a spell...an get acquainted." The effort at speech clearly winded her, and she mopped her forehead with a man's hanky fished from her apron pocket. "If'n ya wanna do that...we'll just show ya where it is. Easier'n tellin'."

"We would love to come." Lisa began. "Uh...Did...did you mean now?"

"Like Bertha says...showin's easier'n tellin'...so we'll just wait on ya ta finish up...'n then go."

Becca, laughed, "Well, this is great.! We were almost finished anyway." She beckoned for the waitress to bring their checks.

As Fred helped Bertha into the car, she hollered at the girls, "Made cake...fresh apple. Hope ya like it."

Fred turned to them and repeated, "She made fresh apple cake. Mighty good. Took a prize at the fair, last year." He went around to his side of the car and nodded to them, "Well, then...just follow us. We'll get'cha there."

They went North on 59 through Clarksville, then back to the east a few miles, pulling in at a rather large farmhouse. "Well...here she be...our little corner of the world!" Fred announced, hurrying around to help Bertha. "Let me help Mama out, here," he said, bracing himself against the open door so she could take hold of his arm and the door to pull herself up and out. "It's hard for her to get around these days." Then he scurried up the kitchen steps to get the door for the advancing party. "This way, now...we'll just go in through the kitchen, here," he said, switching on the light over the sink, then hurrying on to light up the living room. "Come on in...an' make yerself at home. Mama an' I'll just get the cake...an' be right in." He hurried into the kitchen, then popped his head back into the doorway. "Coffee? We don't usually have it this late, but...what the heck...I think I'll live it up a little this evening an' have some myself." Then he popped back into the kitchen. A moment later he stuck his head back in to ask, "Either of you want cream or sugar?" Not waiting for an answer he added, "Well, I'll bring both. Never touch either, myself..." his words just sort of hung there in the doorway, but Fred had vanished back into the kitchen.

Bertha plodded into the living room just ahead of Fred, who was carrying a tray loaded with cake plates and coffee cups. She brought a roll of paper towels. "Fancy napkins," she announced, tearing off pieces for each of them. "Seems like I'm always runnin' outta' napkins. Of course...most of them are so flimsy," she added, breathlessly, "that it takes a handful...to do the work of one paper towel." She handed the girls each a plate of cake, while Fred passed around the coffee.

"Umm, this is...so good!" Lisa exclaimed, savoring her first bite of cake.

"Oh, yes!" agreed Becca. "And…it's so nice of you to invite us out."

Lisa took a sip of coffee, then wiping her mouth, said, "I don't know why, but I never even thought we might have some kinfolk left...around here I mean. It never even entered my mind. So, have you lived here all your lives?"

Fred answered. "Yep." He waved his arm at the wall opposite the sofa, which was covered in pictures. "Thems ours. Got five kids, and they've all got kids."

"Wow...that's quite a family..." Becca started, but Bertha interrupted her.

"Well...what we want to know is...what'er you young'uns doin' around here? Got the whole county buzzin', you know."

"Really?" Lisa laughed. "I can't imagine why."

"Cause...yer strangers...an' ya been nosin' around...askin' questions," Bertha said, finishing off her cake and handing her plate to Fred. "I'll take just a smidgin more...if'n ya don't mind, Poppy."

"Anybody else...while I'm at it?" He asked, getting to his feet.

"Well...' Lisa laughed. "I shouldn't...but, why not?" And Becca handed Fred her plate too. They were both remembering one of their Mama's old adages that nothing flatters a cook like your asking for seconds. And for some unknown reason, they both wanted to flatter these nice people. Maybe it was just because they were both getting a little homesick and it was nice to have someone else to talk to besides themselves. And, after all, these people were, well, relatives...of a sort.

Bertha jumped back in, "So...ya didn't answer my question."

Lisa cleared her throat, "Well…our grandparents homesteaded...out south of Yuma. And since I'm a genealogy buff...I just wanted to know where it was..."

Bertha interrupted, "Yeah...but, ya bought it...the place, I mean." Her frankness was a little un-nerving. "Why'd ya buy it? Ya plannin' on movin' back?"

"Uh..." Lisa, was at a loss for words. But Fred returned with the cake, giving her a welcome diversion. "This cake is really wonderful. I can see how it won a ribbon," she said, reaching for her serving. "Uh...to be quite honest, Bertha, I'm not really sure *why* I bought the place…or why anyone would..." she searched for the right word, "uh...even *care*...why I bought it."

"Don't mind Mama," Fred snorted. "She's about as subtle as a freight train." He settled back into his seat. "Bet yer wonderin' how we know so gol durn much about yer business," he chuckled. Becca and Lisa exchanged glances, waiting for him to continue. "Ya see..." he was obviously pleased at his attempt to keep them in suspense, "that little waitress, Dena...she's one'a ours. Our son Jimmy's youngest. Been keepin' us filled in on yer doin's."

Bertha added, "An that no-good feller she's hangin' onto...that Rob...well, he's fit ta be tied. Wanted ta git his hands on the place...so's they could git married, he sez. Now, he sez they'll haff'ta wait." She washed down the last bite of her cake with a swig of coffee. "If'n ya ask me...she'd be better off ta let that'un go. He's not worth much...if'n ya'd asked me." She laughed, then added, "Course...nobody asked me!"

"I just thought it would be...nice," Lisa said, feeling her way along, "to have the property back in the family. Of course, I had no idea that Rob wanted it...until *after* I bought it." She grinned, adding, "He did seem a little perturbed about it."

Becca interrupted, "Yeah...I'd say it really took the wind out of his sails, wouldn't you?"

Fred slapped his knee, "That it did! That it did!"

Lisa continued, "But to answer your question, Bertha, I don't know exactly what I'm going to do with it. Possibly lease it out, for pasture. There's plenty of good grazing...on the place. But, no, I don't see myself moving back here." She paused, smiling. "Well, let's see, now...did that answer *all* of your questions?"

The old woman laughed, "Guess so." She looked at Fred, "Doesn't she remind ya of her Mama?" Fred nodded. Then Bertha grew somber. "I was so sorry ta hear of her passin'"

"You...uh...remember our Mother?" Becca asked. Then not waiting for an answer, she continued, "What do you remember...about her...about our family?"

"Well now," Bertha mused, "She was...a real sweet person. Always doin' good things fer other folk."

Fred joined in, "That she was. Real sweet. Good." He was quiet a moment, then added, "I'm real sorry she's gone. She never done anybody...no harm."

"No sirree," Bertha added. "Never done no harm. That's why we was all torn up about that car wreck...don't know how she stood it."

"You know about the car wreck?" Lisa jumped in. "What do you know...about it?"

"Well...we knew somthin' wasn't right." Fred answered. "Happened...not too far from here...you know. Just down the road a piece. Awful wreck!" He grew quiet, shaking his head, then added, "We've always said...somebody lied."

"What do you mean, somebody lied?" Becca wanted to know.

"Your poor Mama...she was hurt so bad...couldn't take up for herself...in the hospital so long." Bertha added. "Poor thing."

"But, what do you mean, Fred...when you said *somebody lied*?" Lisa persisted. "Lied about what?"

"Lied about your Mama." Fred answered indignantly. "Heck...they said she was drivin'. An' everbody around here knew that couldn't be!"

"Why...why couldn't it be?" Becca asked.

Bertha looked incredulous, "Why, honey...everbody knew...your Mama didn't drive! An' they charged her with vehicular manslaughter...an' drivin' without a license! Heck! She didn't *have* a license, cause she *didn't drive*."

"We always said yer Daddy, had ta be drivin'. An' he was all liquored up...license suspended, an' all. He and that other fella...*they* put that off on your poor Mama! An' the police bought it. An' her in a coma...couldn't tell anybody what really happened."

"But we knew! All of us...out here..." Bertha swung her arm around to include the neighbors, "We knew...your Mama. An' we knew she wasn't guilty, cause she *wasn't drivin' that car*!"

"What happened, then? Did they actually convict her...?" Lisa asked.

"Naw...they finally dropped the charges. All of us out here, we told 'em. She couldn't've done it...cause she didn't drive." Bertha declared.

"I'm confused..." Becca stammered. "Why did they think she was driving in the first place?"

"Well, ya see, by the time anybody got to the scene," Fred explained, "yer Daddy, an' that Eddie...Eddie Bennetti we always called 'im...they had moved yer Mama...laid 'er out on the driver's side 'a the road, like she'd been thrown out there, instead 'a on the other side." He shook his head, sadly. "An' those poor folks from Holyoke...they never hadda chance."

"Wow..." Lisa whispered. "That must have been awful for Mama." She looked up at Fred, and asked, "Do you have any idea how long she was in the hospital?"

"Oh, I reckon…'bout a month." He answered. But Bertha was shaking her head.

"Huh uh. Huh uh! No...It was longer'n that. Maybe six weeks...even two months. It was an awful long time." She looked at Lisa, "But, honey, you oughtta remember that...you'da been a pretty good sized kid...at that time. Don'cha remember...?"

Lisa shuddered, "Uh...no. No, I don't remember it...at all. I don't even remember the accident...or anything about it." Sometime during the discourse she had begun to rub her temples. "You know...I'm getting a doozy of a headache. Could I trouble you for a glass of water?" she asked Fred, who went immediately to fetch it. She dug around in her purse to retrieve her Excedrin, then took two with the water Fred had brought her.

Becca looked at her watch. "You know what? It's getting pretty late, and we've imposed on your hospitality long enough," she said, getting to her feet. "And when Lisa get's one of her headaches…well... the best place for her is...bed. So, maybe we'd better call it a night." She offered her hand to Lisa, who took it and stood up.

"Yes, I guess we'd better..." she said. "I want to thank you both...this has been really great...Bertha, Fred... but Becca's right...about my headaches. It looks like she might have to drive us back to town. Maybe we can get back out here...again...before we leave," she stammered, moving toward the kitchen.

"Well, you'd better...is all I can say! We'll have ya out fer supper...or lunch...so we can talk longer!" Bertha called after them, not getting up.

Becca turned and smiled at her, "That sounds wonderful, Bertha. Just let us know..." she said, taking Lisa by the arm, half guiding, half propelling her to the back door. Fred walked out with them.

"It's not hard," he said. "Ya just go on back ta 59, turn left...and it'll take ya all the way back ta town." He stood on the back stoop, watching till they were out of sight.

CHAPTER EIGHTEEN

The phone was ringing when they walked through the door. It was Dick. Lisa chatted with him for a few minutes, then climbed into bed with an ice pack on her head. Becca turned out the light and took the book she'd been reading to the bathroom, so the light wouldn't bother Lisa. Some twenty to thirty minutes later she heard a strange noise, and went to check on her sister. It was a pretty unnerving sight.

Lisa was struggling, kicking and clawing, crying out loudly, "Let me go! Please, let me go...I *won't* tell. I *won't* tell! Let me go...please..."

There was a knock on the wall from the adjoining room. "Will ya pipe down in there...I'm tryin' to get some sleep!"

Perching precariously on the edge of the bed, Becca shook her sister. "Lisa, wake up! You're dreaming, again." But Lisa was too far into the dream to be lightly shaken out of it. She struggled all the harder, clawing and punching the pillow. Becca ducked just in time to avoid a wild punch, but she never saw the knee coming, and landed squarely on the floor. The impact of her knee with solid flesh jolted Lisa awake, and she was aghast to see what she had done.

"Oh, Becca...I'm so sorry!" She scrambled out of the bed to give her sister a hand up. "I can't believe...I did that. Are you OK.?"

"Boy...sleeping with you oughta entitle Dick to hazardous duty pay!" Becca exclaimed, rubbing her back side. She pulled a chair over and said, "I think I'll just sit here, for the time being, if you don't mind."

Lisa giggled, "Can't say I blame you! Wow, I must've really...well..." she looked sheepish, "...uh, what was I doing...anyway?"

"Seemed to me you were fighting the Civil War...single handedly," Becca said, wryly. "But, actually...I think you were having a pretty scary nightmare." She sat quietly looking at her sister for a moment, then asked, "Want to...talk about it?"

"Oh, gosh," Lisa said, rubbing the back of her neck. "This just keeps getting weirder all the time. First it was running in sand. This time..." she was pensive. "This time...he caught me."

"Who...caught you? Daddy?"

"Huh uh...it wasn't Daddy. I'm...I'm not *sure*...who..." She left it hanging there, trying to peer into the darkness of her mind, to get a clearer picture. "The dark things...that we don't understand...are sometimes better off...just left there..." she whispered, "...in the dark. Undisturbed."

Becca, shuddered, "But, can you...? Can you just leave them there...undisturbed?"

Lisa's ashen face was pinched and drawn. "Truth be known, sister dear, it is *they*...who trouble us. Not the other way around. Our childish selves always run...like scared little rabbits...to hide from what is too painful to bear. And so, we become locked up inside of ourselves, hiding...thinking we are safe." She thought a moment, then went on, "When, in truth...we are cell mates with the thing we seek to hide from. So it's always there *with us* in the dark... taunting, waiting for just the right moment to pounce. And we are never quite secure. Never truly safe." She got up and straightened the tangle she had made of the sheets. Then she said, "No...It is not we who trouble the dark things ...it is they who trouble us."

Becca nodded, "Yeah, I guess. But...what do we do about it?"

Lisa jumped up, dramatically flinging her arms wide, "We throw open the windows of our minds...and let the light of God chase out every dark thing...every shadow! Jesus said, 'Ye shall know the truth...and the truth shall make you free." She sat back down, feeling a bit foolish for her theatrics.

Becca laughed. "Yes, *I know* the words...but...I'm not sure I really know...what they actually mean, Lisa."

"Well, Becca...I'm not sure if I can fully explain it to you...but I'm going to take a stab at it. When some-thing bad happens to a little child...its natural response is to run away and hide, right?" Becca nodded, then Lisa continued, 'When I was a child, I spake as a child, I understood as a child, I thought as a child: but when I became a man I put away childish things'." She was quiet a moment, then continued.

"Becca, I remember...dark nights...when I was very small and very frightened. I'd lie there in bed, wondering what was there in the room...in the dark...with me. My heart would pound and I would put my back to the wall and lie there awake for hours, watching the darkness, waiting for the sun to come up. When the first rays of daylight came through the window, revealing what was and wasn't there, I could finally go off to sleep. I would be so tired in school, I'd fall asleep at my desk. Finally, one day a very wise teacher talked to me about why I wasn't getting enough sleep. When I told her, she just smiled and hugged me...and told me, that the very next time it happened, I should get up and go to the light switch and turn it on. Then, when I had searched out the whole room, I would be able to go to sleep." Lisa got up and got herself a drink. Then smiling said, "Well...Becca...she was right. When I was able to get up and turn on that switch, I took control of my fear. And I took a little step toward being grown up. *'When I became a man I put away childish things'.* Literally, when I became full grown, I put away childish things. I no longer run and hide from difficulties...but try to face them, as a grown up."

Becca was nodding, "Yeah...I think I follow you...so far."

"Now, that Scripture goes on to say 'For now we see through a glass darkly; but then face to face: now I know in part; but then shall I know even as also I am known.' I think we see life through a glass darkly...our understanding is muddled...until we can let the truth of God...the Light of the World...shine on what we can't understand, and give it clarity."

Lisa took a deep breath, then continued. "Years ago...when I was in graduate school...I had to work through stuff...from my childhood...all grad students in my line of work have to do that, you know. Well...I thought I'd looked at anything and everything...that could possibly give me any problems...in counseling other people. However, after Mama died, these headaches...that I'd actually been having for some time...got worse." She sighed, "And now...these nightmares." Her eyes clouded over for just a moment. "But...I know...that I know, *that I know*...that the same Lord who has always appeared out of the darkness to help me in times past...will also help *me* to get through this." She took a deep reinforcing breath. "It's...just that the little child in me that wants to run...like a scared little rabbit...and hide. But...you see...when I became grown up...I put away childish things." She sat thinking for a bit, then continued. "You know, those words...*put away*...are action words. They require action on my part. That teacher taught me to actively take control over what affects me. And I will *not* let this...rather, I should say the Lord will not let this...make a little child out of me at this stage of my life. The truth...always *liberates*...brings things to the light. It never...keeps one in darkness."

"Let's us see through that glass...clearly." Becca added.

"Right." Lisa, smiled. "Ye shall know the truth, and the truth shall make you free." Then she added, "If the Son therefore shall make you free, ye shall be free indeed'. We need never again be in bondage to the 'dark things'...in our minds...that want to keep us bound and in fear. We are free...indeed." Then she added, soberly, "As long as we act on it...take it for our own. You see, until I acted on the truth that my teacher gave me, I still lay there in the darkness of the night, bound in fear. But, when I accepted what she told me...and got up and turned on the light...I was freed from the power of my fear. And it's pretty much the same with these current memories...I can hide, in fear of what might be there...or I can turn on the light, and see..."

Becca interrupted, "...and see...what really *is* there."

"Right. What *really is there*." Lisa said, emphatically.

"So..." Becca queried. "Who caught you? Who really was there?"

Lisa began, tentatively, "I don't remember much. But, I think his name was Frank. He was chasing me. Then he tackled me...and we both went down in the sand. It was an awful jolt." She paused a moment, then went on, "Like I said, I don't remember much...and what I do remember is not all that clear...but there's one thing I'm very sure of. We were out *there*...at the homeplace."

"But...why? Why...were you out there?" Becca asked.

Lisa blinked, looking curiously at her sister. "That's one thing I really don't know. But...I think...I need for *you* to tell me something."

"Oh, and what would that be?" Becca asked, apprehensively.

"In your memory of what happened at that old house...tell me again...about the man that came downstairs and helped Daddy carry the other man out. And...what did you say his name was?"

Her apprehension growing, Becca answered, "Uh...Hank...his name was Hank...I think."

"OK. Well...please think hard, Becca...and try to describe him for me?"

"He...uh...he was big...tall." She had begun to pace the floor, as if that would help stir her memory. "Yeah, tall. Taller than Daddy. And, uh...he had light colored hair...grey or white. I'm not sure, but...It just *seems* like," she ran her fingers through her own hair, "he had light colored hair. And...he wore glasses. You know, those little old fashioned wire frames?" Lisa nodded, and Becca continued. "And...uh...he was very clean and neat." She racked her brain. "Oh, and he was clean shaven...no beard or mustache...nothing like that." Now she was slowing down.

"Oh, and one other thing...he was wearing light brown...or tan...like an army uniform."

Lisa broke in, "That's gotta be him, Becca! That sounds just like the man who was chasing me!" She was quiet a moment, then said excitedly, "Becca, I want you to do like we did before. You know? Ask me questions. Ask...anything. Anything that might trigger what we were doing out there...or even what was happening before we went out there."

Becca had turned pale, and was clearly shaken. "Are you sure...you want to do this?" She stopped pacing, and turning to Lisa added, very soberly. "I'm not sure I want to. I'm not sure...I can."

"That's OK, Beck," Lisa said in her most reassuring voice. "I know it feels scary to you. It's scary to me...too. But do try to remember, it's only scary because we're dealing with the unknown. Not because what we might find out has any real power to harm us."

Becca looked a bit skeptical. "You're sure about that?"

Lisa smiled. "I'm absolutely sure. You see, Becca...we already paid our dues! Honey, we already lived through whatever it was that happened back there. And...here we are in adulthood, safe and sound...even in our right minds! So...whatever pain is associated with what happened back there...we will be able to bear it...because we *already did.* And we survived."

Understanding registered in Becca's eyes, and suddenly she smiled. "Why yes! Yes, we did, didn't we? And like Bertha, says, *If'n you'da asked me...*we survived quite well!" Her eyes twinkled. "But then, of course, nobody asked me!

Lisa gave her a hug, "Well...I'm askin'...and I'm agreein'...we survived quite well, *indeed!*"

CHAPTER NINETEEN

"All this chatter has made me *very* thirsty." Lisa said, getting up and putting on her housecoat. "I'm gonna go get us some ice. Can I get you anything from the machines?"

Becca shook her head, but then changed her mind as Lisa started out the door. "On second thought...I think I'd like a Coke...and the fizz is definitely gone outta that stuff." She gestured to the liter bottle they had had for several days. She pulled on her robe, adding, "Wait, I'll tag along. Have you got enough quarters?"

Lisa came back in and checked the coke. "You're right, this stuff has had it!" She poured what was left down the drain. "I hadn't thought of it being flat, but we have had it awhile." She searched through her change for quarters. "I've only got two...do you have some? What are drinks here...fifty, or sixty?"

Becca shrugged. "Dunno...might be seventy-five. Well, no matter. I've got a bunch of quarters, here." She laughed, "Will you look at this...no wonder my purse was getting so heavy!" She had dumped it's contents on the bed, revealing a good sized mound of change. "I've just been dumping my change in here, and not taking it out at the end of the day, like I do at home. It sure builds up in a hurry!"

Lisa laughed. "Whoa...lugging that around'll give you a hernia! But then...on the other hand...they say one way to lose weight is to carry an extra five or ten pounds around with you!"

"Well, now, maybe I oughtta put it all back, and just carry it around with me, then!" Becca laughed, digging out several quarters, and heading for the door. "But, for now, let's just go *spend* some of them."

They may as well have not bothered. The drink machine was not working. Though they could see there were drinks inside, it just kept spitting their quarters back at them. Lisa, who had already gotten the ice, rolled her eyes and said, "Oh, well...I *really* only wanted a good cold drink of water, anyway."

"Right...me too," agreed Becca. "Water...give me water lest I die!" she exclaimed dramatically, opening their door.

Lisa fixed two plastic glasses of iced water, and they sat on the bed, savoring it. "Umm...don't know what I was thinking of, wanting a Coke. Nothing satisfies like pure, clear, clean water," she declared. Then turning to her sister, she said, thoughtfully, "Listen, Becca, I know you're not exactly comfortable with the idea of playing forty questions, and I want you to know...that's O.K."

"It is?" Becca asked, uncertainly.

"It is. So don't trouble your head about it." Lisa paused, then added, "I do have another little technique that I can try." Going to the desk, she picked up the notebook she had gotten when they first came to town. "I'll just play around with some word association...and maybe journal a bit. See if that produces anything. So...unless you want to try your hand at the same thing...you are excused, my dear, to do...whatever...read, take a bath, watch TV...go to sleep...just whatever your little ole' heart desires. And, I'll just curl up here and play with words for awhile."

"Are you sure?" Lisa smiled and nodded, and Becca couldn't help feeling relieved...any more than she could help having her interest piqued with Lisa's alternative. "So...how do you do...*that*?" she asked, not exactly sure she really wanted to know.

"Well...in word association, you just write the first word, or phrase, that comes to mind," she thought for a moment, then wrote "Frank", drawing a circle around it. "Then you just write down any words that come to mind associated with it...like...'*big*'," She wrote the word "big", drew a circle around it and made a line, connecting it to her first word. "The next word might be associated with Frank, or big," Lisa continued, waiting for her next association to form. Then she wrote, "bigger than Daddy" and connected it to big. The next thought was, "nervous", which she connected to Frank, then added "tic", connecting it to nervous. "Daddy's friend" was connected to Frank, quickly followed by a question mark, which was circled, then connected to friend.

"What does that mean? That question mark, there?" Becca asked, pointing..

"I'm not sure...but when I wrote 'Daddy's friend', I suddenly wasn't sure what their relationship was. So, it's questionable...at least until something else clarifies it," Lisa explained.

Becca suddenly got a pen from her purse and asked for a piece of the paper. "That doesn't look too intimidating...think I'll give it a try."

Lisa tore off a sheet of paper, handing it to Becca, with a caution, "OK...but the one rule of thumb is to *not* censure anything. It only works if you write the actual words that come to mind...leaving nothing out...no matter how silly or improbable you may think it is."

"I got it!" Becca said, excitedly. "Let's see...I think, I'll start with '*house*'..." she wrote the word, then drew a circle around it. Then quickly followed with the word 'wrong'. "Oops," she said, starting to erase it.

Lisa quickly, put out her hand to stop the erasure. "No, don't do that." Don't erase anything...that's your mind's way of censuring!"

Becca looked frustrated. "But...that was evidently wrong..."

"No..." Lisa laughed. "The *word* 'wrong' came to your mind...so leave it...alone. Just go on to the next word that comes. And remember, *don't censure* it!"

"OK...I got it...*don't censure*." She sat with pen poised, waiting, then wrote, "wrong", then waited, and again wrote "wrong", then again, and again. "Oh, shoot!" she exclaimed, jumping up and throwing her pen up into the air. "This *isn't* working, Lisa! I'm just too dumb to get it."

"What's the matter, Beck...what isn't working?" Lisa asked.

"This!" she shoved her paper at Lisa. "All I get is '*wrong*'! It's obvious to me, that I'm all wrong. Wrong, wrong, wrong, wrong, wrong!" she exclaimed, ripping her paper in half, and stuffing it in the waste basket.

"No! No, *you're* not all wrong!" Lisa exclaimed, retrieving the pieces and putting them back together. "Look, Becca. Each time you wrote the word 'wrong'...what did you connect it to?"

"What? What do you mean...*what* did I connect it to? I connected it to...the house. Oh! I get it...it's not the word '*wrong*' that's wrong...I started with the wrong word, 'house'..."

Lisa was shaking her head, "No, no, no, no, no..." she laughed. "All of your 'wrongs' are 'right', and I think they're telling you...that you got the wrong *house*."

"Oh, man...now what? How could I have gotten the wrong house? That's the house...in my dreams." She sat down and buried her head in her hands. "Oh, Lisa...this is just too complicated. How could I have gotten the wrong house?"

Lisa sat quietly thinking, then asked, "Becca...do you remember...the second time we went to that house? It was almost dark, and you insisted on going out there...because...why?" She paused, letting that soak in, then continued, "Remember? You went inside...because, you said, *'something wasn't quite right'*...do you remember that?"

Becca was nodding, slowly, "Yeah...that's right. So...what was it...that wasn't quite right?" she whispered, mostly to herself. "Let me see that drawing I did of the place from my memory," she said. Lisa handed her the tablet with the drawings in them, which she studied diligently. Finally, shaking her head, she said, "Ah, I don't know. I'm not getting anywhere. Maybe...you should ask me some *specific* questions about the picture." She handed it back to Lisa.

"Ok. Well, Becca...the first thing that comes to my mind, in comparing this picture to the house out there, is that the actual house has no window...here," Lisa pointed to the space just to the left of the front door, "where you show one in your drawing. So...tell me again, how this window fits into the story."

"Well...It's the window that broke...when the gun fired. Little pieces of it fell down on me...and...and I had to move...out of the way! You're right! The way that house is made...there couldn't have been a window there! There isn't...room..." she finished, lamely.

"Is there anything...else...that's different?" Lisa probed. "Now, that your mind is open to accepting differences?"

Becca sat, staring at the picture, "One...one other thing...that I see...is...the stairs are all wrong. You know, the stairs going up to the second floor. See...where I have them, here?"

"Yes, I see." Lisa answered.

"Well...in the actual house out there...they come down this outside wall...instead of the back wall of the room." Lisa nodded, then Becca continued, "But, how...how could I have mistaken the place? I was so sure.."

"That's not too difficult to figure out...if you think about it. That's a pretty standard old house. If we went driving around through the country, we'd probably find several more made pretty much like that one...with minor changes..." Lisa explained.

"Yeah...I guess so. But I..." Becca paused.

"You what?" Lisa asked.

"Well, for a minute there, I started to think, that if the house was wrong...then maybe the whole memory was wrong...maybe none of it happened at all." Her look of dejection turned to determination as she added, "But...*I know*...it all happened! Just the way I said it did."

"I'm sure it did," Lisa said, reassuringly. "*And* just the way you said. That's why...*the house has to fit your memory*...not the other way around. Always remember that." She paused, then added, "Who knows? Maybe *that* house doesn't even exist, anymore, and God just used this house...with it's similarities...as a reminder of the other one."

"So then...what you're saying is…you think *God* wants me to remember it...all this stuff...?" Becca asked, childlike.

"I certainly do," Lisa said. Then, getting into bed and reaching for the light switch, she added, "I also think He wants us to get some sleep...so we'll be able to function tomorrow." Then looking at her watch, she added, "Which, by the way, it already is!"

Becca sat there in the dark for a time, thinking about what Lisa had said. "All right, God," she finally prayed, silently. "If you *really* want me to do this...then, I guess...I can. But..." she climbed into bed and snuggled down into the comfortable darkness of the room, pulling the sheet up under her chin, "but…I can't do it by myself." Then she grinned, sleepily. "OK, so *you* already knew that about me. Whatever."

CHAPTER TWENTY

When they walked into the restaurant Thursday morning Dena met them with a huge smile, "Boy, you guys sure made a hit with my Grandparents!"

"That's nice to know," Lisa answered. "We rather liked them, too."

"And your Grandma's fresh apple cake is to die for!" Becca added, dramatically.

"Oh yeah, it is good! But then, everything my Gram makes is good. Actually," she scrunched up her face, trying to find the right word, "*much better than good.* Somehow *'good'* just doesn't cut it. Anyway, my instructions are to tell you to come for lunch tomorrow...*'If'n you'd care to'*..." It was a pretty good imitation of her Grandmother. "But, I gotta warn you. Lunch with my Gram? Well...it's *the works*... not just a little lunch. So, consider yourselves forewarned." Then, lowering her voice for effect, she added, "And, if I were you, I'd skip breakfast tomorrow!" Then, whipping out her order pad, she said, "But...that's tomorrow. So, what can I get you...today?"

They both ordered the Two for Two Special; two eggs, two bacon, and two toasts, for two bucks. Quick and simple, because, they had already decided, if the micro-films had come in at the Library, they needed a lot of time to work on them. And if they had not come in, then they needed a good chunk of time to go do and do their laundry. It turned out to be the latter. They spent what was left of the morning at the laundromat.

"It's probably a good thing...that we did this," Becca said, loading her clothes into the dryers. "Otherwise, I'd have to wear my birthday suit to Fred and Bertha's!"

"Uh huh...me too," Lisa muttered, absently, starting her dryers. She was engrossed in the word association she had started the night before, having connected many descriptive words to the encircled 'Frank'. To 'hair' she had first added 'silver', then 'sparkle', then 'sunlight'. And to 'uniform' she had added 'neat', then 'tan'. Then she connected the word 'helper' to 'Frank'. After which she seemed to be stumped. She sat drawing and redrawing the connecting line to Frank, making it darker and darker, instead of going on to another word. Finally she stopped, and just sat there tapping the pencil on her pad.

Becca, watching the process, asked, "Why did you stop...? Who was Frank helping?"

"Bingo...that's it! Thank you, Becca!" Lisa said, drawing another line, connecting 'helper' to Daddy... forming a triangle. "He was helping Daddy...to do...what?" she mused, going over and over her lines connecting Daddy...to helper...to Frank...and back to Daddy, until the ever darkening triangle fairly jumped off of the page. "Whatever it was...It must have been a *very* dark business..." she half whispered.

"Why..." Becca started to ask, but suddenly stopped when Lisa wrote the words 'body' and 'dead', connecting them to 'helper'. All of the color had drained out of her face and she just sat there staring at the words she had written. Becca, who had been holding her breath, slowly let it out asking, "Where...where did the body come from?"

And, in answer, Lisa wrote and spoke the word simultaneously, "Home!" She looked up at Becca and whispered, incredulously, "From *our* home?" Shaking herself, as if from a dream, Lisa went to unload a dryer that had stopped. "From...our...home?" she repeated. "Our...home. So...what would they have been doing...with a dead body...at our house?" she asked, mechanically folding the laundry in front of her.

"And...how did you come to know about it?" Becca asked, now folding her own things.

"Good question? How *did* I know about it...?" She picked up the tablet and wrote, "Me!" in very dark letters. Then, grimacing, she suddenly connected the 'me' to 'Daddy', and muttering through clenched teeth, asked, "OK. Daddy...*dear*...just *how* am I involved in this *dark mess of yours*?" Anxiety clawed at her throat. "And...how do I even know it *is* a mess?" Angrily slamming the tablet down on the table beside her clothes, she resumed folding, desperately trying to blink back the tears.

"I'm sorry..." Becca whispered, brushing a maverick tear off of her sister's cheek with her finger. "That must feel...awfully..." she searched for the right word, finally ending lamely with, "Oh...I don't know...what!"

"Exasperating! That's what it is. Purely exasperating! And in the words of our dear departed Mother...'If I was given to cussin' and throwin' temper tantrums....," closing her eyes Lisa struggled to recall her mother's exact words, "Uh...this would be...about the right time to throw me an eyeball scorchin' fit!'..."

Becca chuckled, "Oh, our Mama! She sure had a way with words! Didn't she?"

Lisa nodded, grinning, "Yeah...'an eyeball scorchin' fit'...I always wondered where she got that one. Boy...I hadn't thought of *that* in years."

"And, I certainly hadn't heard it in years." Becca laughed. "You...really sounded like her...when you said it. You know what? I think the older you get, the more like her you become."

"What a nice thing to say!" Lisa gave her sister a quick hug. "Thank you, Becca."

"You are most welcome." Becca said, loading her laundry into a basket to take to the car. "And, I just couldn't help but think what a great idea it was...whoever thought to bring this laundry basket with us. That person sure has brilliant ideas!" she teased, in an effort to lighten Lisa's mood.

"Oh, yes...you certainly do," Lisa agreed, absently, opening the trunk and loading the laundry into it.

"Not me, silly. You. You're the one who brought it with us...from home. Remember?

"Home..." Lisa muttered, clearly preoccupied with something other than the laundry basket. "Our home." She backed out of the parking lot, but instead of turning toward their motel, she headed for the place that they had lived, once...so long ago that it seemed more like a dream than reality. "I just thought...seeing the place..." she said, parking across the street from their old home, "...might jog something loose."

It was a solidly built house, two story, with a full basement under it, and a large front porch. "We used to sit out on that porch in the evening and sing...and talk...till way past bedtime. Then Mama would get impatient and threaten us..." her voice trailed off. "Do you remember it, Becca...at all?" Becca just shook her head, as Lisa continued. "We had a porch swing, you know. And you'd crawl up in my lap and beg me to tell you stories."

"Well, I do remember how I begged you to tell me stories. One was never enough and I'd plead for just one more. Then you'd say, 'OK, but, *just one* more'."

"And then, when I'd finished, you'd say, 'Tum on, Eesie...just one more! Peas!' And you'd make me feel like an absolute cad if I didn't..." Lisa laughed.

"And you'd say...'Oh, all right, Becca, but this is absolutely the last one. Then when you'd finish...I'd start in again...and you'd give in again. And then you'd say 'But, this is absolutely, positively, the one and onliest, very last one! Do you hear me?'...and you'd clench your teeth, and pretend to pull your hair out, yelling 'you're driving me crazy'!"

"And you'd dissolve in giggles," Lisa smiled. "Now, *that's* what I call a very nice memory, all warm and fuzzy."

"You're right about that," Becca sighed, hugging the memory to herself. "Definitely warm and fuzzy!"

"You know, Mama really liked that house," Lisa mused. "For that matter, *I* liked that house. At least what I remember of it." Then she sat quietly trying to see beyond the barriers of the present, into the house of the past. Suddenly she was excitedly pointing at a sign in the yard. "Look, Becca. See that 'for sale' sign? Well...let's...let's go, and get the realtor to show us the house!" Excitement mounting, she pulled away from the curb. "I know we passed that office...somewhere on the main drag. So, Becca, you can help me look for it."

"Realtor? Lisa! You're surely not thinking..." Becca stammered. "Surely you're not going to buy another house! Not here!" Clearly alarmed, she added, somewhat facetiously, "Look, I know money's no object here, but how's Dick gonna feel about your buying up the whole town?"

Lisa giggled. "No, Silly. I don't want to buy it! I just want to...*need to*...see it. The inside, I mean. And...well...it might make those good people feel a bit nervous, if I were to ask them if I could see the inside of their house. And, it would definitely make me nervous, to see it with them present! But, you see..." she said, pulling into the parking lot, "...they won't think a thing about it, if the realtor shows it to me, since *it is for sale*!" She flashed her best smile at Becca, opening the door to the office with a flourish. "After you, sister dear."

"Brilliant!" Becca, mumbled, shaking her head in amazement. "I gotta hand it to ya kid...your brilliance is only surpassed by your moxie!"

Thirty minutes later the Realtor, Madge Philpot, of Philpot and Sterns Realty, was escorting them through the house, having asked the owners to absent the place for that time. They wandered through, room by room, and Lisa was amazed at how little the place had actually changed in all those years. It was hard work keeping check on her impulse to lead the tour and to tell Becca about their life in that house, how they had all gathered around the kitchen table in the evening to listen to the radio and do homework, while Becca played in her highchair along side of them, and how all of their heights had been recorded on the inside of the pantry door, and how she and Barb had made a secret pass through from their bedroom closet into Bill and Scott's room, and how they had always put the Christmas tree in the northwest corner of the living room because that was the area most protected from the bustling activities of five kids, two dogs and a cat.

The first year that they lived there the tree had actually been set up in another location, and was turned over not once, not twice, but three times, before it was moved to that safe corner. She imagined that the present owners also put their tree in the northwest corner of the living room, and in fact said to Madge, "...Good place for a Christmas tree...there." What she really wanted to say to Becca, but didn't, was, "That's were you unwrapped your first baby doll, and I taught you how to change it's diaper." Lisa was amazed that the house had changed so little in all those years. Even with it's different furniture, colors, and textures, when she looked at those rooms time stood still, and she was transported back to 1948. And she was all alone in that house…and her head was pounding.

Then Becca's voice broke through her reverie, drifting in from the kitchen, where she and Madge were about to descend the stairs to the basement. Lisa rushed to join them, but as she began the descent into the abyss below, her heart pounding in her ears, she had to fight the urge to turn and run. Madge was busy making a point about there being a relatively new central heat and air conditioning system, but Lisa wasn't aware of what she was saying, She was busy watching the men who were arguing at the table.

They weren't aware of her presence, and she was thinking that, if she could just slip past them into the washroom, she would be safe until they were gone. But, if she tried to go back upstairs and a creaking step gave her away...she would most certainly be doomed. Holding her breath, she soundlessly, carefully inched her way past, never taking her eyes off of them. Now, just one more step and she'd be safe! Safe, behind the washroom door. Only it wasn't to be. She tripped, sprawling backward over something lying there on the floor, and when she tried to turn herself over and get to her knees, she was looking straight into the fixed and unseeing eyes of a man, a very *dead* man. Lisa had just enough presence of mind to stifle the scream that rushed forth from her memory to break through the sound barriers of the present.

The scream ended up as a choking cough, that had Madge offering to get her a drink of water, and Becca looking very concerned. "Oh, no, thank you...I'll be all right. It's probably just...you know...musty places... Basements, always do that to me. Well, anyway...with this headache...and me getting all choked up, I guess that's a good indicator that we'd better leave."

Later, after they had explained to Madge that the house wasn't what they were looking for, and after they had taken their clean laundry back to their motel, and after they had gotten hamburgers at a drive through, and after they had fed the friendly squirrel at their table in the park, after all these things, Lisa, looking pale and drawn, said in a barely audible voice, "Something terrible happened back there, Becca."

"Uh huh...I thought so. Do you want to tell me about it?"

"Yes...but...first I need you to do something." She took her notebook out and, handing Becca a couple of sheets of paper said, "I need for you to silently write down your description of the man who got shot. And I'll do the same. Remember, just write whatever comes to you. Don't censure! And don't say anything out loud." Becca nodded, then Lisa continued, "We need to give it about five minutes...then compare notes."

They both started by encircling the words "Dead Man" in the center of their pages, and worked steadily for several minutes. The outcome was not a surprise to either of them. Becca described a smallish man, shorter than Daddy, 40'ish, with sparse dark hair, and sallow complexion, wearing a dark blue sort of uniform, with suspenders, and having a thin dark mustache. He also had a tattoo on his right hand. Lisa's description was of a man in his early 40's, with receding dark hair and blue eyes. He was dressed in navy blue, had a thin black mustache, and was smaller than Daddy, built like the old Col. Potter on Mash, small but muscular. He had blue tattoos; one on his right hand of an anchor, and one on his upper arm of a sailing ship with...with...the letters H.M.S. written above it." They sat speechlessly staring at their descriptions.

"It has to be the same guy," Becca finally said, "but, something puzzles me."

"And that is...?"

"How did you know about the other tattoo...the one on his upper arm?"

Lisa was quiet for a moment, staring at the squirrel on the branch just beyond Becca's head. "Barbie said...I was too sick to go to school," she began, haltingly. "I had a fever. And she said for me to stay home in bed. Daddy was at work...and everybody was gone but me. I didn't like having to stay home alone, but she said not to be a big baby...she had to go to school because she was having a test...or something." Lisa paused, giving the memory time. "I...had gone back to sleep, when something...a noise...woke me up. Whatever it was frightened me, so I crept downstairs...and looked through the house, the kitchen and living room...Mama and Daddy's room, but there wasn't anybody there. I thought I had just imagined it, so I lay down on the sofa and went back to sleep. When it woke me the second time, I knew it wasn't my imagination...and I was determined to prove it. Telling myself that the cat probably got itself locked in the basement, and was just trying to get out, I nervously opened the door. When the cat didn't emerge, I quietly worked my way down the steps." She sat there, eyes closed, for a brief moment. "They didn't see me... because they were busy arguing about something."

"They? Who are *they*...that didn't see you?"

"Daddy. Daddy and Frank. They had their backs to me, sitting on that old table we used for laundry. They were arguing...getting loud. Daddy sounded very angry, and suddenly I was very afraid. I thought, 'If Daddy catches me at home, when I ought to be in school, I'll really be in trouble'. I decided to try to hide in the nearby wash room, rather than chance a squeaky stair giving me away. So...I very carefully made my way to the wash room door, just inches away from safety...and I tripped on it!"

"On what? What did you trip on?"

"The dead guy." Lisa barely whispered it. "He was there...on the floor. And then Daddy had me by the arm and I was struggling to get loose. He swore at me...wanted to know what in the name of ... *blank* ...I was doing there, when I should have been in school. Oh, was he ever angry!"

"Wow...What'd he do?"

Lisa was holding her head, rocking back and forth. "Oh, Becca...this is so scary. I...I 'm not sure...I was struggling, trying to get away. And I was crying...and...and *he hit me*...and then, he sent me to get...Oh, God, no...he sent me to get..." She had been working hard to make the memory clear, but now she broke, "Oh, no, Dear God...it's too much..." she prayed. "I really don't want this cup...please. Let it pass. I...I don't want to know any more." She sat rocking, tears streaming down her face, her arms wrapped tightly around herself. Then, after what seemed like a very long while, she whispered, "OK, Lord...not my will...but yours." And then she was quiet. So quiet, Becca became alarmed.

"Are you all right?" Becca asked, wiping the tears from her own face. "I wish I knew what to say...or do..." she faltered.

Lisa wiped her face on her shirt tail. She was calm now. "It's OK," she whispered. "God said His grace is sufficient...and...He's right, it always has been. So...I know...*I can* do this." She took a few deep breaths, letting them out slowly, then cleared her throat, and began again. "He...Daddy...sent me...to get Mama's butcher knife." Becca gasped. "And..." Lisa continued, "I didn't know what to do." She made no attempt to stop the tears now, but let them flow freely. "He said to go get it...and come right back...or the same thing would happen..." she caught her breath, "to me. Oh..." She was rocking again. "Oh, Becca, I thought...I thought...he was going to cut that man up...and...if I didn't get him the knife...he would cut me up too!" Unable to contain herself any longer, she jumped up from the table, heading for the car. "Oh...I've got to get away from here...stop the pain!" When they reached the car, she tossed Becca the keys. "I guess...you'd better drive, girl."

CHAPTER TWENTY ONE

Becca drove around town for a few minutes, then, ending up at the stop light on Highway 34, asked, "Which way...left...or right?"

Lisa said, "Left..." then quickly reversed herself. "No...right. I don't want to go where we've already been. Let's go to…Otis. At least go toward Otis..."

"Right...we'll head toward Otis…into the setting sun. So, I guess, I'm gonna need these." She dug her sun glasses out of her purse.

"Yeah...me too!" Lisa followed suit. They were quiet, each lost in her own thoughts. Then, as they neared Otis city limits, Lisa said, "You know...there's a little cafe here...that has the best pie. At least they used to have the best pie."

"Now, that sounds great! And I could definitely use a bite to eat." Becca slowed the car to comply with the speed limit, and a few minutes later they were ordering soup and salad...to go with their pie. They ordered coconut cream and Dutch apple...and had the waitress cut the slices in half so that they could both try both.

"Now, was I right...or was I right?" Lisa laughed as they headed back to Yuma.

"You were absolutely...positively...right!" Becca exuded. "They were both..." she searched for the right word. "They were both..."

Lisa finished it for her, "They were both...*so good*!"

"Well...in the words of our friend Dena...good somehow just doesn't cut it. No, they were better than good. They were great. And it was a toss up...the pies were both great!

"Ummm, and filling," Lisa, nodded, adding, "And now, all I need is to talk to Dick...and hit the hay. I am sooo tired."

"Me too," Becca yawned. And, although they had turned on the TV to catch the news when they got back to their motel, neither one heard any of it. They were both asleep the moment their heads hit the pillows. Sometime in the night, when Becca got up to go to the bathroom, she turned off the snowy screen.

Around daybreak the wind came up suddenly, slamming a tree branch against their window. Lisa sat bolt upright in bed, screaming, "Noooo!" She was suddenly wide awake, her heart pounding like a jackhammer. She sat there on the side of the bed trying to get her bearings in the dim light, while Becca silently slipped out of bed and came around to sit beside her. "Can I help?" she asked softly, wrapping her arms around Lisa, and rocking her.

After a few moments, after her heart had returned to its normal rhythm and her mind had stopped racing out ahead of the wind, Lisa nodded, "Yeah...I guess you can get me...my writing stuff," she answered, repositioning herself, cross-legged on the bed, with the pillows plumped up behind her. When Becca brought the supplies Lisa laid her hand on her arm, "Thanks, Becca...and...I really am sorry for waking you so early, but I guess I should write this down while it is still clear and fresh in my mind."

Becca laughed, turning on the bedside lamp, "No problem! Heck...I'm starting to get used to it. Who knows...by this time next week, sunrise will probably be my favorite time of the day...or night...whichever way you want to look at it!" She got her nail supplies out of her bag. "Besides...this way I have time to do my nails. So... sister dear, don't think of it as robbing me of my much needed beauty sleep. Just think of it as giving me a manicure.

Lisa wrote in her journal; Friday A.M. Awakened at sunrise, having a nightmare, which seems to be a continuation of what I had remembered yesterday, so I will begin with that earlier memory, then continue with this early morning dream.

I was alone in our house, because my sister, who is six years older than me, said I was feverish and needed to stay home from school. Question: Where's my mother, and why does Barbie seem to be in charge? Answer: My mother's in the hospital. Where's Daddy? At work. Where's everyone else? The boys are at school and Becca is staying with...with...? She closed her eyes and thought about it, then resumed. She's staying with people...from our church, while Mama's gone. I miss my Baby Doll, my Becca. I miss carrying her around and playing with her.

I was awakened by a noise downstairs that frightened me. I had told Barbie I was afraid to stay at home by myself...but she said, 'Oh, grow up! Don't be such a scared little rabbit all the time. You're ten years old, and it's time for you to start acting like a grown up!' She said she was getting pretty darned tired of having to take care of all of us all the time, so I promised I'd help her more. I already do the dishes and help with the washing and ironing. I promised I'd help her cook supper. But I still didn't like being left home all alone, and I begged Barbie to stay with me. She said she couldn't stay at home and *baby sit* me because she had to go take a test at school. Then, lowering her voice, she said, with more than just a touch of venom, that she wouldn't stay home with me...even if she didn't have a test to take! It was time for me to grow up. Feeling abandoned and lonely, I tried to solace myself, winding and re-winding my music box, watching the little ballerina dance around and around in her same circle on the top, until I finally fell asleep.

That's when I was awakened by a noise downstairs, that I couldn't identify. I lay there for a time trying to decide whether I should investigate it, or if it was just all in my head. Then, remembering Barbie's voice calling me a *scared little rabbit,* I decided to be brave and face my fear, like my teacher had said, so I carefully crept downstairs and searched the house, the kitchen, the living room, even Mama and Daddy's room. Greatly relieved at finding nothing, I curled up on the sofa and went back to sleep.

But, I was startled awake again...and this time I was sure I heard, not something, but someone. I heard a voice, a human voice! I lay there with my eyes closed for a time waiting, straining to hear it again, but all was quiet. Finally, feeling quite foolish, I decided that it was probably the cat. Yes that was it! Old Tom had somehow gotten himself locked in the basement, and couldn't get out. After all, I hadn't searched the basement! Carefully I made my way to the basement door, opening it just a crack. But, when Old Tom didn't come out, I decided to go down and find him...so that he would quit scaring me.

Cautiously, with my heart pounding wildly in my ears, constricting my throat, I inched my way down the stairs, hoping to find Old Tom right away, so I could scurry back upstairs. But something I saw made my heart nearly stop. What was it? Oh...yes...two pinpoints of redish light. Red demon eyes, floating, moving about like fireflies in my nearsighted vision, paralyzing me with fear. Then I smelled the cigarette smoke and in the semi-darkness, made out the two forms sitting on the work table. They smoked in silence for a moment, then started to speak.

Oh...what a relief! It was just my Daddy. Daddy and another man. And, just when I was about to speak, to let them know that I was there, cold fear slapped it's hand over my mouth to stop me. Because they were quarreling, and I instinctively knew that they mustn't know I was there. They were getting loud, and Daddy was swearing something awful, sending a cold chill through me. Suddenly it dawned on me that I would really be in trouble if he knew I was there...he would think I was spying on him! And then I had to decide whether to go back upstairs and risk a squeaky step giving me away, or to try to sneak past them in the dim light, so that I could hide in the wash room. I chose the latter, and almost immediately, tripped over a dead man, lying in my path on the floor. The sheer terror of staring into those sightless eyes caused me to scream, giving me away. My father was on me then, and in fury he sent me to the kitchen to bring him a butcher knife...with a warning to come right back, or...the same would happen to me.

The same. The same what? I asked myself over and over. I was convinced that I should run for my life the moment I reached the kitchen...but I was more convinced that I would never escape him. Once when I was five, he had taken the kitten I was playing with in my doll carriage, and gutted it before my horrified eyes, washing the blood from his hands with the water hose...and all because I hadn't done some little thing he wanted. He had said, "You see...I could kill you just as easily! Don't think that you can ever disobey me." And now I was sure that my father was going to cut up that poor dead man...with Mama's butcher knife. Why else would he send me for it? And this one thing I knew, I feared my father's wrath more than God Almighty. I went to the kitchen and got the knife, all the while praying that if he killed me too...God would quickly take me to heaven to be with Him, and not let me scream like my kitten had. All of this I remembered yesterday. My nightmare of this morning seems to be a continuation of that memory.

But, Daddy had actually wanted the knife for the sole purpose of cutting the man's clothes off. They were all bloody. Then he had Frank help him hold the man up, so they could bathe him. There was a shower in our basement, where Daddy cleaned up when he came in from work, and they held the dead man under the shower to get all the blood off of him. Then Daddy told me to run upstairs and get the Indian blanket off of his and Mama's bed. When I got back they wrapped the man up in it, and Daddy sent me to look out the back door to make sure nobody was around. He and Frank then carried their 'package' out and put it in the trunk of Daddy's car.

It seems the man had originally been in Frank's trunk, because there was a lot of blood in it, and Daddy had me get up inside of it with the broom to scrub the blood away as they carried bucket after bucket of water to rinse away the stain. Our hose wouldn't reach all the way from the side of the house to where the cars were parked in back. Then, after we finished cleaning out the car, Daddy had me scrub the blood out of his work uniform, so that he'd have something to wear to work. This I did with a scrub brush on the floor of the shower, so that all the blood would be washed down the drain. When I had finished and hung his clothes out to dry on the line, he sent me to change into dry clothes and shoes, so that I could go with them. I didn't want to go...but feared making him angry again, so I did as I was told.

We headed south out of Yuma, driving for what seemed to me like a long time, before turning west, and again going quite some distance. I was in the back seat, with the two of them in front. It was ominously quiet. I don't recall the radio playing, or there being any conversation...just a grim sort of silence. We finally came to a place, with several big trees and buildings, and Daddy stopped the car. I didn't recognize the place and timidly asked him where we were. He and Frank looked knowingly at each other, then winking at me Daddy grinned and said, "Oh, hell, Baby Girl! We're a hunnert miles from nowhere...that's where. A hunnert miles from nowhere." I had a sinking feeling that we had just dropped off of the face of the earth...and not a soul knew where we were.

Daddy and Frank took the *'package'* out of the trunk and carried it some distance from the car. I had started to follow them, but then decided it felt safer to just stay by the car, so I leaned against it, watching. It was a bright sunny spring day with no wind, and yet the warmth of the sun couldn't penetrate the icy chill of fear in my bones. I stood there shivering, watching, as they laid their 'package' on the ground, and together removed a very heavy concrete lid from off of a cistern, and then, matter-of-factly, heaved their 'package' into the abyss. Then I watched as they made their way down the slope and around the corner of the house, disappearing from view.

I didn't know what to do, whether to get in the car, or go and look for them. I couldn't decide which, so I just stayed there, letting the sun at least try to warm me up. Then they were back, carrying shovels. And together they worked, side by side, shoveling sand into that hole in the ground for several minutes, not saying a word. Finally, they were done. I can still see them standing there...their silhouettes framed above and on either side by the lacey pattern of tree leaves...two men, congenial co-workers, leaning on their shovels, taking a much needed smoke break, as if this was the most normal of occupations. It was truly surreal.

Then the spell was broken. They were talking, arguing again. But arguing...about what? I couldn't quite make it out, but...it felt eerily like they were talking about *me*. Then Frank was looking directly at me, and my frozen heart jolted alive and my feet began to fly back up the road we had just come down...with him right behind me, laughing. And above my hammering heart I could hear Daddy, shouting, "Run! Run, my scared little rabbit, run!"

My feet, that normally were the fastest in all my school, betrayed me now, because I couldn't drag them up and out of the sand fast enough, and he was gaining on me. I felt his hot breath on my neck! Then we were both sprawling, smashing into the hot sand, as he made a desperate flying tackle at my feet. I kicked to loosen his hold, my size four brown oxford soundly connecting with the bridge of his nose, sending his wire rimmed glasses flying over my head to land cock-eyed in the sand out in front of my chin, that had just slammed into mother earth with the sickening crunch of something breaking, and a groaning "whumph", as the wind was knocked clean out of me.

With his knee jabbed firmly in the middle of my back, as he tended to his bleeding nose, I remember thinking, "I'm really in trouble now. I broke his glasses." Then Frank was up and hauling me back to my father who had watched over the whole affair with great amusement. But Frank wasn't amused a bit, and cussing vehemently, said now they really ought to get rid of me, as I was nothing but trouble. And, besides, I knew way too much about their business.

Daddy, actually laughed. Leaning on his shovel, and taking a long draw on his cigarette, he finally said, "Ah, hell, Frank...let 'er go. She ain't gonna tell nobody nothin'! Besides, you're just mad, because she gave you a run for your money." Then, picking up the shovels, he headed back to wherever they had come from.

As soon as he was out of sight, Frank, who had never actually turned loose of me, picked me up and without a word, dropped me into the cistern. Shocked and terrified, I found myself sitting on a layer of sand that was barely covering the dead man, and I began to shriek. "Get me out. Please!" I screamed. "Please...please...please...get me out of here." I begged and I pleaded, promising to do whatever he wanted, but my cries fell on deaf ears. I shrieked and hollered, and begged and pleaded, but to no avail. And I had just come to the conclusion that I was only ten years old, and was going to die there in that cistern, with a dead man I didn't even know, when I heard my Daddy's voice. He was yelling at Frank, cursing. Then nothing. I began hoarsely calling out again, when suddenly, I saw Daddy's outline, leaning into the opening above me.

"You watch out now, Baby Girl, I'm gonna lower this here ladder down to you, and get you out. When it gets close, you reach out and guide it." And then I was crying so hard with relief that I could hardly see the thing, as I guided it past the dead man, to where it was on solid footing. I was up that ladder in a flash, eagerly grabbing hold of Daddy's hand as he lifted me up and over the rim. "Go on, now. You're OK," he said, swatting me on the bottom. Then, turning his attention to Frank, who was standing there with a smirk on his face, he said, "Now, Frank...You shouldn't 'a done that. I told you she wasn't gonna tell nobody nothin'...and...well, you just shouldn't 'a done that!" There was cold steel in his voice, and I turned to watch, glad that Frank was the one in trouble, now.

Daddy stood there, head cocked, taking the measure of his opponent, then he turned and started to walk away. Frank, his lip curled in a snarl, and thinking he had the upper hand, started toward me. And then, in one brief flash of sun on metal colliding with silver hair and skull, he was sprawling forward, surprise registering in his eyes, as he hung suspended before me in slow motion, then crumpled downward like a rag doll, barely making a sound as he hit the sand. Daddy stood there leaning on the shovel. "I said, you shouldn't 'a done that," he muttered. Then dropping the shovel, he leaned over Frank. "Come an' help me, Baby Girl," he said, matter-of-factly.

At that point the journal slid out of Lisa's hands and hit the floor. She was crying, "No...Daddy. I can't. I can't help you. He's too heavy..." Then jumping up off of the bed, she grabbed up the journal and pen, and throwing them across the room, cried out, "I won't do it...*I can't*!" Then she stormed into the bathroom, calling out to Becca., "If we're going to get some breakfast, we'd probably better go now...or the place will be too packed for us to get waited on!"

CHAPTER TWENTY TWO

After they ate, Lisa and Becca spent what was left of the morning browsing in the local stores, then they headed north to Bertha and Fred's place for lunch. Dena was right, her Grandma had really put on a spread. After lunch Fred showed them around the farm, then they settled into the living room for some coffee and conversation.

Before the girls arrived Bertha had sent Fred up to the attic to retrieve a large cardboard box that was the sole repository of the family's recent history. Now Bertha rooted around in the box, producing all sorts of pictures of their mother when she was young.

"Oh, look, Lisa," Becca exclaimed, "She was so beautiful!"

"I know!" Lisa could hardly take it all in. Finally she asked, "Fred...how is it that you have all these pictures of our mother? I thought you said that you were just related to relatives!"

Fred chuckled. "Well, that's right. But ya see, the Bradleys...that's you...and the Johnsons...which is me...have always been tight." He got up and went to the dining room sideboard for a tablet. Then, sitting down by Lisa, continued, "Here I'll show you. Way back when, two young fellers by the name of William Bradley 'n Jedadiah Johnson grew up together near Wichita Kansas. They married their high school sweethearts, 'n headed west to Colorado to homestead. Now William 'n Elizabeth, they settled down over to the west of us here. And Jedadiah 'n Sally Ann, they settled down pretty much on this spot. We tore the old homestead down when we built this house back in the 50's.

Fred turned the tablet sideways, drawing a line down the middle of the page, dividing it in half. On the left side at the top he wrote William Bradley and Elizabeth Harding, and at the top of the right side he wrote Jedadiah

Johnson and Sally Baker. Then he continued the narration. "Now Will and Lizzy, they had three sons." He wrote, "Kenneth, James and Robert, and went on. "Only James died when he was sixteen. So, he didn't continue the family line." He put an X over James, and continued to the other side of the paper. "And Jed and Sally, they had two kids, Mary Jane 'n Alex. Now that's the first generation to be born in Colorado, on both sides. Ya followin' me, so far?"

"Uh huh, so far," Lisa laughed. "I'm getting the picture."

"OK. So now, here we go for the next generation." Fred began, "Now, Will and Lizzy's first son, Kenneth, he up 'n married Amanda Powell, and they had Katherine 'n Henry." He wrote the names under Kenneth. "Got that?'

"Oh yes...that's our Mom and her brother," Becca answered.

"Yep," Fred continued. "Now remember, I said James died. But Kenneth's brother, Robert...the third son of Will and Lizzy...well, he married Mary Jane Johnson..."

Becca interjected, "...daughter of Will's best friend, Jed...right?"

"Right. You got it. And Robert 'n Mary Jane...they just had two...Mary Jo, who married Edward Cooper... an' then their other kid was Jean. And Jeanie, she married Bob Prather, but they never had no kids. An' they've both been dead 'n gone..." He seemed to be calculating the years in his head, then finally shrugged and said, "Well...a long time now." He continued filling in the names as he moved across to the right side of the page. "Now, to Mary Jane we add Robert Bradley...duplicating what we have over there on the left side, only in reverse...and Mary Jane's brother, Alex, here. Well now, he up 'n married Stella Barnes...and they had me, Fred...and I married Bertha Cole. And, last, but not least, they produced my brother, David, who is also dead 'n gone. And...he never married."

"Cause the only woman he ever loved was your poor departed Mama..." Bertha interjected. "An' she broke his heart...when she up an' married your Daddy!"

"Now, Mama...I don't think we ought'ta get inta' that," Fred chided, then went back to what he was saying. "So...that brings us down to your generation...which we don't need to bother with at this time. Now that you see how our families were bound up together..." He tore off the page with a flourish, and ceremoniously handing it to Lisa, continued, "...you can understand...how we *felt like* we were related...even if we weren't. Heck, Kate 'n Henry, 'n Mary Jo 'n Jean...'n me 'n Dave...well, we all ran around together, before we all got hitched."

"And even after we *was* hitched!" Bertha added. "Fer the most part...we all liked each other's mates. That is, all but..." A glance from Fred stopped her before she could say "Joe", but it wasn't lost on the girls. While they had been engrossed in Fred's family tree narration, Bertha had been busy sorting through the box of pictures. Now she spread an assortment out on the coffee table before them, saying, "Now, these here pitchers...that'er mostly yer Mama's family...well...they won't mean that much ta our young-uns. So you girls might as well have 'em."

"Oh my!" Becca exclaimed. "That's...so wonderful of you!" Picking up several, she looked first at one then another, exulting in their good fortune to find this rare treasure trove, until suddenly she stopped short. As the color drained from her face, she tried to speak but no words came out, just a strange unrecognizable sound.

"Becca...are you all right?" Lisa's eyes went from Becca's ashen face to the picture she was thrusting at her sister. "What is it? What did you see?"

"Who...?" was all the startled Becca could stammer. "Who...are these people?" She thrust the picture at Bertha, eyes pleading for an explanation.

"Why...what do you mean, girl? Don't you even recognize your own Mama and Daddy?" Bertha took the picture from Becca. "Yep...that's them for sure. Taken..." She thought about it and shrugged, passing the picture over to Fred. "Looks to me like it was taken out here, before we tore the old house down."

Fred was nodding. "Yep...right out there in the driveway. I prob'ly took it...cause there's my brother...see, there on the left, he's almost outta the picture."

Becca, having regained herself, pointed to another couple standing beside her parents. "But...who's this man...this couple...with our folks?"

"Lands...I wouldn't know," He shrugged, passing the photo back to Becca. "If'n I ever did know 'em...I don't remember 'em now. Must'a been friends'a yer pa. Like I already told ya, we didn't hang around with him...an' his friends. But we was real close to yer Mama...until she up an' married Joe."

"Bad match..." Bertha mused. "And he made durn sure she never had time for the likes of us after they were married. She never shoulda married that man!"

"Now...Mama..." Fred cajoled. "Who's ta say...who should marry who. Ain't none 'a our affair. What's done 's done. Besides...won't no good come of badmouthin' the dead!"

"Oh...I know it! But I just get so..." She sighed a great sigh, then added, "I'm truly sorry...Lisa, Becca...fer talkin' 'bout yer Pa like that. You'll jist have'ta fergive this ole woman. I get carried away, now an' again." She reached over and patted Becca, then continued, "But even the thought of that man..."

"Now Mama!" Fred cut her off sharply this time.

"Now Papa!" Eyes flashing, Bertha met his stern look with a defiant set of her jaw. "These girls know their Daddy wasn't no saint...else their Mama wouldn't've up an' left 'im. An'...I'm entitled...to my own opinion 'a the man!" She was working up a good head of steam, now. "An' I'd appreciate it... If'n you'd stop tryin' to shush me up!"

"Bertha, Fred...please!" Lisa broke in, nervously. "Please...it's OK! Bertha's right, Fred. Becca and I do know that our Daddy was a...first class, royal mess. And, Bertha, of course you are entitled to your opinion of him. But...this whole thing is making us a bit uneasy. Maybe we could just move on to something else?" The older couple just stood there, glaring at each other, eyes locked in silent struggle.

"Right..." Becca jumped in. "We really ought to label all of these pictures before we leave. Since the only people we know for sure are our own folks.

"That's right," Lisa entreated, grasping at anything to break the deadlock, "...and we'll never remember them all, once we leave here!"

Fred was the first to break it off. With a chuckle, he said. "Now, just look look at us, Mama, we're too old to be actin' like a couple'a spoiled kids...each one determined to have his own way...completely fergettin' our guests. Now, why don't you help the girls an' I'll go make us some fresh coffee."

The tension broken, Bertha laughed in embarrassment, and turned her attention, once again to the task at hand. So they spent the rest of the afternoon discussing and labeling the pictures. At some point Bertha had gone to the kitchen and scrounged up some roast beef sandwiches and they continued on. It was getting late and the girls had started to leave when, suddenly, Fred remembered something. He went to the front hall closet and retrieved a dusty old scrapbook.

"Bertha...we 'bout fergot...that we were gonna give 'em...this!" he said.

"Oh, that's right!" she exclaimed. "I'm so glad you remembered, Poppy!"

Fred stuffed the scrapbook down into a grocery bag and handed it to Lisa. "It's newspaper clippin's...from the wreck. We'd plumb fergotten we had 'em. Remembered 'em after ya left t'other night...so...well...we want you girls ta have 'em. They're no good to us." He paused, thoughtfully, then added, "But...I have ta warn ya...it was a really bad one." He shook his head sadly, then added, "A *really* bad one."

"Oh...I should say so!" Bertha exclaimed. "Worst one in these parts in...well...prob'ly...ever. Leastways, I don't remember another one as bad."

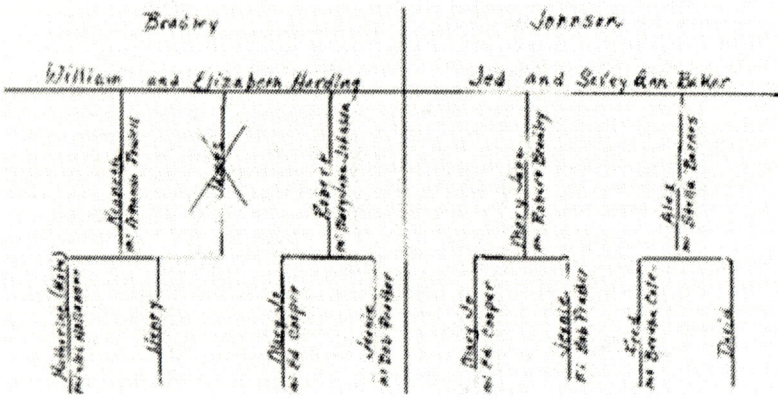

CHAPTER TWENTY THREE

Like a child with a delicious secret to share, Becca could hardly wait to get the car door shut and her seat belt on. "It was him!" she blurted out. "The man Daddy shot!"

"I thought as much." Lisa said, easing the car out of the driveway onto the road. "It was written all over your face. And one thing's for sure...I also recognized him...as the dead man from our house." She drove in silence for a few minutes, then mused, "So, what we have here, is a *lead*. A concrete, visible lead. And...maybe...just having that visual clue will jog something else loose. I can hardly wait to get to our room so we can really study those pictures."

"And the scrapbook..." Becca interjected.

"Yeah...that ought to give us something." She was quiet for a few moments, then added, "Maybe it was just my imagination...but..." She searched her mind for the right words.

"But...what?" Becca prodded.

"Well, like I said, maybe it was just my imagination, but I got the distinct impression that they didn't want us to open that scrapbook there...in front of them."

Becca was nodding, "Yeah...I think you might be right." She paused, then continued, "And...*I* got the impression...well, that maybe they...or at least Fred...*did know* who our mystery couple was. In my esti- mation, that lineabout *'if I ever did know...I've forgotten'*, was pure hogwash! So, what do *you* think, Lisa?"

"Uh...well...I'm not sure what I think about it. But what it *'feels'* like is that...I'm not really sure it's safe."

"What do you mean by *'not sure it's safe'*?"

"Becca, I learned at a very early age that something could look and sound and even smell perfectly all right...but not *feel* all right...and I'd better go with my gut!"

"So...your gut feeling is...that we can't trust Fred and Bertha?"

"I'm not sure. The only thing I'm sure of...is that I feel unsure. Sooo...I guess that means that we just need to be extra careful,"

"But...careful about what?"

"Careful about how much we divulge...how much we take them into our confidence. At least for the time being, I don't want anyone around here to know anything about what we are working on. Let them all think it's just about getting Grandpa's land back...and nothing else."

"Right! I think that sounds like a very good plan." Becca sighed. "And I want you to know...that 'feels' safer to me, too."

Back at the motel they could hardly wait to dig into the scrapbook. While Becca showered, Lisa called home, then she showered, while Becca fixed them Cokes and a snack. Then when they were confident they would have no interruptions they laid the thing out on the bed. Neither one was prepared for the assault on their senses. Both the Sterling paper and the Denver Post had many detailed pictures of the scene. And both described the carnage, leaving nothing to the imagination. They wept openly as they read of the family that had died out there on that open stretch of road they had just traversed.

"Oh...our poor dear Mama. Just think what she must have gone through...to think that she caused that!" Becca choked. "And that poor family...but at least they were all dead and didn't have to live with the memory of it. Oh, our poor Mama." She suddenly felt a tension in her sister and looked up. "I'm sorry, Lisa...I didn't mean to make you feel bad."

"No...you didn't...do anything wrong. It's just that I just noticed this clipping. It was tucked into the back pocket of the album, and ...look!" She smoothed the folded paper out on the bedspread. "Look, Becca, at the man standing there beside the car. I know it's not a very good picture...and his hat rather obscures his face...but..."

"Yeah...I think so too. I think it's the same man. What does it say in the caption under the picture?"

"It says...'A highway patrolman takes a statement from Mr. Edward Bennett, who was a passenger in the Hollander automobile. Mr. Bennett was the only party uninjured in the accident'. Becca! Do you know what this means?" Lisa's voice rose excitedly. "It means we now know the name of the dead man."

Becca interrupted, "Eddie! *Eddie Bennetti*...isn't that what Fred said they called him?"

"That's right. Eddie Bennetti!" Lisa was rifling through the pictures Bertha had so painstakingly dug out for them. "Here...here it is. The one Fred said he didn't recognize...and," she laid it alongside the news clipping, "...bingo! I'd say we have a match! I'd be willing to bet that the people in this picture are Mr. and Mrs. Edward Bennett!"

At that Becca jumped up and danced an impromptu jig, sing-singing "Oh, thank you God! Thank you, Lord Jesus. Thank you, thank you!" Then she plopped back down next to Lisa and whispered, "And see...my hunch was right. Fred...*did*...know...!"

"Yes. At least he knew who Eddie was. However, that doesn't mean he actually knows anything else about any of this. But...we do have to wonder whether there's some hidden agenda here..." Lisa mused.

"You're darned right we do!" Becca exclaimed. "You see? What did I tell you? It all goes back to motive. And that's precisely why...I have so much trouble trusting people. You never can be quite sure why they do the things they do. Why would Fred deny knowing Eddie? It just has to mean something."

"Right...something! But what?" Lisa's question was mostly rhetorical, not meant to be answered. "That's the million dollar question."

They finally settled in for the night and had been asleep about twenty minutes when the phone rang. Lisa jumped like she had been shot, and knocked the receiver to the floor while groping for the light switch.

"Hello...hello...Lisa, are you there...?" came the familiar voice over the line.

"Hello...Dick...Just a minute..." Lisa called out while fumbling for the receiver. "I'm sorry...I knocked the phone off." She stretched out vainly trying for the receiver, when suddenly she fell out of bed, collapsing in a fit of giggles, with the sheet wound around her. And Becca, who was still asleep, suddenly sat bolt upright tugging at the sheet, which only made it tighter around Lisa, pinning her arms so that she still couldn't reach the phone, though she was right next to it.

"Lisa...what's happening? You're there...I can hear you. So...please pick up the phone!"

Laying her face down next to the receiver Lisa giggled, "Hold on Dick...I'll be with you as soon as I get myself untangled." Then she yelled for Becca to wake up and stop pulling on the sheet, which had no effect at all. Becca was out like a light. Finally Lisa decided to just go with the flow. She rolled toward Becca, which released the tension just long enough for her to pop one arm out so that she could grab the receiver.

"Hello, Dick? Are you still there?" she laughed.

"I'm still here...But at this point I'm beginning to wonder if you are all there!" He joked.

"Ha, ha...very funny!" she laughed. "But...whatever made you decide to call me at this ungodly hour of the morning?" She squinted at the clock, trying to see without her glasses. "My goodness...do you realize it's 2:00 AM?" She didn't wait for his answer, "And it's 3 there. Whatever are you doing up at 3 AM?"

"What I'm doing up...is talking to you, silly. I thought that was pretty obvious!" He laughed. "I just had a brainstorm and I wanted to share it with you."

"OK...I'm up! What's the brainstorm?" Lisa yawned.

"Guess!"

"Oh, Honey...not at 2 in the morning...please..." she groaned.

"OK...I won't make you guess. I'm really missing you...so I decided to come up there!"

"That's nice..."Lisa purred, half asleep. Then, as it registered, "You're what? You're coming up here? When?" Now she was fully awake. "How are you going to do this, and when?"

"I thought that would get your attention!" he laughed. "I'm flying in tomorrow...or later today, actually. I'll be at the Denver airport at 4:30...think you can pick me up...or should I rent a car?"

"No...don't rent a car! I...we'll...pick you up. What airline? Now, listen, I have to extricate myself from this bed sheet so I can get something to write with. Hold on...don't hang up...OK?"

"OK...I'll still be here."

Later, as Becca sipped her breakfast coffee, she said, "Boy, I had the weirdest dream last night!" Lisa raised an eyebrow and grinned, waiting for Becca to go on. "Yeah. I dreamed we were being held prisoners in an old castle tower, and I had to hold on to the bed sheet while you lowered yourself out the only window to go and get help."

"And...? What happened? Did I get help...and come back for you?"

"Uh huh," Becca said, spreading jelly on her toast. "At first he looked like the Lone Ranger...you know, with a mask, and riding a white horse..." she giggled, "but, when I looked again...it was only Dick."

"Hum," Lisa said. "Then it probably won't surprise you to hear that the Lone Ranger called last night... and wants us to pick him up at the Denver airport this afternoon."

"No...really?" Becca was clearly stunned, and just sat looking at her sister, toast poised for a bite. "When did he call? I didn't hear the phone." She started to take a bite, then withdrew the toast. "You're *not* joking...are you?"

"I'm not joking," Lisa laughed. "And your dream about the bed sheet? Well, that was just me, falling out of bed to answer the phone!"

CHAPTER TWENTY FOUR

It was Saturday morning and Dick was flying in. That, in and of itself, was enough to make Lisa radiant, but the prospect of his *surprise* had her almost giddy. He had said, just before they hung up, that she and Becca should go into Denver and pick up bathing suits because he had booked them into someplace very special for the weekend, and he was sure there would be a hot tub. So, that's what they had done, and now they were watching for his plane to taxi up to the terminal. Lisa felt like a schoolgirl, tingly all over.

Becca sat watching her sister then laughed, "I swear, Lisa...you are positively glowing! It must be wonderful...to have what you two have."

Lisa blushed. "Oh, it is that. Can you believe it...after thirty two years! But the truth is, I love him more today than I ever have. It just keeps on getting better and better. And I can't even *imagine* life without Him." Having said that, she took a piece of paper from her wallet. It was yellowed and starting to fall apart from years of folding and unfolding. She handed it to Becca. "I wrote this for Dick on our twenty fifth anniversary...and it's even truer today. I wouldn't change a word."

Becca carefully unfolded the paper on her lap and read,

He and I

He and I. For all these years together.

It is not good for man to be alone.

Me neither! I need Him.

Need our togetherness,

Our couple-ing,

Mr. and Mrs.

> Even when we're apart we are joined.
> Together. A oneness in duality.
> Neither subjugated by the other.
> Comfortable in silence,
> Ecstatic in love,
> Warmth seeking warmth,
> Touching, connecting, knowing.
> He is both essential and luxury.
> No, it is not good for me to be alone,
> So there is he!

Transfixed, Becca read and reread each line, then awestruck, she whispered, "Oh, Lisa...that is so beautiful!" But Lisa didn't hear her. Dick's plane had come in and she was wrapped up in his arms at the gate. Becca watched them in wonder. "What must it be like to love...and *be loved*...like that?" she asked herself. "Will I ever know?"

Dick's surprise was that he had booked them into a two bedroom suite at the Broadmore in Colorado Springs for the weekend. So as soon as they had collected his luggage, they headed south, arriving in time for a wonderful meal and a good soak in the hot tub before calling it a day.

Later, as Lisa lay snuggled in Dick's arms, she purred, "Whatever made you think of this wonderful treat?"

"Well, the other night when we talked you sounded so..." he searched his mind for just the right word.

"So...what?"

"So...I started to say down, but that's not the right word. Maybe forlorn...or dejected. I don't know exactly. There was a trace of sadness in your voice and I just wanted to reach out and hold you. I got to thinking how hard it must be to go through what you've been dealing with...alone. And I just wanted to be here with you." He kissed her very tenderly, then added, "And...I wanted to do something to show you how much I care. How *very much* I care. I can't begin to know how painful it must be to have to work through all that stuff about your Dad...but at least I can be here."

"Thank you," she whispered. "Sometimes I think it is absolutely the worst kind of pain there is...because it creates such cognitive dissonance." She chuckled, "Now, that's the therapist talking... *cognitive dissonance*? The child in me calls it pain, pure and simple. There is a part of me that hates him and everything about him...because he was so purely evil."

He started to agree with her, but she cut him off, saying, "But, you see, Dick, nothing is so *purely* anything! There's good and there's evil, yes...but usually it's all mixed up together. It's not an either or proposition. Like my Dad. Most of what I recall about him is truly evil...and it's easy to hate what we can clearly see is evil." She repositioned herself, so that she could watch Dick's face, then continued. "But then... I remember little things. Things that were actually sweet and good...untainted by his corruption. Like the first time he took me up behind the waterfall...to what he called *the beginning of the world,* where time stood still, and there was just he and I, and the God of the universe was in the air and in the water and in the trees...all around us, and it was so good...and I loved him so...so purely." She tried to hold back the tears, but couldn't, so she buried her face in his chest and let them come.

"It's OK. Go ahead and cry," he whispered, running his fingers through her hair. And then they were making love, melting into each other until they were truly one flesh, and nothing else remained.

They awoke clinging to each other, and lay there talking until they heard Becca stirring about in the other room. Finally Lisa got up and headed for the shower. "Oh, I meant to thank you for getting a two bedroom suite...so Becca has a room of her own and doesn't have to sleep on the couch."

Dick grinned, following her into the bathroom. "You could say, I had an ulterior motive."

"Well...that's quite all right...I'm sure we all slept better for it." Lisa murmured, turning on the shower.

After breakfast they went to Church, then took a long leisurely drive up to Cripple Creek. The girl's Mother's Mother had come from there, so they spent some time looking for the old house on Bennett Street where their Great Grandmother had run a boarding house during the gold rush. They found where the place should have been, but the current residence was much too modern looking to have actually been the original, which was a big disappointment. Laughing, Becca conceded that it probably was a good thing that the original wasn't there...so that "Lisa wouldn't be tempted to run down to the courthouse and buy it!"

Then they drove up the hill to Mt. Pisgah Cemetery and after a long search they finally found the old family plot. It was badly overgrown. "Boy! This sure needs some work." Lisa declared, rummaging around in the trunk of the car for some tools. However, all she came up with was an old pair of work gloves, a claw hammer and a small screwdriver. So Dick decided to go down into town to see if he could locate something a bit more suitable. While he was gone Lisa and Becca went to work with what they had on hand, but it was slow going.

Soon Dick was back, and he brought the one thing they were most in need of, bottled water. The hardware store had gone out of business, but a man at a service station had taken pity on him and loaned him a couple pair of work gloves and a small hand scythe. Now that they all had gloves, they went to work in earnest. First Dick would cut a patch of grass and weeds, then the girls would dig out debris and rocks, using the claw of the hammer. They worked hard, restoring the overturned tombstones, carefully scraping around the inscriptions with the screwdriver. It took a couple of hours of concentrated effort, but finally they sat down on a low wall and surveyed their efforts.

"We did good," Lisa declared, wiping her brow. Becca nodded, tiredly.

"Yep...we did." Dick agreed, slipping his arm around his wife. They sat there another half hour or so, making small talk about the gold rush and the people who had lived and were now buried there, then Lisa began to sing, softly, reverently, *"Sweet hour of prayer, sweet hour of prayer! May I thy consolation share, Till, from Mount Pisgah's lofty height, I view my home and take my flight:"*

At the chorus Becca and Dick joined her. *"This robe of flesh I'll drop and rise, To seize the everlasting prize; And shout, while passing through the air, Farewell, Farewell, sweet hour of prayer."*

They sat quietly watching the sun descend in a brilliant display of color, then silently, preserving the mood, they likewise descended to the town below. Evening was coming on, and the town was coming to life, but they went on through, after returning the gloves and scythe to the man at the service station. Heading on down, they stopped at Divide and had some of the best trout they had ever eaten, at a little place that had Hummingbird feeders every couple of feet across the front of the glassed in building. And the hummers, as thick as mosquitoes, and in several varieties, squabbled, and dive bombed and chased each other, in a dizzying display of machismo. It was delightful and they couldn't take their eyes off of them. Finally, when it was completely dark out, they left, winding their way back down to the Broadmore...and that wonderful hot tub.

CHAPTER TWENTY FIVE

Monday was a gorgeous day and the trio decided to spend another day in the mountains before heading back out to Yuma. They had the kitchen prepare them a lunch before they checked out of the Broadmore, and headed up Hwy 24 with no real plan in mind, but a vague thought of possibly having lunch at *the beginning of the world* on Hwy 119 if the weather held. They took Hwy 9 from Hartsel into Fairplay and then to Dillon where they picked up I-70 heading east. At Idaho Springs they turned north to Central City, where they stopped to wander around for about an hour and a half, and then headed on to Nederland. By the time they got there it was looking quite gray out, so they didn't tarry, but headed on down the canyon to find the donut rock and the waterfall. By the time they got there, it was really raining, so they just parked and ate their lunch in the car.

"Oh, well, we tried...to get here in time," Lisa sighed, handing out the sandwiches.

"It was the stop at Central City...now that was our downfall." Becca said, between bites.

"Downfall...or blessing?" Dick asked. "I'd rather call it a blessing. 'Cause...if we had been here before the rain started, we'd have been caught...out there," he waved his hand at the obscured windshield, "Right smack in the middle of it! And besides...this way we don't have to share with the ants..." He laid his sandwich down to pour coffee from the thermos.

"Or other critters," Lisa laughed, holding out her cup for a fill. "Besides, if experience counts here, I don't think it will last long. I've *been* in a lot of these afternoon showers, and they hardly ever last any time at all."

"Well...since we don't have to be anyplace...at any given time," Becca muttered, working steadily away on her sandwich, "I reckon we can wait a bit...and just see what it does...or does not do. Right?" Then, not waiting for an answer, she added, "And...In the meantime, I think I'll catch me a little nap..." Then, stuffing her sandwich wrap down into the trash bag, she chuckled and added in her best Bertha voice, "If'n you don't mind."

"O.K. by me." Lisa laughed.

"If'n? Did she say '*If'n*'...?" Dick asked in an exaggerated whisper.

Lisa nodded, grinning, "You heard right. I tell you, Dick, she's only been gone from home two weeks...and she's a changed woman!" But the humor was lost on the sleeping Becca. Lisa and Dick chit chatted awhile about things at home, but soon they nodded off too.

With the rain droning on the roof Lisa was soon drifting off to another time and place. And in her dream she was riding comfortably along in the rain, when suddenly, there was a horrible wrenching as the car shuddered across the road into the path of an oncoming car, right into it's blinding headlights and chaos. Somewhere a woman screamed, and she heard a sickening crunch of metal on metal, but nothing touched her. She was safely floating away from it all on a very soft cloud, seemingly lifted above and beyond by what she thought were her mama's strong hands. Then she was lying out in an open field with the rain falling on her face. Everything was blurry, but in her daze she could finally make out people moving about in the rain. And with the steady beat of the rain came the voices, "Is she dead?" Lisa was struggling, trying to answer them, but they just went on like they didn't hear her.

Like she wasn't even there.

Then Dick was gently shaking her, "Hey, Honey...wake up! The sun is shining and we can go for our hike if you want to. Becca's already out there climbing around on the rocks." Lisa straightened up and blinked, trying to reorient herself. She took a sip of her cold coffee and shuddered. "Did I horn in on a good dream?" Dick asked, opening her car door.

"No...I wouldn't call it...a good one. Boy," She shook her head. "I really don't know what that was all about, but..." she slipped her hand into his and headed for the path to the falls, "I think...I'd much rather go hiking, than try to figure it out"

Since the ground was wet and slippery, they very carefully made their way up above and beyond the falls, then sprawled on an enormous flat boulder to soak up some sun. Lisa sat with her arms wrapped around her knees, watching a Nuthatch busily work over an area of dense pine needles, coming back again and again, despite the fact that a bossy chipmunk kept chasing it off.

Dick put his arms around her, snuggling against her back. "Kinda reminds me of someone I know."

"Think so?" She grinned. "Which one...the bird or the chipmunk?"

Becca had been sitting with her back to them. She turned, her eyebrows raised, anticipating the answer. When it didn't come right away she laughed. "Hey! Definitely not the chipmunk!"

"Are you accusing me of tenacity...or stubborness?" Lisa laughed, getting to her feet and pulling Dick up with her. "Come on, you two...let's go upstream...to the beginning of the world!"

"Well, OK..." Dick said. "But, we'd better keep an eye on the sky. We really don't want it to be the 'end of the world' as we now know it." They picked their way up the swollen stream for about ten minutes, when suddenly a dark cloud passed over the face of the sun. "Well, I think that's our cue. We'd better be heading back, Lisa."

Looking disappointed, she conceded. "Yeah...I do think we're pushing our luck a bit." Low thunder punctuated her remark. "And, though I hate to admit it, as slippery as that mountain was coming up...we'll probably have to slide back down it." She was right. Dick started down first so that he could help Lisa and Becca, but when he lost his footing, they both did too, and by the time they reached their car they were well plastered in mud.

"Wait," Lisa said breathlessly, as Becca reached the car. "We've got a couple of old throws in the trunk. They'll protect the seats...at least from the mud." Dick was already getting them, and Lisa continued. "When we get into Boulder we can clean up at that big truck stop on the edge of town. I don't relish the idea of riding all the way out to Yuma in wet muddy clothes!"

Becca, winded from their fast pace, didn't say a word. She just grinned and, raising her forefinger, made a 'chock one up for Lisa' sign. The truck plaza actually had showers, which was even better than they had anticipated, and after freshening up they headed on out.

"Will you just look at that sky!" Dick whistled through his teeth. "I think there's practically every color..."

"Wow! And look...over there," Lisa interrupted, pointing, "A double rainbow!"

"I don't think I've ever seen anything like it!" Becca exclaimed. "And will you just look at those formations! That one looks like a giant turtle...and a minute ago it had an elephant riding on it's back!"

"Yeah, I saw that," Lisa said. "But, look now, Becca. Your elephant is turning into something else." She paused, then added, "Looks more like a buffalo, now. Oh, and speaking of buffalo," she continued, absently, "We're coming up on the Hudson exit. Let's stop at the Pepper Pod, for a bite to eat."

"OK by me," Dick said, slowing down for the exit. Then he laughed, "By the way, Lisa. I didn't quite make the same connection you made back there."

"Huh?" Lisa asked. "What connection?"

Becca giggled, then mimicked her sister, "Speaking of buffalo...let's stop at the Pepper Pod? You must be really hungry, Lisa!"

"Yeah," Dick laughed, "Maybe...I can't afford to stop at the Pepper Pod!"

Lisa looked like she was on a different wave length, "Huh...what ever are you two talking about?"

"Wake up, Silly," Dick said, pulling up to the stop. "What you said, in essence, was..." he made the turn into the parking lot, "Speaking of buffalos...let's eat! And I..."

Lisa started to laugh. "Oh, I didn't think...of course you two don't know the connection!" Getting out of the car, she explained. "When I was a little girl, there were buffalo...here. Yes, real live buffalo...at the Pepper Pod. It was always our stopping place, coming and going. We would use the restroom...and have a soda pop at the Pepper Pod. And then, we'd sit on the rock wall, and watch the buffalo chew their cud."

"Well, I want to do more than just chew my cud," Dick laughed. "And...I definitely want more than a soda pop!" He ushered them inside.

"Well, I think the restroom sounded like a pretty good idea," Becca added, following the sign inside. "You two go ahead and be seated. And I'll be right with you."

To their amazement and delight they found the Pepper Pod actually served buffalo steak, which they all decided to try. And then they were back on the road to Yuma, ooh-ing and ah-ing over that marvelous Colorado sky.

CHAPTER TWENTY SIX

Dick and Lisa had planned to get another room at their motel and let Becca stay put, but the motel didn't have another king room available, so Becca moved instead. They were all exhausted from their exploits of the day and turned in early. But they had only been asleep about an hour when Lisa was jolted to her senses. She was replaying the dream she had had earlier in the day, and again she was sailing through the air, with the rain falling on her face, and those awful words droning in her ears. "Is she dead?" the voice kept asking over and over, while she was trying her best to answer. Then she heard another voice answer for her, "Ah, hell...I don't know." It was the voice of her father. "But...we'd better move her," he said, "Before anyone comes."

"Oh, good...they're going to move me...at last," she thought, sinking into blackness. When she again opened her eyes, there were other cars, and lots of people milling about, but nobody came near her. And try as she might, nobody heard her calls for help, because everyone was focused on that other car. She knew it must be pretty bad, for she kept hearing the word *dead*...over and over.

"We're all dead..." she heard herself say, but nobody paid any attention. And then she felt herself sinking, sinking into oblivion. She was fighting now, struggling for consciousness. "No, I'm over here. Come...find me!"

Then Dick was shaking her awake. "Lisa...it's OK, Hon. You're having a dream...but you're OK. You're safe...with me!"

Startled, she struggled against him, "I...I'm not dead! They're all dead...but I'm not dead!" She was staring wide eyed into the face of her beloved Dick. "Oh, my...they're all dead," she moaned, dissolving into tears.

"Who?" Dick asked, wrapping his arms around her. "Nobody's dead, Lisa, Honey, ...it was just a dream." He rocked her gently, saying over and over, "You're OK. It was just a bad dream. Nobody's dead."

When she was fully awake, Lisa, got up and splashed cold water on her face. "Oh, I do wish I'd stop dreaming about that stupid wreck. You can't imagine how real it all seems." She came and sat down on the edge of the bed, rubbing her temples. "Gosh, Dick...It's just like I was...actually there."

He got up and came around to sit next to her. "Well...in the light of all this *other stuff* that you've been dealing with...what's the probability that it's *not* really just a dream?" He gave that a minute to sink in, then added, "Maybe...maybe you really were there."

"No...it's not possible!" She got up and retrieved the scrapbook, tossing it onto the bed. "Look there!" She rifled through the pages. "See...all the accounts are the same. *I'm not there*!" She sat staring at the pictures, then added, "The only thing I can conclude about these dreams...is just...that I've gotten so caught up in all of this...that I've...*somehow*...put myself there."

"Can you *really* do that?" Dick asked, incredulously.

"Well...I didn't know that I could. I've never done it before." She was quiet for a few moments. "And I've never known anybody else to do it...but *it's the only answer I have*. The only *logical* explanation there is," she finished lamely, while Dick just sat shaking his head.

"You're saying...in all the years you've been counseling...that you've never known anybody to do it? I mean deliberately put themselves into a..."

"Nope," she shook her head. "Never. Well, not *normal people*..." She laughed. "And...I assume that I'm a normal person..." She got back into bed and, pulling the sheet up under her chin, prayed, "Now, Dear Lord, please... help me get back to sleep...and not dream about that darned wreck!"

Dick was saying his own prayers for his wife. He wasn't at all convinced that she was just dreaming, and he was praying for *mercy.*

There had been a message at the desk for them when they came in. The Librarian had received their newspaper copies, so the first thing after breakfast the next morning they headed straight for the Library.

"Well, there doesn't seem to be anything new here," Lisa mused, quickly scanning each page. She paid the Librarian and turned to Dick. "So, this is your day, my Love. What do you want to do first?"

"I want to go see the house I bought!" He laughed, taking Lisa's arm and propelling her toward the door. "If that didn't beat all...calling me on the phone to say that you had bought a house...and I should pay the man!"

Lisa giggled, "I thought you'd like that!"

And then Becca joined in, "I tried to warn her. I said, Lisa...Dick's not going to be any too happy about you being up here, buying up everything you see. Hey...I really had to work hard...to keep her from buying that old family home we lived in. It *is* for sale, you know!"

"No...I didn't know!" Dick laughed. "And, believe me, I don't even want to think about it!"

They went directly to the old home place and gave Dick the walking tour. He was fascinated by the antique machinery in the barn. "Wow...you were right, Lisa. You really did get a deal, you know. Why...there's enough old stuff in there to buy and sell this place ten times over!" he exclaimed. "Or...to start our own museum. And I wonder just what treasures might be in that old shed? I see it's padlocked."

"Well, to be exact," Becca said. "There are two shovels...one with the blue paint almost all gone, a ladder, and a wheelbarrow! And you want to know something spooky?" She didn't wait for an answer. "Your psychic wife, here, knew all that...without even looking!"

"She did?" Dick asked, rather mechanically. Then, when it registered, he turned to Lisa, "You...did? You knew all that?"

"I did," she nodded sadly. "Come on up to the house where we can sit down, and I'll fill you in on the particulars." They sat on the front stoop, in the shade of a wonderful old oak tree, and Lisa recounted the story. Up to the point where her Dad had called her to come and help him.

"And did you?" Dick asked, putting his arm around her shoulders.

"Uh...I don't really know," she said, squinting as if to see more clearly. "I get to that point, and..."

"And?" Dick prompted.

"And...well...I have this overpowering need to just run. Get completely out of the picture."

"And does that work?" he asked quietly.

"No! No, it does not!" she yelled, getting up and heading around the corner of the house. "It happened...up here," she called back over her shoulder, "...where the old road came onto the property." Dick scrambled to catch up to her, with Becca trailing him up the slope. Lisa stood there facing them. "If...if I could only *see*...what happened next! It's so exasperating!"

"Well, what if..." Dick was searching for some way to help her. "What if Becca and I act it out...for you. Maybe that would help."

"Yeah," Becca joined in, "we could do that, Lisa."

"Well, I don't know. I guess it couldn't hurt to try," Lisa answered.

"OK...so...I'll be your Dad...and Becca will be you. And… you're just a neutral observer, see?" Dick started. "Now, Lisa, show me where I would have been standing...after I just cold cocked this guy in the head."

"OK...well, I think the old cistern was about there, so you'd be standing about here," she marked the spot with her foot, and Dick moved onto it.

"And, Becca...you...you'd be standing over here, not too far away, and...and facing him, uh...Dick." She moved her sister to the right distance.

"OK...so I'm you," Becca began, "and I'm standing here...facing Daddy...and the guy that's laying there...and...?" The question just hung there.

"And what?" Lisa asked.

"So, I'm you...and I'm standing there...doing what?" Becca prodded.

"Well, I'm...I mean you're very nervous. Uh, maybe...rocking...back and forth." Becca started to rock. "And...and wringing your hands. OK. That's right. And Daddy...Daddy's leaning over the man...uh, Frank...and hollers for me to come help him."

Dick asked, "OK, so was I standing? Or kneeling...like this?"

"Uh...kneeling. Yes, like that."

"And...what, exactly, did I say?"

"You said, Come here. Come here, Baby Girl. Come and help me..."

Becca looked up at Lisa. "Well...what now? Do I go over there?"

"Uh, yeah. Go over and...and pick up...uh, try to lift the man's arm up..."

"Like this?" Becca asked. Lisa nodded. "And so...then what do we do? Do we drag the man?" Becca paused, waiting for Lisa to answer.

"Uh...yeah...I think..." she started, then dropping to her knees, cried out, "No! I can't do it, Daddy...I can't hold it. He's too heavy!" Tears were running down Lisa's face as she once again relived the trauma. "No...Daddy...no! I tried. Honest, I tried! But, he's too heavy!" Then she sank to her knees, throwing her hands up in front of her face. "No, Daddy...please! It's me...your Baby Girl!" she screamed. "Don't hit me....please! I'll try again!" Then she was sobbing and Dick and Becca were holding her. When she could finally speak, she sobbed, "He...just said...get the hell and gone out of my face!"

After a pause to let her compose herself, Dick asked, "And...did you?"

"What?" Lisa struggled for air. "Did I what?"

"Did you leave?"

"I...I guess so. I guess I did leave." She thought for a minute, then whispered, "He...he almost hit me...with that shovel! His eyes were wild...like a crazy person's. It was like he didn't even recognize that it was me! Then... then he just threw it down and screamed at me...Get out of here! Get the hell and gone out of my face!" All the color had drained out of Lisa's face. "And I...I just got up and ran."

"Where? Where did you go?" Becca asked.

Dazed, Lisa stood up and walked toward the house, then she turned and started to run. She ran back up the slope where she paused for just a split second to look back in terror, then she just kept on going, faster and faster, putting as much distance as she could between her Daddy and Frank, and that dead man in the cistern. Then shifting into second gear, she ran even faster, cutting off across a pasture and coming out on the main road about a mile and a half from the house. Dick and Becca saw where she was headed and drove down the road to wait for her. Dick held the barbed wire up so that a very bedraggled Lisa could slip through.

Becca started to scold, "Lisa...whatever got into you? There are,."

"I know...rattlesnakes..." Lisa panted, breathlessly. "But...I just had to do it. I had to retrace my steps...to know what I really did." She climbed in limply beside Dick, and whispered. "Thanks for coming for me. I couldn't have made it back under my own steam," she panted. He kissed her on the cheek, and started to turn the car around.

Just then a very old black pickup pulled up alongside of them. "Everthing OK?" asked the weathered old face leaning out the window. "Saw the missus, cuttin' across the pasture, there, and..." he made an attempt to spit some juice from the wad of tobacco he had tucked into his cheek, but it didn't get far enough out and ended up running down his door. "S'cuse me." He took a swipe at his mouth with a very dirty old red rag, squinting to get a better look at who was in the car. "Why...I seen you two before."

Lisa flashed him her best smile, "Yes, you gave us directions the first day we were here. When we were looking for our grandfather's property."

"Well...are you OK?"

"Yes, I'm fine. Used to run track in school...and every now and then I just have to run...get it out of my system." She laughed.

Her lightness angered him, and he stomped down on the accelerator, revving the engine, but going nowhere. "Lady! Now that's a dang fool thing to do around here! There's snakes all over this cussid place! You want to run, go on in to the High School and run around the track...or run around the cemetery," he spit again, "but...don't be running across my pasture! Besides snakes, it's plumb full o' prairie dog burrows. Break a leg...and the snakes'll get you for sure!" He was clearly very put out with them. "Besides..." he revved the engine again, "you get hurt in my pasture...and I'm the one that'd haft ta come and carry ya in. An' I don't have time to play nursemaid to no fool city folk!" He spit again. "Now...ya got that?"

Dick and Lisa spoke in unison, "Yes, sir...we got that." Then Lisa added. "It was really nice of you to be concerned...and you can be sure I won't be running in your pasture again."

Seemingly appeased for the moment he sat there blinking, then slowly cut himself another plug off of his tobacco, and asked, "Well...is there anything I can do for you...now that I'm here?" He took another swipe across his mouth with the rag, and tucked the new plug into his cheek, all the while looking expectantly at the trio in the car.

"Can't think of a thing." Dick smiled. We do thank you for being concerned. Sometimes we city folk get a little too rambunctious for our own good."

For some odd reason, *that* pleased the old man, and his face lit up with a tobacco-liquidy smile. "Well... can't say I blame you." He punched the steering wheel, and let out a funny sort of old man's laugh, "Whew-ee! I guess some would say I was a leetle bit rambunctious in my younger days, too!" He sat there grinning at some far away memory, then, clearly back in the present, added, "So…well…if ya don't need me fer anything, I guess I'll just be a moseying on back now." He started to pull away, then backed up. "Hey, I heard ya bought the place! So... then...I guess I oughter be a' welcomin' you to the neighborhood!" He punctuated that with another spit of tobacco, put his truck in gear, and roared off down the road in a cloud of dust.

They sat there bemused, watching their neighbor's dust cloud, until finally, Dick turned to Lisa and asked, "What do you think...had enough trauma for one day? Or…do you want to go back to the house for awhile?

"Oh, I think...I need to give it a rest…for today. Let's just go on back to town."

CHAPTER TWENTY SEVEN

"I talked to Gram awhile ago and she told me to tell you to be sure to bring Dick out to meet them," Dena said as she took their lunch orders. Then she giggled, "What she actually said was, "Tell that Lisa I said *'Now, girl...don't you make me hafta come in there'*!"

"Yes, and I could just hear her say that!" Lisa laughed. "She's quite a character."

"I'd like to meet your Grandparents, Dena," Dick said. "And we really don't have any plans for this afternoon." He looked from Lisa to Becca. "At least that I know of." They both said that it was OK by them.

"Great! Soon as I get these orders turned in, I'll call her and tell her you're coming," Dena said, heading for the kitchen.

Lisa called after her, "See if Bertha needs anything from Alco. We're stopping there first...before we head out." Dena acknowledged she heard with a wave of her arm as she disappeared into the kitchen.

When she returned with their orders, she said, "Gram said you could bring her a can of that coffee they've got in their sale flyer...she couldn't remember which brand it was, but they've always got their flyer posted on the front door. Just get the three pound one that's on sale, and she'd prefer that regular stuff to the 'unleaded'. But if decaf is all they have, then it's OK." She consulted her order pad to see if she had brought everything. "Anything else...before I go?"

Well...when you have time, Dena, I'd take another cup of that regular stuff, myself," Dick said. "I don't much care for the *unleaded* kind, either."

"Just started a new pot, 'n I'll bring it as soon as it's ready," Dena tossed back at him, as she scurried off to wait on another table.

Their trip to Alco was quick. Becca needed toothpaste. Lisa needed hand lotion, gum, and tissues, and while they were there Dick decided he was running low on aftershave. They were already checking out when it dawned on them that they hadn't gotten Bertha's coffee, so Dick hurried to get a can. They were in and back out in less than twenty minutes, heading North on Hwy 59.

Becca was telling Dick all about Fred and Bertha, and how they figured into the picture, and Lisa was just enjoying the ride. Watching a circling hawk, she remembered some lines from when she played the part of a mama hen in a childhood play. "Chicken hawk, chicken hawk, do fly away! I'm tired of..." She searched her memory for the lost word. "Running? No, not running. Hiding? Yes, that's it, hiding. I'm tired of hiding...and...? And what?"

Closing her eyes, she tried, vainly, to peer into that long ago classroom, to once again see the oversized words that had been so carefully drawn, to accommodate her nearsightedness, on the seldom used side blackboard of Miss Austin's room. She could make out the room, and Miss Austin, and the blackboard. But there were no words written there. "Darn..!" she thought, "I just wanted a little peek." And just about the time she was going to give it up, there they were. Not on the board, but crystal clear in her mind.

"Chicken Hawk, Chicken Hawk, please fly away!
I'm tired of hiding in my house all day,
And my wild, unruly children pay no heed to what I say.
With you circling about, they think they can run and play,
They laugh, and flirt with danger night and day!
And have no fear, till they've been caught away.
Oh, Chicken Hawk, Chicken Hawk, please fly away!

Smiling, groggily, at the memory, she felt herself being lifted, soaring upward with the hawk. Drifting dreamily off to a place where she was lying out in the cold rain wishing someone would come along and find her. It seemed like she had been there for such a long time. People kept coming and going. Flashlights and car lights played against the sky, and she heard many voices, and even a siren at some point.

"I'm over here!" She didn't know if she actually said it...or if it was just a thought. "Please, please, come and get me." But still no one came. Then all the cars were gone and, except for the groaning of a nearby windmill, it was very still. She struggled harder to get the words out, to rouse herself. "Come back," she screamed. "Don't leave me! I'm not dead!" Then gentle hands were touching her, and she opened her eyes. A very tall lean figure was bending over her, and although she wasn't sure if it was a person or an apparition, the moment he spoke, she was no longer afraid.

"Hey, Missy! Where in the world did you come from?" The voice was deep and rich and warm, and his movements were slow and methodical as he carefully checked her arms and legs for breaks. Then, wrapping his coat around her, he gently lifted her off of the remains of the haystack that had cushioned her fall. Safe at last, she stopped struggling, and allowed herself to just go, drifting away, sinking serenely into the warm security of his arms.

Suddenly, Lisa was aware that the car had stopped, and Dick was opening her door. Then, leaning in, he stroked her face. "Honey...it's OK." he said. "Was it that same dream again?"

Dazed and disoriented she looked into his concerned eyes, "What? What are we stopped for? Are we there?"

"No, Lisa...you seemed to be caught up in that dream again. You were screaming about not being dead, and wanting someone to come find you."

Then he was kneeling there beside the car looking up into her face with such concern that she was suddenly embarrassed.

"Oh, Dick, I'm sorry. Yes, I guess it was that same dream again. I wish it would just go away! Why does it...keep hounding me?" Stepping out of the car, Lisa shuddered, as if to rid herself of a heavy weight. Then, closing the car door, she leaned against it.

Dick positioned himself next to his wife. "Was it just the same? Or, was there anything different...or new...this time?" he asked.

"The same..." she began, then looking surprised, added, "No! It was different. There was a man...and he came and carried me away," she answered.

"What man? Did you know him?" Dick prodded.

"Huh uh...I don't think so. But he seemed so kind...I wasn't afraid."

"Where did he take you?"

She just shook her head. "I don't have the foggiest notion. He was carrying me away...and I felt safe. That's when I woke up." Kicking at some loose gravel, she looked squarely at her husband, "But, something puzzles me?"

"And that is...?" he asked.

"Well, I assumed, before, that I couldn't see any of the people clearly, because it was a dream...because I wasn't really there. I had read the articles...but I didn't really know any of the people, except my parents, so I wouldn't have had faces to put with the sounds." She stopped, gazing off into the distance, but Dick was sure she wanted to say more.

When she didn't, he prodded her, "So...how has that changed? Or has it?"

"No...I guess not...except..." She put her hand up to shield her eyes from the sun.

"Except what?"

"Except...that was a *real* man! I didn't know him, but he was a real flesh and blood person...with a recognizable face. I'm sure if I saw him...whoever he was...walking down the street today I would recognize him! And *that* makes it feel more like..." She was having trouble saying it.

"More like a memory...than a dream?" Dick asked.

"Yeah. It really does, now. But I don't know…how…it can possibly be..."

They hadn't been aware of the car that was coming toward them until it pulled up and Fred got out. "Hey, ever'thing OK? Saw you was stopped here...so I just came on down." He came around the car. "You OK, Lisa?"

"Yes...I'm OK. What makes you ask?" she answered.

"Jest wondered," he said, with his head cocked to one side like he was sizing up a situation. "How'd ya know it was here?" he asked, rubbing his chin.

"What? What was here...?" Lisa started, then his words registered. "Do you mean to tell me that the wreck...was here? Right here...?"

"Yep...pretty close...if'n I remember it right." He looked around. "Yep...pretty durned close…if not on this very spot. You see that old windmill and cattle tank over there..." he waved his arm. "Well, it was right in line with that, so this has to be pretty close."

Lisa came around the car. "Show me...show me how it happened, Fred! Please…show me...where the cars were…and where Mama was." She walked out into the middle of the road. "I need to see it...feel it!" Now she was pulling him along with her. "Please…Fred…just show me!"

"Yeah...Fred," Becca said, getting out of the car. "I want to know, too."

They spent the next several minutes discussing the wreck, with Fred telling them everything he could remember. Finally, they drove on up the road to introduce Dick to Bertha. It was a pleasant afternoon with Bertha insisting that they stay, while she rustled up a supper of leftovers, after which they retired to the living room with their coffee. Fred was happily showing them their photograph wall, with all the kids, grandkids, and sundry relatives, mixed together, when Lisa stopped him.

"Who are *these* people?" she asked.

"Who? Oh, those are my cousins...on my Mother's side. Barnes. My mother's brother's kids. They all went further west in the mid fifties. The whole family. Settled in Arizona, up near the Nevada line. Now the girls down front there are, Dodie, the oldest, and Millicent, Millie, we called her. She was the youngest. And that one there is John. He was the second one." He pointed each one out. "And that's Jake, and Justin, the twins, there on the hay wagon. Our Dad used to tease their folks. Said they needed to have at least one more, cause it wasn't right for Millie to be the end of the line, the fish hook, cause she was too pretty for that." He laughed. "When Millie got older...he took to calling her fish hook and she'd get so mad she wouldn't speak to him!"

"Ok...and so, who's the tall fella...in the cowboy hat, sitting astride the horse there in the back?" Lisa asked.

"Oh, *you know*...that's David...my brother." The look he gave Lisa made her uneasy, but she didn't know why. And that made her even more uneasy. In fact, she was beginning to wish they'd left an hour ago, before she had started to get such a headache. Dick saw that she was having a bad time of it and came to her rescue.

"Well, folks, I hate to break up such a wonderful party, but I'm bushed. I think it's time this old man hit the hay. What do you say, girls, shall we call it a day?" They didn't need any persuading.

Back at the motel, Lisa quickly spread out all of the materials they had on the wreck. "Darn!" she said. "I was almost sure..."

"Almost sure of what," Dick asked, wrapping his arms around her.

"Oh...I don't know...exactly. But, when I saw David's picture...I was almost sure I'd seen him before. Like...at the wreck...but he's not in *any* of these pictures. And there's no mention of him in any of the accounts. But...there was just something...so familiar about him." She picked up the clippings and piled them on the desk so that they could go to bed. "I don't know. I guess he just looked...familiar."

"Well then, there's a reason he looks familiar...so lets just sleep on it. It'll come to you... when the time is right." Dick buried his face in her shoulder. "But, right now...you're the one who seems very familiar to me. And I'm having vague recollections of a past life with you...before any of this existed." He picked her up and deposited her on the bed. "I just want to get lost in you...and forget all about that wreck out there on Hwy 59, and Fred and Bertha and David, and your parents. I just want you and me...us."

"Anybody ever tell you what wonderful ideas you have?" Lisa asked, turning out the light. "You could probably market them."

"I'm not interested in marketing them..." he laughed, "just putting them into practice!"

CHAPTER TWENTY EIGHT

Lisa woke before dawn, her heart pounding like she had been running a marathon. She lay there for some time trying to figure out what had awakened her. Perhaps it had just been the sound of the birds coming to life in the trees outside her window, but as soon as she had the thought she dismissed it. No, she loved the birds, and no matter how loud their singing was, it wouldn't have frightened her. No. It was something else. Something within the house. She squinted at the ever lightening room. There was nothing amiss. So she climbed carefully out of bed so as not to awaken Barbie, and slipped soundlessly out into the hallway.

There...there it was again, coming from downstairs. Perhaps it was just the old Tomcat crying to be let out. She rushed down the stairs, her bare feet making hardly any sound at all on the smooth hardwood, but at the foot of the stairs she stopped cold. The sound was coming from her parents room, and it wasn't old Tomcat. She turned to go back upstairs, but couldn't. Her mother was crying and maybe there was something she could do to help, so Lisa turned around again and headed for her parents room.

The door was slightly ajar and instinctively Lisa knew that she dare not go in. Her mother, clad only in the casts she wore on one leg and one arm, lay sprawled face down on the floor, while her father easily held her down with a foot in the middle of her back, wildly swinging a set of crutches over her head. "You want to leave? Well, let's see how far you get without these!" He shouted, flinging the crutches across the room. Lisa winced and ducked out of sight as her cursing father stormed out of the house. His parting words struck terror in her heart. "And don't think you're going to take my kids away from me...I'll see the whole lot of you in hell first!"

As soon as the back door banged shut behind her father, Lisa sprang into the room to help her mother. First she got a fresh gown from the bureau drawer, but as she tried to help her mother turn over she realized that it would take more than her ten year old strength to really help. "Don't worry, Mama," she cried. "I'll get Barbie. Together we can get you back in your bed."

"No...honey. I think it's going to take more than my girls to help me up. I'm hurt bad. Get Barbie...but don't wake the boys. I don't want them to see me like this."

Lisa was crying, "I'll get her, Mama." She started out the door, then turned, "I won't wake the boys, either, Mama...I promise!" Tears streamed down her face as she ran for the stairs. "I'm hurrying, Mama, see?" She took the stairs two at a time, hoping her mama knew what an effort she was making.

"Oh, that's my good girl, Lisa," Kate whispered, sinking down into her pain.

Together, the girls were able to get the gown on their mother, but despite all their efforts, they couldn't get her back into bed. Finally, in complete exhaustion she sent them to a pay phone to call for help.

Then Lisa was waking up. Dick was shaking her, calling, "Hey sleepyhead, I'm ready to go get some breakfast. How about you?"

"Noooo..." Her mind was saying. "I need to stay with this just a little bit longer..." But it was too late. She was already too much awake to recapture the dream. Or whatever it was. She told Dick about it while she dressed. Then, after breakfast, they told Becca about it while they fed the squirrel in the park.

"Well..." she mused, "I wonder who it was that you called for help." She paused, then added, "And...I wonder what they were fighting about in the first place!"

"Well, obviously...she had just told him that she wanted to leave..."

"Yeah...but I mean before that! They must have been having a fight. You said her crying woke you up! So...I wonder what set it off."

"I wouldn't know," Lisa said, absently. She had dumped the manila envelope of pictures that Bertha had given them onto the table to show Dick. Suddenly the hair on the back of her neck stood up, and she handed a picture to Becca. "It was David!" she whispered. "Remember this picture of Eddie Benetti...and his wife...with Fred's brother, David, in it?"

"Yeah...but what does it have to do with anything?" Becca asked.

"See...you can see him better in this picture...than in the one on their wall. And...Becca, Dick...it's him. I know it's him!"

"Ok. So it's him...but what *about* him are we supposed to be impressed with?" Becca asked.

"He's the one who got me...after the wreck."

"Uh, excuse me, but did I just hear you say...that you *now* believe this to have been really...real," Becca asked, "and *not* just a dream...*about* the wreck?"

"Well, I wasn't sure...until I saw this picture just now!" Lisa exclaimed. "But, it certainly...feels real at this moment!" She closed her eyes and took a deep breath. "I tell you...I can almost smell him. Old Spice...mixed with pipe tobacco!"

"That sounds pretty real to me," Dick smiled. "Didn't know you had a thing for Old Spice, or I'd have gotten me some at Alco when we were in there yesterday." He laughed, then asked seriously, "What clinched it for you?"

"Just now...seeing this picture. It also made me remember who Mama sent us to call." She was quiet a moment, wanting to be absolutely sure. "It was him. She sent us to call David." They all sat there in stunned silence a moment.

"Well...Bertha kept trying to tell us that David had this gigantic crush on our Mama," Becca offered. "But, she never said...it was mutual!"

"Whoah...wait a minute," Dick jumped in. "We don't know that there was anything between them...except that David had a crush on her. We don't know what your Mama did about that...if anything! So let's not jump to conclusions."

"Right..."Lisa answered, getting up from the picnic table. "No jumping to conclusions. But, this is making me really anxious. I feel like I need to run...or at least walk." She was stuffing the other pictures back into the envelope. "Here, let's leave these in the car," she said handing the packet to Dick, "so we can go walk around the pond. I need to move my body! Walk...run...something. Just so I'm moving!"

Grinning, Dick looked from the packet to Lisa, "That's...let's...as in let *us*?"

She nodded, grinning back. "Uh huh, and your half of *'us'* just got elected. If you will, please?"

"Then I guess my half says...OK...I'll be right back," he said, lightly kissing the top of her head, as he headed for the car.

They started out slowly, but soon Lisa, lost in thought, was pushing pretty hard, and it was a challenge just to stay up with her.

"Uh...Lisa...just let us know if you don't want our company," Becca yelled, stopping to catch her breath. Dick stopped too.

"Huh?" Lisa asked, turning toward them, absently. "What did you say?"

"I said..."Becca, repeated, "Just let us know if you don't want our company. I didn't know this was some kind of a race!"

"Oh...I'm sorry! I was totally zoned out...thinking," Lisa offered, lamely, waiting for them to catch up.

"Yep...that's my Lisa. Always thinking, thinking, thinking." Dick said, catching his breath. "And where has all this thinking gotten you, my dear?" He asked, laughing.

"Nowhere. Nowhere at all," Lisa shook her head. "Too much stuff..." she pointed to her head, "...in there! I do wish I could make sense of it all."

Dick put his arm around her shoulders, "You will, my Love. You will."

"Do you really think so?" she asked. "It seems like I just go from one memory to another. About the time I think we've figured this thing out...bingo! I have another dream...and nothing is the same." She threw a pebble into the pond. "Surely there can't be much more...it has to stop somewhere."

Becca nodded. "Yeah. Who would have thought that all of this stuff was tucked away up there..." she pointed at Lisa's head, grinning, "in that punkin head of yours."

"Oh, no you don't," Lisa laughed. "You can't lay this all off on me! Seems to me that you started this whole thing, with your, 'Eesie, stop the car. I have to see that house'!"

They resumed their walk, taking it much slower this time, each caught away in their own thoughts. Finally Lisa spoke. "You know, guys, it's pretty scary...not knowing what we're going to turn up next. Sometimes I wish we'd never started this."

Becca thought about that for a few seconds, then added, "Well...nothing says we have to stay and finish it. We could just leave."

"No...we can't...just leave!" Lisa said. "At least, I can't. I may be in way over my head, but I can't turn loose of it. At least not at this point."

"Well, Mama always did say you were the bulldog of the family," Becca laughed.

"Ah, yes, she told me that, too...on our wedding day, if I remember it right." Dick said, smiling wryly at the memory. "In fact, now that I think of it, she told me you were part pit bull!" They all laughed at that.

"I'm just...tenacious." Lisa said, grinning. "And sometimes it pays to be tenacious!" Then she added, sadly, "But I just wish...we were at the end of this. It's...so...so..." Blinking back the tears, she just threw up her hands in a huge sigh. "Oh...I don't know what...!" They were back at the picnic table and Lisa plopped down, burying her face in her hands and let the tears come. After a few moments she stopped and asked Dick for his handkerchief. "Thanks. I guess I was just needing a good cry."

Becca was trying to coax the squirrel to the table but it wasn't cooperating. "OK, be that way," she said, turning her attention to Lisa. "Have you remembered anything else, Lisa? About David, I mean?" Lisa shook her head. "Well...then, do you want us to ask you questions? Do you think that would help."

"I guess it can't hurt," Lisa said, shrugging her shoulders. "And...it really might jog something loose. Yeah, go ahead."

"Well, I was just wondering...where he took you. You know, after the wreck. Do you remember where you went." Becca asked.

Lisa was pensive, searching her mind, "Hum, well...he picked me up..." She closed her eyes, trying to get back into the scene, "and carried me..." She was very still, concentrating. "Nope...nothings coming. I don't remember where he took me," she said in exasperation. "I can't seem to stay with it! When I try to visualize him carrying me, I just get other stuff crowding in!"

"Other stuff?" Dick asked. "Like what other stuff? Maybe it's connected. Why don't you just let the other stuff take over and see where it goes?"

"Yeah," Becca said. "Maybe it is connected. Can't hurt to check it out."

"Well...I don't know *how* it's connected...but we'll give it a shot." Lisa was quiet, eyes shut, "I see a very old lady...in an apron."

"Old? Like how old?" Dick asked. "And where is she...your house...or somewhere else?"

Lisa was very concentrated, now. "Uh...she's really old. Like late seventies or eighties. Very little and shriveled up...with a hump on her back."

"And what's she doing?" Becca asked, excitedly.

"Well...she has something in her hand...like...like a wet cloth. Yes, it's a washcloth. And... and she's coming toward me. She's wiping my face with it. Now...she folds it, and puts it on my forehead."

"Can you see where you are?" Dick asked.

"I'm on a sofa...I think..." Lisa started.

"Oh, this is neat," Becca squealed. "Look around, and tell us about the room."

Lisa was quiet a moment, "OK...The flooring is linoleum...with a gray feathery pattern on it. It's a very small room."

"Is there anybody else in the room?" Dick asked.

"Voices...I hear voices...but I don't see...anybody..."

"Take your time," Dick said. "We're not in any hurry."

"Gee, you're good at this!" Becca whispered to him. "I guess it pays to be married to a therapist, huh?" Dick just grinned at her.

100 MILES FROM NOWHERE: murder remembered

Lisa started to talk again. "I see…uh…there's an old man. He's looking at me, checking my hands and fingers. Now…he's listening to my chest. Why, he's a doctor! Concussion…he said. I have a concussion, and they shouldn't move me! They're going away, now. Through a door…and now it's…dark! No!" Lisa became highly agitated. "No! Don't go! Don't leave me…I'm not dead!" She began crying again, "I'm *not* dead. Don't leave me, please!"

Then Dick was holding her, whispering over and over, "It's OK, Lisa. I'm here. And I'm…never going to leave you!"

After lunch they took a drive up hwy 59. Back to the place of the wreck. As they sat there watching the old windmill groan out it's meager trickle of water Lisa whispered. "Thank you, Lord, for not letting me die out there. Now, please just help me figure out the rest of this mess…so we can actually put it to rest…and go home." Then she looked at Dick, "Believe me, home never looked so good…as it does at this moment!"

CHAPTER TWENTY NINE

They had been parked by the side of the road for several minutes, each one lost in thought, when Becca ventured, "Well...what now? Where do we go from here?"

"I think..." Lisa began, weighing each word carefully. "I think we need to go see Fred and Bertha." She straightened up in her seat, as Dick put the car in gear. "I don't know what they can add to what they've already told us...but...there's something there that I just can't quite put my finger on. I think...I *feel*...that they might know more than they know they do."

Dick grinned, "Well...let's go see if they do." Then he added, "Actually, I'm a bit surprised that Fred didn't come to see why we were sitting here so long."

Becca laughed. "Me too! And, if I'm not mistaken, that sorta looks like a Fred dust cloud coming toward us now...don't you think?"

"Yep...It definitely is a Fred dust cloud," Lisa laughed, just as the black pickup topped the rise before them. They stopped as Fred brought his pickup along side, exchanging greetings.

"Were you going somewhere?" Dick asked. "We were just on our way to visit you, but if you're going somewhere, we can come back later."

"Nope! I wasn't goin' nowhere...jest bein' nosey. Saw you was stopped down there...'n thought I'd see what you was up to," Fred, grinned congenially. "Go on, 'n I'll jest get turned around 'n folla ya in."

Pulling into the driveway Dick chuckled, "I'll just bet he doesn't miss much."

"Yeah," Lisa agreed. "I was thinking the same thing."

"And Bertha, too," Becca added. "If something did get past Fred's antenna...she'd most certainly catch it." She laughed. "They're like...the community watchdogs!" As Fred pulled in along side of them, they got out of the car and followed him up the steps to the kitchen.

"Hey, Mommy...look what the cat drug in. I found these folks just sittin' in their car in our yard. Figured they must be hungry...to show up at our doorstep so close to supper time!" He rambled on, in spite of the protestations from his guests. "You got any of that meatloaf left from last night?"

"Oh, I figured they'd be coming on up to the house, when I saw their car down the road...so, I'm one step ahead'a you, Poppy. Already got it in the oven, warmin'. Figured we could make hot meatloaf *slam itches*." That's what our kids called 'em when they was little," she chuckled. "An' I got salad fixin's. Come on...you girls kin help me git it ready...while the menfolk visit." Breathless, she slumped into a kitchen chair, content to let the girls be her arms and legs.

After their meal, as they lingered lazily over dessert and coffee, Lisa suddenly brought the party back to life by asking, "So, Fred...where did David take me...after the wreck?"

"Uh..." He was clearly taken off guard. "Uh...I'm not sure...what you're asking..."

"Well...it took me awhile to figure this out...since not one article even hinted that I was in that wreck. But, I have finally pieced it together. David...found me...out there," she gestured, "in the field. And I need to know where he took me. There was a very old woman...with a hump on her back...and I was in a house with linoleum on the floor...with a gray feathery pattern." She paused, looking at Fred, then Bertha, "Surely...you *two* know... where he took me."

Fred stared at her a moment, then blinked and said, matter-of-factly, "Well, he took you to our Grandmother Barnes. That's where David was livin' at the time." He downed the remains of his coffee, then continued. "You had a concussion...I believe...an' so he an' Gram took care o' you."

"For how long?" Lisa asked.

"Well...I don't rightly know how long it was." He looked at Bertha. "What do you think, Mommy? How long was she there?"

Bertha shrugged. "Seems like several days. That's for sure. Maybe a week. Finally your Pa came an' took ya home. It was prob'ly about a week." She shrugged again, furrowed her brow, then added, "But...maybe longer."

"That night...when I told you I didn't remember the wreck, Bertha...when you said I was old enough to remember..." Bertha nodded. "well...why didn't you tell me all this...then?"

The old woman shrugged. "I dunno...why I didn't. It seemed kinda strange...that ya said ya didn't remember...an' you was prob'ly nine, or ten...certainly old enough ta remember. I just felt like I shouldn't say anything...at least till we knew ya better."

"We didn't know if we could...trust you." Fred added, gingerly. "Remember...we'd just met you. You and Becca were complete strangers...to us." He got up and poured more coffee. "An'...when you asked me who David was...that *really* had us puzzled. I couldn't figure how it was that you didn't recognize 'im...as much as he helped your Mama...an' all." He finished, lamely, then after a moment added, "We was jest bein'...uh...cautious."

Becca, picking up on the thread about David, asked, "How do you mean...he helped our Mama? What exactly did he do?"

"Why, he helped 'er get away from Joe...that's what!" Bertha snorted. "Fat lotta good it did 'im! After all he did for her, she up and left 'im flat!" She stopped to catch her breath. "An' then, he up and takes off...for God only knows where!"

Lisa stopped her, "Whoa...whoa, slow down there...a minute!" She took a moment to clear her thoughts, then began again. "Fred...I thought...in fact I'm sure...that you said...that your brother, David, *was dead*. Am I right? Didn't you tell us...when you were giving us that genealogy lesson...that David was dead?"

He sat nodding, staring into his cup of coffee. "That's right, I did. And I'm sorry for misleadin' you. But...you see...I was tryin' to find out if you knew anything...about where he was. After your Mama took you kids and moved away...he was supposed to go there...wherever it was that you all had gone to. He told me they were going to get married...as soon as her divorce was final."

Lisa looked incredulous, "So...you're telling us...that he just *disappeared*? And that you don't know *what* happened to him?"

Nodding sadly, he said, "That's right. He had all 'is stuff boxed up..." He took a sip of coffee. "an' we were supposed to send it to 'im...soon's he got settled."

"But he never did let us know," Bertha added, "where to send it. Oh, his stuffs all up there..." she motioned to the attic. "After Gram died...we finally just put it up there...ta git it outt'a the way." She sat quietly, eyes downcast. "Might as well be dead...fur all *we* know."

"Did you..." Becca started, tentatively. "Surely...*you did*...try to find him?"

"Yeah...but not right away," Fred answered, sadly. "You see, we just figured he was too busy gittin' settled into 'is new life...that we'd hear from 'im soon. An' then...well, time has a way of gittin' away from you...you know?" The old man was looking older and sadder by the minute. He was quiet for a time, and then continued. "Then...one day Gram called an' asked me to come by. She wanted to show me somethin'. It was a letter *to David*... from your Mama...from somewhere in Texas."

"Abilene...it was from Abilene," Bertha interjected.

"Yeah. Yeah, I do believe it was Abilene. Anyway, we thought that was pretty strange...that she'd be writin' to 'im...if he was out there with her. So...we figured...he must'a left to come back here for a visit, or somethin'... and he'd be along any day, but..." Fred's eyes misted over, "he *never did show up*." He paused to blow his nose. "After some time passed...I don't rightly know how long, maybe a few weeks, maybe longer...I went inta town an' talked with the sheriff. He said he just figured things prob'ly didn't work out between David and yer Mama, an' he'd be back when he got ready...not to worry 'bout it. Said, in the meantime, he'd poke around...'n see if he could come up with anything. Well...if he did, he must nott'a found nothing...cause he never got back ta me."

"And you...never pursued it further?" Dick asked, gently.

"Nope. I jest came to the conclusion that...if a man doesn't wanna be found...he won't be. Then, when Gram died we just moved 'is stuff inta our place...the attic." Fred looked out the kitchen window. "All these years I've hoped that one day I'd look up an' see 'im coming up the drive." He got up and stretched, "An' when he does, 'is stuff'll be there waitin' on 'im...jest like he never left." With this, Fred excused himself to go do his chores.

"Don't mind 'im..." Bertha said. "When he gits down...he's always got 'is *chores* ta do. It helps ease 'is mind."

After they helped Bertha tidy up the kitchen, the trio headed back to Yuma. And that night Lisa had another dream. She was once again awakened by her mother crying, and once again she worked her way silently down the stairs to cringe outside of her parents room. She wanted to be close in case her mother needed her. In fact, she had armed herself with a large heavy flashlight, *just in case*...she didn't dare let her mind go to wherever that was headed ...just, just in case.

Katherine was huddled in the corner of their room, her bruised face filled with terror as her husband menacingly started toward her, a knife in his right hand.

Lisa screamed, "No...Daddy, no!" At the sound of her voice, Joe turned and lunged at her. Frozen with terror, she dropped the flashlight. Her mind kept saying "run" but her feet weren't getting the message. Then she saw the light of recognition come into her father's liquor crazed eyes, as he dropped to the floor in front of her, sobbing.

"Now...baby girl...you know your Daddy wouldn't hurt you..." he sobbed, dropping the knife onto the floor beside him. "You *know* I wouldn't hurt a hair on your head..." He reached out for Lisa, but she stepped back into the doorway, clearly still terrified.

Pulling a robe around herself, Katherine hobbled across the room, and scooped up the knife. Then, pulling Lisa into the shelter of her arms, she told Joe to leave.

"You...can't throw me out of my own house!" he cried, a pathetic, broken man. "Think about what you're doing, Kate!"

"I am thinking..." she said, clearly, determined, "and you either leave, now, or I'll make your life hell!"

He sneered, looking at the knife in her hand. "You wouldn't never use that..." he started.

"No? Well...just don't you push me! Besides, I have something much more harmful to you than this knife."

"What...? What could *you possibly have*...?" he sneered, but she cut him off.

"I have names, Joe! And places...*bodies!* You...you...talk too much when you're drunk."

Clearly stunned, he blinked, then started toward her, snarling, "*You'll...never live* to give anybody any names...or places..."

Holding the knife out in front of her, she screamed, "Don't...come any closer! Did you honestly think I'm fool enough to sit here and take all this...and never do anything to protect myself...or my children? If you did, *you're the fool*, Joe! You see...I've got *it all written down*...in just the right places...and if anything...*anything at all*...happens to me...or my kids...it *will* fall into the right hands. You'll never get away with hurting me or my kids again...ever!" She was screaming and trembling and nearly choking Lisa as she clung to her. "Now...go on...get out of here...while you still can! And remember...if anything at all happens to us...*you're going down*!"

His look was one of incredulity, "I can't believe that *you*...are smart enough...to..."

"You'd better believe it, mister! And remember it's not just one copy...but several! Did you hear me, *several*!" she screamed. "You might find one...but you'll *never find them all*! Oh, yeah...it's *all* written down, Joe! It's *all* written down!"

Then Lisa was waking up, her heart pounding like a sledgehammer, and for a moment she didn't know where she was. She saw daylight pouring in around the edges of the drapes, and gradually remembered that she was lying beside her sleeping husband, in a motel room in Yuma, Colorado. Her parents were nowhere to be seen, but her mother's words kept playing over and over in her mind, like a broken record. "It's all written down. It's all written down. It's all written down." She got up and went to the bathroom, thinking, "Ok...so...it's all written down. *But...where?*"

CHAPTER THIRTY

Lisa cupped her breakfast coffee with both hands, musing as she stared into the hot steaming liquid, "So, it's all written down," her voice was barely audible, "But...where?"

Becca and Dick looked at each other and then asked in unison, "What's written down?"

"Huh?" Lisa asked, looking up. "What did you say?"

"It's not what we said...but what *you said*. And you said, *It's all written down*," Becca offered.

"Yeah," Dick added. "So, what's written down, Lisa? You've been in a fog all morning, have you had another memory?"

They no longer questioned whether they were dreams or memories, but just accepted them as a given. In fact, Lisa had begun to anticipate them, even welcome the relief they brought. She nodded, answering them. "Uh huh, I have. Mother and Daddy were fighting again. He had beaten her, badly...but she was able to turn the tables on him...with a threat of exposure. She said it was *'all written down*...names, places...*bodies*...and, that she would use it against him...if he ever bothered her or us kids again. He must have believed her...because he left. And as far as I know, he never contested the divorce...or tried to take us kids away from her." She sipped her coffee. "But, I wonder...if she actually did have *real evidence*...if it really was written down...or if she just played a fantastic bluff...and won."

"Well...who might she have given the information to...a relative...a lawyer?" Becca asked. "If she had had a safety deposit box, we surely would have learned about it when she died...right?"

"Well, yes...I would think so. Even if she had some secret account, with a safety deposit box... there would have been statements, or rent due...or something. Right, Dick?" Lisa asked.

"Yeah, I'd think so." Dick answered. "Besides, you didn't find a safety deposit key in any of her belongings, did you?" The girls both shook their heads.

"Huh uh," Lisa said. "I'm *sure* there wasn't one." Then she continued, "Well, one things for sure, whether it was for real, or just a bluff, it worked." She sipped her coffee. "Probably because she told him the record was in more than one place. He *dared not* disbelieve her."

Dena came and refilled their coffee, and asked if everything was alright...since Lisa had hardly touched her meal. "Oh, yes...everything's fine. I'm just not very hungry this morning. Too many things on my mind."

Dena laughed, "Gram said to tell you...not ask, mind you, but tell you... to come out after lunch. She's made another fresh apple cake and doesn't want it to go to waste...*her waist*, that is!"

"I've heard a lot about that apple cake." Dick answered. "So you can be sure we'll take her up on her offer. Better *my waist* than hers!"

"I'd think they'd be getting tired of us by now." Becca said.

Dena laughed, "Not hardly! They love to have company...and you know they don't have a lot to do anymore. Gramps putters around with his machinery and stuff, but the sons do most of the heavy work on the place... 'cause of his heart problem." She started to clear another table, but continued talking to them., "And Gram...well she does pretty much what suits her...but not anything like she used to. Man, when I'd stop by to see if I could help her with anything she'd be knee deep in cannin', or sewin', or she'd have all the blankets out on the line airin' out. I couldn't keep up with her." She started to the kitchen with a pan full of dishes. "Workin' here's a breeze, compared with tryin' to keep up with that old lady!" The door swung shut behind her.

Lisa grinned, "Yeah, I think she's right. I'll just bet that Bertha was a regular whirlwind in her heyday. And as for them getting tired of us...just you remember, Becca, they came looking for us, not the other way around. I think we're a welcome diversion." She busied herself, putting jelly on her toast, "And that's good...because I've certainly enjoyed them."

"Yeah," Becca agreed. "So have I."

Lisa finished a bite of toast, then, looking mischievous, ventured, "So, do you think they trust us enough by now...to maybe let us take a peek at David's stuff?"

"And why would we want to do that?" Becca asked.

"Well, obviously our mother *trusted him*...and she just might have confided in him what she had on our wonderful loving Father."

"Now *that's* brilliant!" Becca effused. "And just why couldn't I have thought of it!"

"It probably depends on how invested he is in the dream that his brother is out there somewhere." Dick said, ignoring Becca's question, and getting back to Lisa's about Fred and Bertha's trust. "You know...we wouldn't want to destroy what little hope he..."

"Not on your life!" Lisa interrupted. "We certainly wouldn't! And if I thought there was *some chance* that David was going to turn up...well..." she sighed, "but, you know, my hunch is..."

Dick finished for her, "That he's not ever coming back." She nodded, sadly.

"Why?" Becca asked. "Why *don't* you think there's a chance that he really will come back someday?"

"Because, I think David was...very solid. And he was a homebody. He lived with his old grandmother, so it doesn't fit what we know of him...to just *'up and leave'*, as Bertha put it, and never even let his family know where he was. Sure...he might have been disappointed in love...but he wouldn't have left his support system. He was a kind man...and a people person. That type doesn't do something so out of character...at least not for long."

"I'm not sure I understand what you're getting at." Becca said. "Lot's of people take off...when they can't handle life's disappointments." As soon as the words came out of her mouth, Becca blushed. "Well...maybe not lots...but *some people* would. Wouldn't they?" She might as well have said *'I would'*, because she knew that Lisa knew what she was thinking.

"Yes, some people would...and even David might have left for a short while. But, my point is, that he'd never have *stayed gone*...for a long time. He'd have worried that his grandmother couldn't make it without him living with her. Or...that he wasn't doing enough for his brother." Lisa answered.

"But...how do you *know* this?" Becca asked. "I don't know it...so how do you?"

"Oh...it's not so hard, Becca. Just think about it..." Dick jumped in. "What Lisa is saying is that David is a caring, giving person. Remember? *He's* the one who rescued Lisa from the wreck, and then helped take care of her until your Daddy came and got her. And...*he* was the person living with an old Grandmother, making sure she was taken care of."

Lisa laughed, "Yep, that's right. He was a caregiver. Once a caregiver, always a caregiver, I always say. You see, Becca, he might have taken off for a while...to clear his head. But he'd never have stayed gone this long. Nope...something happened to him. And I don't think he's ever coming back. I also think Fred and Bertha really know this, deep down." She sighed.

"But...for some reason...they need to hold on to the hope of his return. You can rest assured that I wouldn't just yank the rug out from under them...and cold heartedly announce that I don't think he's coming back...but I actually might be able to help them come to terms with their loss."

"Yep," Dick drawled, "Once a caregiver...always a caregiver." They all laughed at that.

Then Becca added, "Or you might say, it takes one...to know one?"

"Well, whatever..." Lisa chuckled. "But, I'd rather be a giver than a taker any old day! And speaking of giving...Husband...please leave a little bigger tip this time. Waitressing is hard work and Dena is very good at her job."

"Yes, ma'am," he gave her a mock salute. "Nobody's ever accused me of being stingy, I'll have you know, madam. I resent the implication!" He pretended to be insulted, but Lisa just grinned as they made their way to the register.

That afternoon as the trio sat enjoying apple cake and lemonade with Bertha and Fred in their shady back yard, Lisa said, "Fred, David sounds like a very nice man...rescuing me the way he did. I'd like to know more about him." She sipped her lemonade, waiting for Fred to pick up the strand. When he didn't, she added. "He just seems like someone I'd really like to know. Please tell me more about him."

Fred squinted longingly down the road, then looked at his feet. He scratched a mosquito bite on his arm, then shifted uncomfortably in his seat, and just when Lisa had about decided to try Bertha, he spoke. "Well," he cleared his throat, "he was...*is*...a good brother. And a good man. Always helpin' somebody. Jones, over there..." he nodded toward a house barely visible down the road, "got burned out, 'n David rounded up the neighbors ta help 'im rebuild." He paused so long that it was hard for Lisa to keep quiet and wait, but she did. Finally he started up again. "Our young'uns loved 'im. Always wanted a family of 'is own."

"An' he'da made a good daddy," Bertha interjected. "But...Kate...your Mama...was the only woman for him. Wouldn't even consider anybody else."

Fred resumed. An' she know'd she'd made a mistake...but she was a stubborn one. Kept hangin' on, tryin' ta make it work. An' he jest kept a'waitin'...said he know'd she'd come at her senses...sooner er later. An' sure enough, she did. But it took that wreck. He told me it took her durn near losin' her life...an' the life'a one'a her babies...ta wake her up." Fred squinted at Lisa, "Why yer Daddy never even came ta check on you...said he didn't even remember that you was in the car that night!"

Lisa flinched, and Fred blinked, "Oh...oh, now I'm the sorry one...ta be tellin' you this about your pa." He reached out and took her hands in his. "I'm so sorry to have caused you such pain." he said, as the tears flowed effortlessly down her cheeks. Then that very gentle old man reached out and pulled the middle aged woman to him, comforting her as a father comforts his child. "Fergive me," he said, rocking her gently. "An', God, fergive this foolish old man." He held her for a few moments, then gently tilted her face up. "Now, tell me...what can this sorry old man do to make amends?"

"Nothing," she stammered, feeling foolish herself. "There's nothing to be done, Fred. I know you weren't telling me that out of spite or meanness. And remember," she tried to laugh, "I actually *asked* for it!" She fetched a tissue out of her purse and blew her nose.

"Well, you asked me to tell you about David...not your pa. An' I shouldn't'a gotten inta all that. Nobody should have at hear...stuff *like that* 'bout their pa. An' I really mean it. I'm sorry fer havin' done that."

Lisa smiled at him, "I know you are. Now...let's get back to David, shall we?"

He smiled back. "Well...I don't know what else ta tell. Is there somethin' *specific*...that you want to know?"

Lisa was quiet for a moment, then praying silently for help, she took the plunge. "Well, Fred, before my folks split up...they had a terrible fight," she began.

Fred nodded. "Yeah, David told me. Said he beat 'er up pretty bad."

"Well," Lisa continued, "Mama threatened to expose him...if he didn't let us go. She said she had the goods on him...and that there were several copies...and, well...it must have worked. It really must have worked, because he actually did let us go...after threatening our very lives if she left!"

Fred was shaking his head, "No, no, no, he *didn't mean it*...that was the liquor talkin', Lisa. People say mean nasty things when they're all liquored up...but, no, he didn't mean that. Sorry as he was, I don't want to believe that he would have actually harmed his children. And you mustn't believe it either, Lisa."

"Well, be that as it may," Lisa resumed, "we do believed that he *was* capable of doing...uh...what he said he would do. And, not only was he capable of it, but I...*we*...do believe that he would have followed up on his threat...if pushed. So... to us, the fact that he *did back off*...and actually let us go...meant that he took Mama at her word. He *believed* what she told him."

Fred was still shaking his head, "No...I don't want you to go through your life thinkin' your papa would have harmed you in any way. Now...no rational man would harm..."

"Fred," Lisa said, in a very authoritative voice, "stop!" She laid her fingers across his mouth, smiling gently at him. "I know you mean well...but, we're not talking about a rational man, here. Our father.." She looked at Becca and Dick for support, "was...anything but rational. And yes, it hurts terribly to say it, but he *was* capable...of doing away with anyone who got in his way!" She wasn't sure if Fred was more shocked by her forcefulness, or by the knowledge that a family man can actually contemplate such mayhem, but he was clearly shocked. She continued, "Now, our Mama trusted David...and I think she may have given him that information...for safekeeping." She let that have time to sink in, then went on,. "And what I'm wondering is...did David ever mention anything... anything at all...that might lead you to believe that he had that information?"

Fred puzzled on that for a bit, then, sadly shook his head. "No...I can't say as he ever did. But... if'n he had said somethin'...I might'nt'a caught it. You know what I mean?" Lisa nodded. "But...you know...that *letter* she sent? The one I mentioned before?" She nodded again. "Well...do you think that might'ta been it? We just assumed...or speculated...about it. We didn't actually have any idea what was really in it. An' we never opened it." He got to his feet, sort of in a daze. Then he turned to Bertha, "What'd we do with that letter, Mommy? Is it upstairs with t'other stuff?"

"I dunno..." she mused. "Never thought no more 'bout it. Prob'ly is, though, now that you mention it."

"Well, I 'spose we could take a look...and see if it is." He turned to Lisa. "I don't think David would mind us pokin' in 'is stuff...ta help Kate's girls. Come on...let's go see what we kin find."

Bertha sat rocking herself in a double rocker that Fred had made her so there would be plenty of room for grandkids to crawl up beside her. She fanned herself with her apron. "Think I'll just stay put, if'n ya don't mind." Then, not waiting for an answer, she continued, "But, I have ta warn ya, the stuff in that attic hasn't been disturbed practically since we put it there. Hard tellin' how many layers 'o dust you'll have ta wade through." She waited until they were almost to the door, then called after them, "An' it'll be hotter'n blazes up there, ya know!"

"It'll be OK, Bertha. And don't worry about us...we're dust proof!" Becca called back to her.

"Al'right, suit yerself." Bertha said, more to herself than anybody else. "Suit yerself."

CHAPTER THIRTY ONE

The attic bore testimony to the fact that this house had been well lived in, and that it had watched over the raising of a considerable brood, accepting the cast offs of each generation with equanimity. Becca lagged behind as they made their way carefully to the farthest corner of the room. "Wow...what a treasure trove!" she exclaimed, whirling around and knocking a box of toys off it's precarious perch. The ensuing dust cloud sent her into a fit of sneezing. Lisa made her way back to her sister.

"Are you all right?"

"I will be...achoo!...just as soon as...achoo!...I quit...achoo! ...this...achooing!" She was laughing as hard as she was sneezing. "Ah...the price of antiquity!" She held up a little stuffed bear, calling out, "And what am I offered for this magnificent...achoo...little bear? Let's open the bidding at twenty five dollars and fifteen achoos!"

Lisa giggled, "Oh, no...that's much too low. Twenty five dollars and thirty achoos...would be more like it!"

Dick and Fred were oblivious to the girls silliness. They had located the pile of things that constituted David's stuff, and were busy moving boxes so that they could get to it. "Ah...here we are!" Fred exclaimed. "Right where we left them."

The first and second boxes they opened contained only clothing, and Fred was completely unprepared for the flood of emotion that seized him when the opened the third. It contained David's military effects, and the old man suddenly needed to sit down. He very gently lifted the Marine dress jacket from the box, and whispered, "He looked so handsome in his uniform." Then, clearing his throat, he said, "I was Navy. We had a great rivalry going. Dad, too! *He* was Army...in the Great War!"

"Great family legacy..." Dick said.

"Yeah." Fred nodded, laying the jacket aside and picking up a box containing David's medals, he gently fingered each one, then closed the box without comment, and moved on to another box. It contained some letters from their Mother, written to David while he was overseas. He took one letter out, but it fell apart from age and much handling. Gathering up the pieces he carefully put them back into the envelope and put it back. The box also contained some pictures of David and his outfit, both in the States and overseas, and one very dog eared picture of Kate. "You see..." he said, handing the picture to Dick, "he always loved 'er." Dick nodded, passing the picture over to Lisa and Becky, who had finally joined them. Fred took out a picture of David in front of the Eiffel Tower. Looking at it sadly he said, "But, you know, he made a really big mistake...prob'ly the biggest mistake of 'is life."

"What was that?" Lisa asked.

"He never told your Mother how he felt about 'er. Said he didn't want her to be devastated...if anything happened to 'im over there." He handed the picture to Lisa. "This was taken in France. An'...you see," he continued, "That wuz 'is big mistake. While he was over there...Joe stepped in. An' that one never let any grass grow under 'is feet! No sir, not that one. He caught 'er off guard and kept 'er that way until he got a ring on 'er finger!"

Fred continued rummaging through the box, commenting on various objects, until he got to the bottom. "Well, doesn't look like we've got anything more here." He packed the jacket back into the top and closed the lid. "Well, let's see what this one has ta offer," he said, lifting another box up to where he could go through it easily. Near the bottom he found a packet of letters tied with a blue ribbon, and one lone letter postmarked November 23, 1949. It had never been opened.

"This...must be it," Fred whispered, reverently, turning it over in his hands. "I don't think...I kin open it, though." He passed it over to Lisa, who sat staring at the envelope, with her mother's handwriting on it.

"I know what you mean." she said. "It feels almost sacrilegious." They all sat quietly lost in their own thoughts. Finally Becca broke the silence.

"Well, what now? Do we put it back...or...what?"

Lisa looked up at her sister. "I'm trying to decide. This letter was meant for David's eyes only...and it was never opened. I'm not sure...what to do next."

Then Fred stood up and started for the stairs. "Maybe we should jist go downstairs...an' have some coffee...an' think about it."

"Good idea," Dick exclaimed, following Fred's lead toward the door, with Lisa and Becca falling in behind.

"Well, did ya find anything?" Bertha's voice boomed at them as they entered the kitchen where she was preparing coffee. Lisa handed her the letter. "Well, my goodness, you all look like you jest stepped on a grave or something'!" she exclaimed, taking the letter from Lisa.

"We're having trouble opening it," Lisa offered. "It feels strange...like reading someone's diary."

"Oh, nonsense!" Bertha reached for a knife and slit the top open, before anyone could stop her. "Now...are ya gonna read it, or am I?" They all looked aghast, as she took the white paper out of it's cover. "Oh...sit down, all'a you...an' I'll read." Everyone hurried to get their coffee and sit down at the table. When they were situated, Bertha began to read.

"My Dearest David, At last I am a free woman. The divorce has been final for some months, now, and I haven't seen or heard from Joe since we left Yuma. I am beginning to be able to breathe freely again, and not feel like he is in every shadow...just biding his time.

Now that I feel somewhat safe again, I think it's time to address the question of us. When you asked me to marry you, I was desperately trying to get away from Joe...to make sure my children were safe. So at that time I couldn't focus on the future. And when I told you that I had to have time and space to figure things out...it was never about us, I felt sure of us...it was simply about Joe, trying to figure out if he really would make good on his promise to kill all of us. Thank God my bluff worked. I told him I had hard evidence against him...and that I had given it to several people...so that if anything happened to me or the children, they'd come after him. Much to my surprise... and delight...it seems to have worked.

So, now, let's get back to the big question...us. You and me. God is my witness, how I've loved you since I was a girl. But when you went off to war...without ever letting me think that I had a chance with you, I lost hope. And then Joe stepped in. I can't say that I didn't love him...I did. At least I was infatuated with him. But, I didn't know all the ugly, devious things he was capable of. When I was in the hospital, after the car wreck, he told me that he had a plan...to help pay for the hospital, he was going to sell our baby. Can you believe it? He was going to sell my Becca!..." Bertha stopped and looked at the stricken faces around her. "That bastard!" she exclaimed. "He was plannin' ta sell his own child! He was even worse than I thought he was!"

Becca was openly weeping, "What...what else does it say?" she asked, wiping her face. "What else does our Mother say?" She leaned closer to Lisa who wordlessly wrapped her arms around her little sister, nodding for Bertha to resume reading.

"It says", she continued, "That was absolutely the last straw. It boiled down to this, not only was he a drunk, who blamed me for killing all those people, when he was the one driving... and left our Lisa, injured and lying out there, where you found her...but he seemed to be completely without any morals whatsoever. Once, when he was drunk, he told me that he had run over a man on the side of the road in the mountains, and when I asked him if he got help for the man, he said, 'The guy was dead, so what would have been the point?' He said, he couldn't help the guy, and it would have just meant trouble for him, so it was best to just let it go. The awful thing was...it didn't seem to bother him at all, that he had caused someone to die. And he said that I was stupid to be upset about it...because, to him, it didn't concern me.

It was at that point, David, that I first realized what I had gotten myself into. This is really serious stuff, and I've come to believe that Joe is actually crazy. Then, that day, when he said that he had made plans to sell one of our children...it was just too much, absolutely the last straw! I knew then, that I had no choice but to leave him. And that brings us to the present...and what to do about us.

When you told me that you loved me and my children...and wanted to take care of us for the rest of our lives...I couldn't comprehend that kind of love, David. And, I also couldn't help but wonder if you had really thought it through. My children are Joe's. His blood, as well as mine, courses through their veins. And knowing all you know about him now, can you really say that you want to be their father? You need to be absolutely sure...because my children are my life. They deserve a daddy who will love them and cherish them just because they are...not for whose they are. Could you do that? Now, I'm sure that you think you could...but, please give it a lot of thought. And...if, after giving it a lot of thought, you still want us, then we'll be here waiting for you to come for us. But, if you decide you were too hasty...I'll understand...and I won't hold it against you. Only...if you decide you can't take on this load, then let's agree to just break it off cleanly. No hard feelings. If I don't hear back from you, I'll understand. Just remember, I'll always cherish all you did to help us. You are forever in my heart. Love eternally, Kate."

They all sat quietly sipping their coffee as Bertha finished the letter. Finally she handed it over to Lisa. "I really think you girls oughta have this. After all this time," her voice broke, "I don't think David's ever gonna come back." She looked at Fred, "What'dya think, Poppy?"

He just sat looking sadly into his coffee mug, then slowly began to shake his head. "No...I don't recon he is." He stood and stretched. "Well, if'n you'd excuse me...I got my chores ta do."

"That's OK, Fred," Dick said, rising. "We really should be getting back to town.

They were halfway back to Yuma before anyone spoke. Then, Becca, choking on the words, cried out in great pain, "He was going to sell me!" At which point Dick pulled the car off the road and stopped so that Lisa could comfort her sister.

"I know, Honey," she said softly, stroking Becca's hair. "I know...but...he didn't! If you can just grab onto that, Becca...for whatever reason...he changed his mind. He didn't go through with it!" She continued to stroke her sister, letting her have as much time as she needed.

Finally Becca looked up at her sister and said, "Right! He changed his mind...and now we finally know what I was doing out there in that strange house with those strange people!" She sighed a huge sigh. "So...he changed his mind...and that's supposed to make me feel better." She blew her nose. "The truth is...I still feel terribly unwanted!"

Dick, feeling the need to help, made an awkward attempt to make Becca feel better. "Hey, Sis, please don't think I'm trying to make light of your distress...but you might look at it another way." When Becca glanced up at him, he continued, "It seems there were people willing to pay a large sum of money to get you...so, I'd say you were wanted...a whole lot."

Becca sighed, "Oh, please! Sorry Dick. I know you're trying to help...but that doesn't. The idea that total strangers were willing to buy a baby...*any baby at all*...from some sleazy characters Dad was hooked up with, doesn't lessen the pain one bit!" He looked embarrassed, apologetic, and she made a half hearted attempt at a smile. "Oh, they might have been perfectly nice people...or they might have been just as rotten as the men they were dealing with. God only knows what *their* motives might have been." Then as the tears started anew, she groaned, "Oh, Lisa...what kind of a monster was he, anyway? Daddy's are supposed to love their babies...not sell them to the highest bidder!"

Lisa had no answer, but feeling herself swallowed up in the vast sea of her sister's grief, she simply shrugged, letting her own tears flow freely.

About that time a highway patrol car pulled up along side of them. Dick rolled down his window as the officer approached, asking, "What seems to be the trouble?"

"Ah...bad news, Officer. The ladies were just overcome...for the moment." Dick offered.

"That so?" The officer walked around to the passenger side of the car to make sure for himself that everything was on the up and up.

Becca rolled down the window and choked out the words, "Uh...yes, Officer. Family tragedy..."

Then Lisa, working to regain her composure, added, "Yes...uh...we just found out a few minutes ago...and, well...it just hit us awfully hard. But...we'll be OK."

Becca continued, "Yes, we'll be OK. It was...It was just a shock...a horrible shock… that's all."

Seemingly satisfied, the officer got back into his patrol car and drove off.

When they finally did get back to town they opted for hamburgers, which they took to the park, so they wouldn't have to worry about people noticing if they cried or not.

After they ate, Lisa took out the letter and read it to them again. Then, putting it back into the envelope, she got to her feet. "Hey, come on...I need to walk." They made sure things wouldn't blow away, then started around the pond. "So...what happened to David?" she brooded. "We know he left here...according to Fred...and that he left his stuff at his grandmother's...because he was planning to send for it..."

"Yeah." Dick agreed. "But, what could have possibly happened? He took his car...and it's never surfaced anywhere that we know of. So..."

Becca jumped in, "So...he probably was in an accident somewhere...and couldn't get back. Maybe he drove off a cliff in the mountains, and was never found. It happens, you know."

"Yeah...it happens." Lisa mused, then added, wistfully, "I just wish..."

"What...what do you wish?" Dick asked, drawing her close to him.

"Well...it's obvious that Mother never knew that he had disappeared...or she wouldn't have sent that letter. I really do wish that she had known that he was planning to come for her...for us. She went to her grave thinking that he had changed his mind, and I just wish to goodness that she could have known the truth."

Becca nodded. "Right. He didn't answer her letter because he couldn't. He simply never got it!"

"Yeah," Dick said. "That is sad."

Later, as Dick and Lisa snuggled in their bed, she sighed. "You want to know what I think is really sad? I think it's sad...that my Mother and Father never had what we have."

"Honey, I'll just bet not too many people out there have what we have!" Dick answered, kissing her on the neck.

"Right! And I'm sure all deliriously happy couples think that nobody else in the whole wide world could possibly have what *they* have." Lisa said, smiling with the smug assurance that comes from loving and being well loved in return.

"Oh...so now you're calling me delirious! And I suppose, the next thing I know you'll be wanting to have me committed!" he teased. But Lisa was much too sleepy to answer. She simply smiled at him and drifted off.

Friday morning they woke to gray skies. As Lisa came out of the shower Dick had just turned on the TV. "Calling for scattered showers," he said, handing the control over as he headed for the shower, himself. "Don't know why I think I need a shower, since it's going to rain, but...I really do. So, I guess I'd better just get it over with," he laughed.

Lisa, oblivious to what he was saying, scrunched her face nearsightedly at the TV screen. "Darn, I wanted to go out to the home place today," she muttered. "Darn rain!"

"You could probably see better...if you put your glasses on," Dick teased, reappearing to get his shampoo. "Works better for me, anyway!" he added, popping her with his towel.

"You're so busy making with the wise cracks..." she raised her voice as the bathroom door swung shut, "that you probably didn't hear me say that I wanted to go out to the home place today!"

Later, as they sat down to breakfast, Becca said, "I've been thinking...it's about time to be heading home, don't you think?" Then, not waiting for a reply, she added, "I can't think of anything that's left for us to do here, can you?" She was trying for a detached, nonchalance...which came off more like depression than anything else. "I mean...we found Grandfather Hollander's homestead...and now we know why I was at the old house...and so, what's left to do?"

Lisa looked thoughtfully at her sister, then responded casually, "Well...I did want to go back out to the home place once more...and I really need to make arrangements with someone to oversee the place." She turned to her husband, "What do you think, Dick?"

"I'm with you...ladies. Your wish is my command," he said, with a mock bow and a flourish of his hand. "Or something like that," he chuckled. Then finishing his toast, he added, "But, Lisa, you're right. Now that we are land owners in this community...we really are going to need someone to oversee things for us here."

"Well, since they're calling for rain...and you want to go back out there," Becca said, listlessly. "I guess we probably ought to hit the road..." Pushing her chair back from the table she headed moodily toward the cashier. "before the rain sets in."

CHAPTER THIRTY TWO

Dick and Lisa kept up a running conversation as they headed south out of town. But after a few minutes, Lisa said, "Becca...what's up? You're never this quiet, so what's going on with you, girl?"

Becca tried to grin but it came off more like a grimace. "Nothing...I just don't have anything to say, that's all. Besides...I'm just listening to the two of you." She looked out the window, then added, "So...what's wrong with being quiet, anyway? I thought you guys would jump at the chance to visit...without me butting in all the time."

"Well, first of all, we don't consider conversation with you to be *you butting in,* and secondly, you seem kinda down...today." Lisa gave that a moment to soak in, then looked directly at Becca. "Am I right? Are you a little bit down this morning?" When Becca shrugged instead of answering, Lisa added, "Maybe a bit dejected?"

"More like *rejected*," Becca said, turning her face toward the window so her sister couldn't see the glimmer of tears that she was valiantly trying to hold back. "And...yes, I guess you might say that makes me feel...a little bit down." She mulled that over a bit, then added, "Yeah...I guess *dejected* is probably the right word for it."

"Anything we can do to help?" Lisa asked in her very best therapy voice.

Becca shook her head. "No. You didn't do it, and so....you can't fix it. I don't guess anybody can. That's just how it feels to be rejected...not wanted. It's pretty awful, you know?'

Lisa nodded. "Yeah...but we want you, Becca. We're not trying to get rid of you. Don't forget...I'm the one who *asked you* to come? I'm the one who thought you wouldn't want to come with me... remember?"

Becca gave her sister a slight grin, "Yeah...you did." She said, in a barely audible voice.

"Well...I can't begin to imagine how devastating it was for you to hear that our daddy was actually going to sell you. It makes my blood run cold, just thinking of it! And you're right...there's not anything I...or anybody else, for that matter...can do to take away that pain, that feeling of rejection. But...maybe I can help you refocus."

Becca looked puzzled, "Refocus? Like...how? And what good would that do anyway?"

"Well, Becca, it's like what happens when you've been looking at a picture in a semi-dark room, and then you take the same picture out into the sunlight. You see things that you didn't know were there." Lisa stopped there to let Becca determine if she wanted to run with it.

"So, you're saying...there's *another way* to look at what Daddy did to me?" she asked. "OK... so...I'll bite. How...can I *refocus*...this?"

"You can start by looking at the other players in this picture? There's you...and Daddy...and who else?"

"Well, I guess Mama. Even though she wasn't there at the time...I guess she *is* a part of the picture."

"Right!" Lisa exclaimed. "She was very much a part of the whole picture!" Taking their Mother's letter to David out of her purse, and handing it to Becca, Lisa continued. "Now, Honey skip down...to the part where Mama talks about you...and tell me what she said."

Becca quickly scanned the letter. "Here it is. She says, 'When I was in the hospital, after the car wreck, he told me that he had a plan...to help pay for the hospital, he was going to sell our baby." Tears started afresh as she looked at Lisa. "How...can I make something different out of *that*? He was still going to sell me!"

"Go on, Becca,"Lisa urged. "Read on. What else did Mama say?"

"C...can you believe?" she read, "he was going to sell my Becca."

"And then? Go on...what did she say then?" Lisa prodded.

"Well, she said...'that was absolutely the last straw'..."

"Yeah...and read on, Becca. She says it again...twice! See...a little farther down the page."

Becca read, haltingly, "I've come to believe that Joe is actually crazy. Then, that day, when he said that he actually had made plans to sell one of our children...it was too much. I knew then, that I had no choice but to leave him'..." Becca paused, and Lisa jumped in.

"Becca, think about it...what was the straw that broke the camels back? What was that last straw?" Lisa coaxed. "That...very last straw...?"

The light dawned in Becca's eyes, and she attempted a smile, through her tears. "*Me*!" she whispered. "She was going to leave him...because...of *me*!"

Lisa smiled, "Right on! Think about it. She had put up with a lot of bad stuff because she didn't want her marriage to fail...but she left when he threatened you, her Becca. That is what she called you, isn't it? *My Becca*?"

Becca almost laughed, "Well...not just me...all of us kids. She wanted to protect all of us kids."

"Right...but she was talking *specifically* about you, Sis. 'My Becca', she said...didn't she?" Lisa drove her point home. "And then...later in the letter...where she talks about us having both of their blood in our veins..." Lisa took the letter. "Here, here it is. She said, 'My children are my life. They deserve a Daddy who will love them and cherish them...just because they are'. Oh, I love that part, Becca! Not because of whose we are...but just because we are! Oh, I'm sure our mother loved us. And I know beyond a shadow of a doubt that she loved you too...enough to leave him...to protect you!"

Becca was dazed, letting it all soak in, but her face was literally glowing, lit from within, like she had just discovered the pot 'o gold at the end of the rainbow. "Wow! And all these years I was looking for some...some kind of tangible proof...that my mother loved me. And, now...I have it...in writing! Somehow, that makes it more...believable. She *really did* love me!"

"Yes, she did! And any time you get to thinking that nobody loves you...you need only to remind yourself of that. *You have it in writing*!" After a moment, Lisa added, softly, "And...when you get to wondering if God loves you...remember...you have *that in writing too*! For God so loved Becca...that He gave...his only begotten Son..."

Becca closed her eyes, basking in the warmth of those words, and just let the tears flow. "Yes," she whispered. "Thank you, God...for so loving me...and help me...to never doubt it again."

They were hit with a shower just as they turned west off of 59, but it was a little one, and was already over by the time they pulled into the driveway of the home place. "Boy...that was a quick one!" Becca laughed, getting out of the car.

"Yeah, hardly enough to settle the dust." Dick added.

"Oh, but doesn't it smell good?" Lisa asked. "I love the smell of summer rain on the baked earth! It's so..."

"Earthy!" Becca finished. "It's so earthy! So...what are we doing here today?"

"Well, I brought my notebook. You know, we started an inventory before, but we kept getting side-tracked," Lisa said, heading toward the barn. "We really do need to get an antiques dealer out here to appraise this stuff."

"And...where exactly do you think we'd have to go to find one of those there critters?" Dick asked. "Do you think Yuma...or Wray...? Or would we have to go into Denver?"

"Oh, I'd think we should be able to get someone locally. You know they have that Old Threshers thing...at the fairgrounds, I think. And that's all about "old" stuff. You know...we saw those signs in town." Lisa was thoughtful, then added, "But, Fred and Bertha might actually be our best bet in that area. They seem to know everything and everyone in and around the county, so I'm sure they could help us there."

Dick nodded, "Yeah...they probably could," he said as they pushed open the heavy barn doors. "I think it's pretty amazing that all of this stuff is still here...after all this time."

They worked their way through slowly, cataloging all the tools that were hanging on the walls, first, then going to the floor items. Lisa even drew a layout, to show where each item hung, or was sitting. By the time they finished it was raining again, so they just decided to wait it out, sitting on the dusty fender of the old tractor.

"So where's the little boy who looks after the sheep?" Becca sing-songed, "He's under the haystack fast asleep."

"Now *what* brought that on?" Lisa laughed. "Boy, you run the gamut...from way down in the dumps...to singing nursery songs!"

Becca chuckled, "Yeah...I do, don't I? But, I couldn't help but notice that big haystack back there in the corner, thinking...if it was a bit fresher...we could take a nap in it. However, it looks like it's been back there as long as most of this other old stuff. I believe...you called *them* antiques, but, frankly...I never heard of antique hay!" She giggled.

Dick got up and walked to the back of the room. "Yep, I'd say this stuff has been here a long time. I wonder if it has any nutritional value at all left in it." Bending down, he grabbed a handful of the stuff, that promptly fell apart in his hand. "It's pretty old, and, like most antiques, falling apart!" he laughed, carefully scooping up another handful. "Whoa...what's that?" he asked turning to the girls. "It looks like there's something under the haystack...and I don't think it's little boy blue."

"Gosh!" Becca exclaimed. "Come on, Lisa, let's see what it is." So she and Lisa joined Dick by the haystack.

Lisa stuck her arm into the stack near where Dick had gotten his hay. "There is something. Something really hard...under here!" she said, excitedly. "Let's clear some of this hay off, so we can see what it is." She started to move the hay but it was so dry and dusty that it flew up in her face, and she backed away, sputtering and spitting. "Oh, my gosh...be careful. This stuff is almost disintegrated. Don't get it in your eyes!"

Dick looked around for something to work with, and found some old gunnysacks hanging over a feed bin. "Well, this might do," he muttered, and laying the sacks on top of the hay to hold down the dust, he very carefully pushed some of the hay out of the way.

"Yes!" shouted Becca, "that's working!" as she jumped up and down. "Look, there's something kinda shiny...like..."

"Like a car bumper," Lisa finished. "Why...it is, Dick. It's an old car under there!"

Dick stepped back to see what he had uncovered. "Well, I'll be darned! So it is!" He kept replacing the sacks and carefully moving the hay until he had most of the car uncovered. "Who would have ever thought...that a car would have been under here?" He opened the door on the driver's side. "Looks to me like about a 1947 Buick. I wonder who it belonged to."

"Well, there should be a registration," Lisa said. She had climbed in on the passenger side and was pointing to the steering column. "Look...there. There's the registration. This car belonged to..." she leaned closer, to make out the faded writing, "...to David Johnson, of Clarksville, in Yuma County!" Lisa and Dick looked at each other in total amazement. "Well for heaven's sake! Who would have ever thought to look under the haystack...in an old barn?"

Becca had opened a rear door and let out a whistle. "Suitcases back here! He was definitely headed somewhere!"

"Yeah...but how'd the car end up here?" Dick wondered aloud. "And...where is David?"

Suddenly all the color drained out of Lisa's face. "I...I've got a pretty darned good idea...where David is," she said, climbing out of the car.

"You do?" Becca asked, following her, as she headed for the barn door.

"Yes, I think I do! Dick...can you help me find something to break a padlock off of the old shed?" she called back over her shoulder. "Yes sir, I'd almost lay money on it!"

Dick, having joined them, asked "What's up. Why do we need to break a padlock?"

"Because, my dear husband...that's where the shovels are." It was still raining, but Lisa left the shelter of the barn and sprinted to the nearby shed. She checked the door and the padlock still held tight. Running back to the barn, she said, "Look around, Dick...do you see anything that we can use to hammer that lock open...or...or... something to pry it with?" She searched frantically, but the best she could come up with was a pair of hedge lopers. Turning to Dick she asked, "What do you think...will this work?"

I don't know...but we can give it the old college try," Dick answered, taking the instrument from her and heading back to the shed. But when the lopers didn't do the trick, Lisa found a good sized rock for him to hammer with, still to no avail. "That's one stubborn lock!" Dick exclaimed.

"Here...give me that rock," Lisa said, taking it around to the side window and breaking the glass. "There!" she said, making sure there was no glass left to get cut on. "Mama always said there's more than one way to skin a cat! Now, Dick...see if you can reach far enough in to get the shovels." He could, and after retrieving them they waited in the barn for the rain to abate before setting out for the hill behind the house.

"How...how will you know where to dig?" Becca asked, trying her best to keep up with them.

"Don't you worry your pretty head about that, Becca. I think I know just about where to try." It took only a few minutes of probing the sandy soil before she heard what she was listening for. "Bingo!" she exclaimed. "We'll dig here! I'd be willing to bet that klink I just heard was the top of the old cistern." The rain, having loosened the soil, actually made their job easier, and within a few minutes they had uncovered the square cement top of the old cistern. "All right! We did it!" Lisa threw her arms around Dick's neck. Then leaning on her shovel, she mused, "And so...now what?" She looked from Dick to Becca. "How are we ever going to get that top off of the cistern itself...?

Dick wiped the sweat off his brow and said, "Well...why don't we go have some lunch...while we try to figure that one out?"

"Sounds good to me," Becca laughed. "I've kinda worked up an appetite...watching you two work!" She started for the car, then turning toward them, added, "But I really think we ought to go back to the motel and freshen up first. You two look like a couple of drowned rats...and I'm not sure I want to be seen in public *with you*!"

Lisa and Dick looked at each other, then started to giggle. "Yeah...I guess we do!" Lisa said. "I guess we do." Just then there was a loud clap of thunder and they made a mad dash for the car and headed for town.

Back at the motel, Becca called in an order for pizza, while Dick and Lisa got cleaned up. Then, since it was still raining, they got Cokes from the machine and went to Becca's room when the pizza came.

"So..." Becca started, "Lisa...what I'm wondering is...how are we going to tell Fred...what we found in the barn?" She reached for another piece of pizza.

Lisa took a big breath and let it out slowly. "I've been thinking about that."

"Yeah...me too." Dick said. "Of course he'll have to be told."

Lisa nodded. "Yes...but I was trying to decide...if we should say anything...*before* we actually look in the cistern. And that leads us to another problem...getting the top off of it. That won't be easy." She looked at Dick. "Do you think we could pull it off with our car?"

"Maybe...but...I'd hate to mess up the car, trying." He rubbed his chin, thinking.

"Hey! Maybe we could rent something...to do it!" Becca offered. "Like...maybe a tractor?"

Lisa went to the desk to get the telephone directory. "Let's see if there's a rental place here," she said, going to the yellow pages. "Doesn't look like they have anything that rents farm equipment here in Yuma. And the towns around would be awfully far..."

"Well we might consider just getting a wrecker to come out..." Dick added.

"Hey...Fred! Fred has equipment..." Becca jumped in. "But then, of course...we'd have to tell him what we want it for."

"Yeah..." Lisa said. "No matter what...he has to be told, anyway...so..." She looked up their number in the directory. "Maybe we should just go...there...and...well...play it by ear." She dialed the number. "Hello, Bertha. This is Lisa. We were just thinking...if you're going to be home, we'd like to come by in a little bit." Bertha was thrilled with the idea of having company. She said rainy days kinda got her down because she couldn't get out in the yard, and would love to have them. Lisa told her they didn't want her to bother with cooking anything, that they would stop and pick up a watermelon on the way.

It had stopped raining and the sun was trying to peek through, as they made their way north, and by the time they got to the Johnson's it was out in full force. Bertha was delighted that the sun had come out, so they could have the watermelon in the back yard. She had Fred cut into it right away. "Oh, now *this* is good!" she said. "We had one the other evenin' with the kids, but it jest didn't have no flavor."

"It's a black diamond...out of Oklahoma," Lisa said. "At least that's what the clerk said. And she was surely right about it having a lot of flavor."

"Yeah," Becca added, helping herself to another piece. "It's sooo good!"

They sat around making small talk for quite awhile, then Lisa, praying for God to help her, said, "Fred...I need to tell you something. And...there is no easy way to do it, so...please bear with me. OK?"

He looked concerned and put his fork down. "Well, OK...Lisa...what is it, girl?"

"We...we were taking inventory in that old barn on our Grandfather's place...there's a ton of antiques out there...and...well...we noticed something shiny sticking out from under the hay at the back of the barn."

"Something shiny?" he repeated. "What was it?"

"It...was an old car...that had been covered up with hay. When we uncovered it...we...oh, I'm so sorry to have to tell you this...but, It's David's car."

"Noooo..." It was almost a whisper. "How do you know? I mean..."

"It's an old Buick...and it has his name on the registration...on the steering column," Dick said.

The old man sat there in stunned silence, his face trembling. He just kept drumming his fingers on the table. "It has his name...on the steering column..." he repeated.

"Oh, my dear God!" Bertha cried out, tears streaming down her face. "Oh, my dear God, help us!"

"Was he...in the car?" Fred asked, working hard at composure.

Lisa shook her head, sadly. "No...he wasn't. But, his suitcases...are in the back seat."

"His suitcases? Then...he never even left at all...?" The questions were rhetorical. Fred got to his feet and went to the kitchen sink to look out the window. "That's incredible. To think he's been here all these years...but where?" He turned to look at Lisa. "Do you...do you think he's out there...on the property somewhere?"

She nodded, "I'm so sorry...but yes...I do. If his car is there...then he probably is...too."

Fred slammed a fist down on the countertop. "Well...if'n he's out there...then we'll danged well find him!" His face crumpled in pain. "We...I...have to find my brother!" He lunged for the keys hanging on the wall beside the back door. "He deserves to be put to rest...properly!"

"Wait, Fred...wait just a minute, please. I...need..." Lisa reached out and took the old man's hand. "I need to tell you...something else. So, please sit back down...for just a minute more, and...then we'll...we'll all go with you. Please?"

His mind racing, he was hardly able to comprehend what she was asking him to do. "Uh...what's that...you want to tell me something...else?" He slumped into the chair.

"Fred, Bertha...this isn't easy for me to say, but..." She choked on the words, then cleared her throat and went on. "We told you...that we knew our Daddy was capable of really bad things...like killing people who got in his way." She looked from one to the other, making sure they were with her. "Well, it seems obvious...to me, at least... that Mama had something on him...so...he wasn't able to hurt us." She stopped, briefly, choosing her words carefully. "But, when we found David's car...out there...on the property...I couldn't help but think, *Daddy*. How else could David's things...his car...and his suitcases...end up there...on our grandfather's property?" She gave them a moment to think about that, then continued.

"Now, that car was well buried under the haystack...in the farthest corner of the barn, with an awful lot of hay between it and daylight. So, what I'm saying is...it was deliberate! It had to have been put there by someone. Someone...who was banking on it never being found. At least, not in his lifetime." She paused briefly, "Now...our Daddy...is the only person...who has had access to that place all these years. He leased out the property, yes...the fields and pastures...all but the buildings. He didn't live there, but he didn't allow anyone else to either. So...it sat... virtually untouched...until he died three years ago. And even then his secret remained safe...because the young couple who bought it, never got around to moving out there! And, when they divorced, it just went back to the bank...where we were just lucky...actually, blessed is a better word for it...enough to be able to buy it back. Now, Fred, I have a hunch...where David is." He was struggling to stay with her.

"Go on..." he whispered. "You have a hunch...where he is."

"Yes, well...we uncovered an old cistern on the place...and it makes sense to me...that if you don't want someone found...you don't leave them anywhere somebody might accidentally find them. So, I think...well, I actually have reason to believe...uh...that David is...in that cistern."

Fred jumped up and pounded his fist on the table, "Then...then let's go and get him out!"

"Yes...yes, we will." Dick said. "But, Fred, we need your help. We need equipment that's heavy enough to lift or pull that cement top off of the cistern, so we can get to it."

Bertha had stopped crying. Now she asked, solemnly, "Did...did ya, by chance, go ta the sheriff with any o' this?

"No...no we haven't, Bertha. Because it is just a *hunch*," Lisa said. "But...if we can get a look into that cistern...and it does turn out that David is there..." She faltered. "Well, regardless, we will go to the authorities, anyway...because we have found the car, there. But...I just wanted...*needed*...to see if the body is actually there, before bringing them in on it." She looked pleadingly at Fred and Bertha. "So...will you help us, Fred...*before* we call the sheriff?"

"Well, o' course! I want ta find my brother...whatever we haffta do!" He stood up. "I've got some heavy chain in the shed...and I think my pickup would do...ta git that lid offen that cistern." He headed for the door. "Well...come on...while there's still daylight, an' it's not rainin'."

Bertha struggled to her feet. "I'm a'goin' too, Poppy! I gotta be there! Gotta see this for m'self." Fred started to protest, but one look at the set of her jaw and he thought better of it. If they were going to find David, Bertha did, indeed, need to be there. So, taking along her oversized wooden rocker and a straw hat to protect her from the sun, Fred helped her into the pick up. Then, after throwing the heavy chain, a pick ax and shovel into the truck bed, the procession was off, with Dick, Lisa and Becca leading the way.

They stopped in town only long enough to restock their supply of bottled drinking water, then headed straight for the home place.

CHAPTER THIRTY THREE

When they reached the home place it didn't take long for Dick and Fred to hook the chains onto the old cistern top and yank it off with Fred's pickup. Lisa and Becca were busily getting Bertha situated, so that she could keep an eye on the action without being in the way, or getting a lot of dirt thrown on her.

"Wow," Dick let out a whistle. "Looks like the top several inches, at least, are rock fill. We'll have to work cautiously...to make sure we don't destroy any..."

"Evidence," Fred finished. "Yeah...an' it looks like we're gonna haffta move all those rocks by hand... before we can do any diggin', anyway."

Lisa and Becca jumped at that. "Well, we can help move those rocks," Lisa said, getting down on her knees by the opening to the cistern. "Here Becca, I'll hand them over to you." She strained to move a large one, that Dick promptly took away from her, and moved himself. "Well! Find your own rocks, if you don't mind!" she bristled.

"Now...don't get your hackles up," he laughed. "You ladies may have us out done in the brains department, but, remember, God did make man stronger for a reason. And besides...we don't want anyone throwing their back out down here. We still have to ride all the way back to Texas, remember?" He moved another large rock aside to get to some more manageable ones. "And…that's in a car...remember? Now…it won't be any fun...traveling…if you mess your back up out here today!"

"OK...so I'm not as strong as I thought I was," she feigned a pout. "But, there are plenty of smaller rocks... and I'm...*we're*...not too proud to move *them*! Are we, Becca?"

Fred laughed. "C'mon...there's plenty'a work here fer everbody! Let's jest git it done!" He hefted a pretty good sized stone out, then stood up to catch his breath. "Let's jest git my brother outta here." After that, they all worked silently for awhile.

About twenty minutes later Fred hoisted himself out of the hole, saying, "I need to take a break...so...why don'tcha show me where that car is? I'd...I'd like ta see David's car."

Becca got water for them all, and they started down toward the barn, going slow enough for Bertha to walk with them. The old barn was cool and dry, a blessed respite from the blazing afternoon sun. Fred, helping Bertha along, followed the trio into the cavernous barn, and went straight to the hay at the back, barely aware of anything else around him. He was stoic, nothing but a slight quiver of his chin betrayed the deep emotion he felt as he ran his hand lovingly over the exposed grill of his brother's car.

"I'll never ferget the day he came home with this car," he said, in a voice barely audible. "It was 'is pride n' joy." He climbed in and looked at the registration on the steering column, running a rough finger over it. Then he looked at the luggage in the back seat. "It's incredible," he whispered, "...that he was here all this time. Right here...all this time." Lowering his head to the steering wheel, he wept, unaware of the others around him, alone in his anguish of soul. "Oh, my God...why? Why'd you let 'im die out here...all alone? Why did you...?" The others moved back, taking up residency on the old tractor, to give him space to grieve. All but Bertha. Though she could hardly stand unaided, she managed to stand stoically by the car, tears streaming down her face, quietly waiting for her husband to emerge from his black hole of grief.

After several minutes Fred and Bertha rejoined the others and they made their way back up to the cistern. Fred seemed to have been re-energized. He went at the removal of those rocks with a fury. Finally Dick took him by the arm, "Fred, come on, now...we'll get it done...but *not* if you push yourself into a heart attack...right?" Fred looked at him blankly. "Look, man...you gotta hang around here to look after Bertha. I'm telling you...slow down and take it easy." That seemed to have registered, so he pressed on. "Now, look, you just sit yourself down here by Bertha...there on that rock. We're getting close to having these rocks gone, and then you can help me with the dirt. OK?" Fred nodded, and allowed Dick to help him out of the hole. Sitting next to Bertha he lowered his head onto her lap and wept, while she rocked him tenderly humming "I Must Tell Jesus", as the tears rolled down her cheeks.

Finally they had the top layers of dirt and rock out of the hole, and it looked as though they were into sandy loam. "We'll have to be really careful, here," Lisa said. "It would be very easy to overlook something...a button, or anything small."

"Say...I think I remember seeing an old screen-door in the basement of the house," Becca said. "I think...I'll just go check it out." She started toward the house. "I think it would make a great sifter."

"Yes," Fred said, suddenly energized. "It might, at that! But, it'll be awkward for you to handle... so wait a minute, Becca," he scrambled to his feet, "and I'll help you...bring it up."

The screen-door worked perfectly. Held up on either end by a pile of rocks, the diggers carefully lifted shovel after shovel full of dirt onto it, then Bertha sifted the dirt out onto the ground below. They worked steadily for several minutes when suddenly the sun went under a cloud. "Oh, Lord...Lisa prayed aloud, "Please...don't let it rain now! Not now...when we must be so close!" Just then her shovel clanked on something solid. Looking down, she gasped, "Dick, stop! Look...there's...there's something there...at the tip of my shovel!"

Dick reached down and dusted the sand off of a skull. "Well...it looks like we've hit pay dirt." he said, with a grimace. Lisa ran and got a soft bristled brush from the trunk of her car, and then carefully began to brush the dirt away from their find. The skeleton was of a very tall man, dressed in a well rotted dark blue serge suit, with a white shirt and blue patterned tie. They all stood back and looked in horror, then Lisa and Dick climbed out of the hole and sat down with the others to decide what to do next.

"Lisa looked at Fred, "Well, Fred...what do you think? Is it David?" He sat speechlessly nodding.

"How can you be sure?" Becca asked, lamely, then regretted opening her mouth.

Just then the sun broke through the gathering clouds and sparkled off of something in the hole. Lisa jumped in and picked up a set of keys, half exposed in the sand. "Well...here are his car keys...as if we needed any more proof." Climbing back out she said, "But...you know what? It's getting ready to rain again. We'd better find something to uh...cover him back up with...until we can get the sheriff out here. Rain now could do a lot of damage...and we dare not move him."

Fred nodded. "But...what's that?" he asked pointing into the hole. "I saw somethin' flash in the light..."

"What? You mean these keys...that I just found?" Lisa asked.

"No...after...you found the keys. I saw another glint of light...when you were getting out." The sun was well hidden now, and Lisa didn't see anything.

"Wait...I've got a flashlight in my truck." Fred said, running to get it. When he returned, they all watched carefully as Dick passed the light back and forth, systematically, over the corpse.

"There!" Fred shouted. "I saw it again." Climbing down into the hole, he carefully brushed the sand off of the partially submerged right hand, and uncovered a class ring still on the bony projectile of a finger. "It's David, all right! He always wore that ring." Fred started to remove it, but Dick stopped him.

"No, Fred! Leave it there!" Dick cried out. "For identification." It suddenly grew darker, and Dick offered Fred a hand up out of the cistern. "I think we'd better do what Lisa suggested, and get this thing covered up before it starts raining again," he said, heading for the barn. "There ought'a be something in there...that we can use."

Leaving Bertha at the sight the rest hurried to the barn to search for a cover. After a few minutes, Fred said, "Here...this corrugated metal...here on the side o' this stall...it'd do the job all right...if we kin jest git it off."

"Yeah, you're right," Dick said, joining him. Without anything to pry the nails out, the men decided to throw their weight against it...while Lisa and Becca pulled from the other side. After a few body slams, they had their new top for the cistern. Hurrying to get it installed before the rain hit, they piled rocks on top to keep the wind from blowing it off.

Finally, Dick stepped back. "Well, that oughtta hold it for now, and," he looked at his watch, "And, I think we can just make it to the sheriff's office...before he goes home for supper...if we leave *right now*."

Sheriff John Ruger was just locking the front door as the two vehicles pulled up. Seeing the familiar faces of his old friends, he waved, "Hi, Fred, Bertha! What brings you two hurryin' in just at closin' time?"

"Well, John," Fred said, stepping down out of his pickup. "Bad news, I'm afraid. Mind givin' us a few minutes o' yer time? It's real important." When John nodded, Fred went around to help Bertha out of the truck and into the office. The trio followed.

As soon as they all crowded into the little office, John asked, "What's up, Fred." For a minute the old man, overcome with a fresh wave of grief, couldn't say a word.

"It's 'is brother, David," Bertha intervened. "We found 'im."

John was clearly confused, "You mean...he's come back?"

"Huh uh," Bertha said. "We found 'is body." It was quiet enough to hear a pin drop.

Finally John gasped, "What? Where...did you find...his body?" He stumbled over the words. "Where... for heaven's sake...did you find him."

Fred, having finally composed himself, said, simply, "Out...on their property. Out at the old Hollander place. Been there all along. Only...we jest didn't know it. Never had no reason to think...he might be out there. But, he was there all the time...since the first day he disappeared." The old man slumped down in a chair. "Since that very first day."

It took time for Lisa to tell the story, how she had come back here searching for her grandfather's homestead, and had not only located it, but had also bought it. How her mother's family was intertwined with the Johnson family, and how they naturally got acquainted with Fred and Bertha. How her parents had split up, and how David had rescued her after the wreck that claimed five lives, and how he had helped their mother escape from a very abusive situation...and then just vanished. And how, while they were doing an inventory of the old barn they just happened to find David's car...leading them to believe that her father had done away with him...somewhere on the property...since that's where the car had been all this time. When she finished, John's head was spinning.

"You say...you actually have found a body...out there...in an old cistern."

"Yes...and we found these keys...beside the body in the cistern. And they fit...the old car that we found in the barn," Lisa calmly explained.

"OK, folks...Here's what I think we should do. It's late...and it's shore enough gonna rain this evening, if you can believe that rumbling that we keep a'hearin'. So...let's just go home, for tonight. You come in here in the morning and take me out there." He lifted the keys off of his desk, turning them over in his hands, then growled at Lisa, "Lady...I hope you didn't move...or re-move...anything else...from that cistern!"

"Oh, no," she shook her head. "No, sir. We didn't remove anything else. It's...he's...still there...just like we found him."

He chewed, thoughtfully, on a cigar that had actually been out for hours, then, thinking that he needed to do something official like, he said to the strangers, "An'...don't you be takin' no trips outta town...till we git this all sorted out."

CHAPTER THIRTY FOUR

Sitting thoughtfully at his desk after Fred and Bertha and the strangers had left, Sheriff John took out a yellow notepad and jotted down everything he could remember about the old Hollander place...which wasn't much. Picking up the phone he called his part time deputy, Andy Metcalf.

"Andy, what in blazes do you remember about that old geezer Joe Hollander? Yeah, that's right...the one who died about three years ago." The sheriff listened to Andy tell him what he didn't know, then proceeded. "Well, you're not gonna believe this, but his kids 'er here...with the strangest tale!" They talked for some time, then Sheriff John told Andy to be sure to report in the next morning, as they would be making a run out to the old place. After he hung up, he wondered for just a minute if he should have reminded the deputy that this was official business and not to talk about it. But just then his wife called to remind him that supper was ready, so he rushed out without giving Andy another thought.

"What was that all about?" Sarah Metcalf wanted to know, as her husband got off the phone with his boss and rejoined her at the supper table.

"Ah...not much. Now, Honey, this is the best pot roast you've ever made...I do believe," Andy said, helping himself to more mashed potatoes. He was painfully aware that she was not eating, and was waiting for him to fill her in. Well...his boss hadn't *said* to keep it under wraps, like he usually did, and what could be the harm, just this once? He looked up into her icy cold blue eyes and knew they wouldn't thaw out until she was satisfied, so he told her what he knew...just the barest of facts, mind you...no elaborations.

"Oh, Andy! How exciting! Why it's a real mystery...right here in little ole Yuma! She got up from the table and came to sit on his lap. "Are you ready for some desert, now, Sweetie?" she purred. "I've got strawberry shortcake!" He was drowning in her warm blue eyes. Nobody he had ever known had eyes like hers.

After supper, while Andy lounged in front of the TV, Sarah went to call her mother, who lived in Otis, because nothing that grand ever happened in Otis. And Sarah's Mother just had to call her best friends, Shirley and Mildred. Of course she told them to keep it to themselves. Her daughter hadn't *said* that it was official, or anything like that, but she liked to be discreet.

Mildred wondered if her son, who was a bank trustee in Yuma, knew anything about it, so of course she called him, and Shirley wondered if her daughter, Emily, who was married to a car dealer in Yuma had anything to add to what she had just found out. She didn't…but said she'd make some discreet inquiries, and if she learned anything new she'd call back.

Emily thought the best person to call would be Patsy, over at the Yuma Pioneer. Patsy was intrigued, but hadn't heard a thing about it. She said she'd get back to her as soon as she made a few calls. Now, Emily never liked to be left out of anything, so after talking to Patsy and learning *nothing*, she called her pastor's wife who was completely in the dark, but promised to check it out. Next she called the High School Principal…who would surely know something, if anybody did. He was also in the dark, but clearly didn't intend to stay there, now that he knew something was afoot. By the time Fred and Bertha Johnson turned out the lights and went to bed, virtually all of their neighbors and most of Yuma had heard that David had turned up at long last.

Fred and Bertha arrived at the restaurant the next morning just as Dena was serving up the morning special for Dick, Lisa and Becca. "We'll take a couple of those, Sweetheart," Fred said, giving Dena a peck on the cheek, as he helped Bertha into a chair across from Lisa, and positioned himself across from Dick. "An' keep the coffee comin'."

"All right, Gramps," Dena laughed. "I'll keep it comin'!" She hurried off to turn their order in, then, grabbing a couple of mugs, returned to the table to pour her grandparents some coffee. "What brings you two into town so early in the mornin'?" she asked, cheerfully.

"Oh...jest business," Bertha said. "Jest business."

"And...has that business got anything to do with a skeleton turnin' up in some ole' cistern?" Dena asked.

Taken off guard, Bertha winced and looked first at Fred, then at the trio seated across from her. She didn't answer, but sat there blinking.

Fred picked up the ball and asked, "An' wherever did you git such a notion as that?" He looked sternly at his grand daughter.

Dena faltered. "Uh...well...it's been the buzz all morning!" Now she turned defensive. "I couldn't help but hear it, Grandpa."

"You...didn't mention it to us," Dick reminded her.

"Well, of course not!" She refilled his coffee mug. "I wouldn't be talkin' about somethin' like that...to total strangers!"

Lisa was taken aback, "I wouldn't call us *total* strangers!"

"Well...not *total*...I guess. But, I don't really know you!" Dena retorted. "Now...do I?" She filled Becca's and Lisa's cups. "I mean...yeah, like we've been friendly...but, I don't *really know* you, an' you don't *really know* me. An', for that matter, you don't *really know* my Gram and Grampa. After all...we all just met...a few days ago!" She walked stiffly back to the kitchen.

"Wow...what a change!" Becca said. "Wonder what brought all that on."

Fred chuckled, "Well...I'd say...she's just tryin' to be protective. Of her Gram an' me. She'll come back around."

Lisa raised her eyebrows, "Protective? Nobody needs to protect you...*from us*! Do you think we're up to something...that you need to be protected from?" she asked.

"Oh, no...o' course not. We don't think nothin' o' the kind," Bertha said. "But,it's obvious that *she's* been hearin' some talk." Bertha patted Lisa's hand. "She'll be OK."

As the group left the restaurant and headed for the sheriff's office it seemed that the eyes of the whole community were on them. People stopped whatever they were doing and watched, solemnly, as they passed.

The first thing Fred said as he walked into the sheriff's office was, "Well, John...I'da thought you'da kept this news under wraps...leastways till we had it all cleared up! Now...you had no right ta git the whole town a'buzzin' like this. I'm surprised at you."

The deputy jumped to the defense of his chief. "I'm the one to blame...for everbody in town knowin'. The Sheriff didn't have nothin' to do with it. It was me...an' my big mouthed wife!" he said, apologetically. "And... well...I'm truly sorry."

The Sheriff nodded, "And a *good morning* to you, too, Fred," he said amiably. "Sorry 'bout all that Hubbub. But, you've lived around here long enough to know that you don't keep news like this under wraps for long." Rising, he donned his hat and started for the door. "Now, why don't you good people just show me where we're a'goin'." He nodded toward Lisa and Becca. "Ladies, let's go see what this is all about." Then, turning to his deputy he said, curtly, "Stay here, Andy, and man the phone...in case I need anything. I'll keep you posted." He started out the door, then turned back. "Oh, an' don't tell anybody anything...just say we don't know anything yet...*if you're asked*!"

When the party emerged from the sheriff's office, there were already news people gathered there, asking questions. The sheriff stopped and looked at them squarely, then, deciding that evasion would not get him anywhere, he raised a hand to silence them. "I'm goin' to tell you what I know. Then I hope you'll have the good graces to leave it alone, until we know more. Fair enough?" There were chuckles and nods from the crowd.

"All right. This is what we know. Yesterday afternoon, these good people found a skeleton on their land. And...for reasons that I won't go into at this time...they believed the skeleton to be the remains of Fred Johnson's brother David, who disappeared over fifty years ago." As the crowd came alive with questions, he held up his hand. "Now we had a deal! No questions, until I know more than just speculation. And...I'm dead serious when I say, If you expect me to be forthcoming...when I do know something...then you must abide by my rules." He started to get into his car, then stopped and faced the crowd again. "Oh, and one other thing...the place we are going may very well be the scene of a crime. So, naturally, I will expect you to treat it as such. You will...again I say, you *will*...abide by my rules...and the boundaries that I impose...or *you will be*...arrested on sight! I trust I've made myself clear." With that, he motioned for Dick to lead the way, and the whole entourage headed south out of town.

When they reached the farm, the Sheriff stopped their followers at the road, explaining, "Until I have looked things over and decided where you can and can't be, you will remain here. I'm sure it won't be terribly long. But...if it tires you to wait, you may leave to go back to town at any time. Is that clear to all of you? You will *not* set foot on that property...until you have the go ahead from me. Understood?" Grumbling, the crowd gave assent, and Dick led the Sheriff onto the old homestead.

Disembarking from their vehicles, Lisa and Becca, told the sheriff again, how they had first found the car... so they thought it would be best to start with the barn. He agreed, and they led him inside. He was astonished to see the vehicle sitting there at the back of the room...*in plain sight.*

"Now...how is it that you didn't see this...earlier?" he asked, shaking his head in disbelief.

Dick explained that it was completely covered with old hay, showing him how he had reached into the stuff and come up with a handful of nothing, because it was so rotten on the surface, and how, digging down deeper into it he had hit something hard. Then he demonstrated how he had used the old gunny sacks to remove the hay and uncover the car.

About that time Fred and Bertha caught up with them. Fred opened the car door and showed the Sheriff the registration and the suitcases in the back. "I couldn't believe my eyes, at first," he said. "It seemed so unreal. But," the words caught in his throat, "this is...David's car. And those are 'is suitcases...there in the backseat."

"So...did you look into the suitcases, Fred?" the sheriff asked.

Fred shook his head, "Huh uh, John. We didn't touch 'em. I was too broken up to think of lookin' into 'em."

"I'm sure you were, Fred. I'm sure you were." The sheriff looked around the vehicle. "Why didn't you go ahead and finish takin' the hay off?" he asked Dick.

"I...I just didn't think of it," Dick answered. "We were...uh, overwhelmed...with what was staring us in the face...and I guess we just didn't think of it."

"Well...about that time..." Lisa said, "it dawned on me...that...I might know where David was...and...and we went to check it out. And after that, we didn't really think of going back to the car...to look for anything else."

"OK...so, now show me...what you did next...then...after you found the car," the sheriff said.

Lisa took him through their next steps, showing him how they broke the glass window of the shed to get the shovels and went up the hill behind the house to look for the cistern. Then, upon finding it, how they had decided to tell Fred and Bertha, to enlist their help in opening it up.

After the party finally made its way back up to the old cistern, Bertha plopped down in her chair, thankful that they had left it there the day before, and the sheriff leaned himself against the old tree, breathing hard. He was quiet, collecting his thoughts.

"One thing puzzles me," he said, squinting at Lisa. "By your account, you never looked anywhere else...not elsewhere in the barn, not out in the fields or pasture, and not in the old house...that right?" She nodded. "Well, then ...how did you decide it was the cistern? How did you even know there was a cistern here?" He let her ponder her answer a minute, then added, "And, I thought you came back here to find your grandfather's homestead, because you didn't know where it was. So...if you didn't even know where it was...how is it that you know so durned much about it...that you could go straight to an old cistern, that had been buried for...God only knows...how long? And...had all this" he motioned with his hand, "wild grass growin' on top of it."

Fred bristled at the tone his friend had taken with Lisa and stopped him. "Now...John, you wait jist one gol durned minute..." Lisa interrupted him.

"It's OK, Fred. Of course this all sounds strange to the sheriff. It sounds strange to me! And he's just doing his job." She turned to the sheriff and said. "You know, Sheriff, I'll be glad to answer any and all questions you have for me...but don't you think it would be a good idea to at least take a look at the...uh...skeleton...before those news people get tired of being left in the dark, and come trampling all over everything in sight?" She gestured toward the cars now sitting partially in the driveway instead of all the way out on the road. "*They* have gotten a bit closer than where we left them."

The sheriff swore, "OK...let's have a look, before they're all down our necks." With that the men removed the makeshift lid from the cistern, and John let out a low whistle. "Well, I'll be..." he mopped his brow. "So, you all..." he swept over them with his hand, "So you all dug all those rocks out of here?" They nodded assent. "Rough work..." he mused. "An' you never found anything...else...but those keys...that can identify him as David?"

"Look there, John," Fred said. "Look at 'is right hand. That's gotta be 'is class ring. He always wore it. I saw it glint in the sun light...but we left it there for identification."

"Good thinkin', Fred. Thanks for not disturbin' it." He hauled himself out of the hole. "Well, the scene seems to be intact." He took a roll of yellow crime scene tape out of his pocket, and starting at the tree, he asked Bertha to hold on to the end, as he made a circle out around the cistern. "Now, Fred, you and Dick go on down to the barn and rope it off." he said, handing them the roll of the tape. "Maybe this way we can keep 'em back...till we get it all sorted out." John then got a bundle of stakes from his car so that he could make a boundary around the cistern to attach the tape to. Lisa and Becca helped him pound them into the sandy soil with rocks. "Thank you, ladies," he said, politely, as he dialed Andy on his cell phone. "Andy, get ahold of Sam Davison at the coroner's office and get him out here right away. And tell him not to stop to jaw with any of the onlookers out by the road."

Having gotten the coroner business out of the way, the sheriff got out his camera and proceeded to methodically photograph everything in site. When he finished with the cistern and it's immediate surroundings, he went down to the barn. Lisa and Becca tagged along, while Bertha sat perched like a sentinel, guarding her brother-in-law from invasion by the crowd that was inching its way ever closer down the driveway.

After John had photographed everything in and around the car, he carefully lifted the two suitcases out of it. "These are David's?" he asked Fred, who nodded, gravely. "All right you all will be my witnesses." He motioned them to gather around, then opening one, he photographed all of it's contents. When he was satisfied that he'd gotten it all, he opened the other and repeated the process. Having finished them both he asked Fred, "Can you see anything amiss, here?"

"Nope," Fred shook his head. "It looks like what David would'a had with 'im." Then he scowled and added, "Cept'in...I didn't see no money. Now, I'da thought he'da had some money in there." He scratched his head. "Maybe...not. Maybe he had it on 'im."

"Well...we'll look," John said, "when we bring him up...OK?" Fred nodded.

"I jest know that...he'd never'a gone without no money," Fred added, solemnly. "An'...another thing...I know that he closed out 'is checkin' account at the bank."

As the coroner turned into the drive he hit his siren to let John know he was near. And the group in the barn went out to meet him. "What's up, John?" he asked, getting out of his vehicle, and unloading the stretcher.

"Looks like we've finally found Fred's long lost brother, David," John said, nodding at the rise behind the house. "Up there. We've tried to keep the crowd back, but don't know how long they're gonna be willing to just sit on their hands...so let's get at it. Fred, you and Dick can help us here. We'll have to carry this thing up through that sand. It'll never roll on it's own."

At the top of the rise where Bertha still kept watch, softly humming to herself, Sam jumped down into the hole. "Oh my Lord God Almighty! He's sure been down here a long time!" he exclaimed. Then looking up at the group, he said, "Thanks for not disturbing anything else." Then he went to work, carefully brushing away the dirt with a very soft brush. He lifted the skull out first, and laying it on the bier said, matter-of-factly, "Looks like he had his head caved in."

At that moment Lisa remembered again that other flash of sunlight on metal as it colided with silver hair and she almost fainted. "Oh Dear God," she prayed silently, grabbing onto Dick's arm for balance. "Oh Dear God, say it isn't so! I didn't want to believe that it could really be so... that it could have happened again."

"C'mon," Dick said softly, putting an arm securely around her waist. "Let's go down to the car...for a drink of water." She let him take her to the car, because she didn't want to fall apart in front of anyone, but as soon as they were out of sight, she let the tears come. Dick let her cry, shielding her from the prying eyes that were ever encroaching on their privacy, so close to the car now that you could almost feel them. As soon as she had regained her composure, they once again made their way back up the hill.

Sam had lifted all of the bones out onto the stretcher, and was now carefully digging in the dirt beneath where the body had lain, just to make sure there wasn't anything that had come loose and worked it's way downward. He was very methodical, slowly lifting small shovels full of soil onto the screen-door, to be sifted. "Great idea...that screen door," he said, placing another shovel full onto it. Then, turning, he pointed his shovel downward ever so slightly and tried to push it forward...but it couldn't go forward because it had hit something. "Must be a rock," he mused," bending down to brush the soil away. But it wasn't a rock. "Uh oh!" he exclaimed. "What have we here?" Turning it over in his hands, he looked up at the sheriff. "It's appears to be another skull, John. Were we expecting another one...another skeleton...down here?"

John stood there in stunned silence, looking first at Fred, then at Lisa. "I'm sure I don't know...were we?" Lisa looked on in horror, not saying anything. "OK...I'll ask you one more time, Ma'am...were we?"

Lisa nodded slowly, "Yes," she whispered. "We were." She struggled hard to maintain her composure. "Maybe...maybe even two."

John looked at her in stunned disbelief, blinking as if trying to clear his mind of irrelevant information, "What did you say?"

"I said," Lisa struggled with the words that were barely audible. "I said...there may be two more bodies...uh, s...skeletons...down there." She was totally drained and looked for a place to sit down. John wasn't stunned for long, though. He immediately bombarded Lisa with half a dozen questions, not giving her time to answer any of them. She looked like she was on the verge of running away when Bertha intervened.

"Here, Lisa girl, you come over here...and sit down by me," she said. "This has been a terrible thing for you to have to go through." As soon as Lisa sat down on the rock beside her, Bertha pulled her head down onto her ample lap. "Now, you jist rest here a bit," she said, rocking back and forth. "You jist rest...an' Bertha'll take care o'you." She looked hard at John. "Now, John...really! Questions kin wait. This girl's been through too much!" She rocked back and forth. "An' it's not like she hasn't been tryin' ta cooperate. Why...she's the one that brought us all out here! Have ya fergotten that?" She paused, briefly, then added, "Yep, I think any more questions kin jist wait. Ain't that right, Poppy!"

"Oh, yes...I agree," Fred answered. "You jist git on with findin' them skeletons down there..." He motioned for John to get down into the cistern with the coroner. "An'...like Bertha sez, the questions kin wait til later.

We'll *personally* vouch fer Lisa. She'll answer yer questions, John, but...later."

Just then someone yelled, "Two...they got two skulls up there on that stretcher!" And Lisa was aware of running footsteps, and people crowding around. "Who's the other stiff, Sheriff?" someone asked from behind Bertha. "There are two skulls there on the stretcher...so who's the other one?"

"Well...we knew we couldn't hold 'em off forever," John said to Sam. "Let's go face the music." They helped each other out of the hole.

"Keep back of the ribbon, folks!" John insisted. "Or…you can just go on back to your cars. We still set the rules...and the boundaries...here."

CHAPTER THIRTY FIVE

"Better you than me!" Sam whispered to John, as they faced the curious onlookers. "You keep 'em busy, while I go get a couple more sheets from my vehicle. Gotta keep those bones separated." With that, he ducked through the crowd.

"OK, Sheriff, let's have it," someone shouted. "Exactly how many people are there anyway...down there in that cistern?"

"All we know at this time is that there may be as many as three...but we aren't sure of that yet. And...as to who these other people are...your guess is as good as mine." He mopped his brow. "It stands to reason that if David has been down there about fifty years, and he was on top of the others...then they've been down there at least that long...maybe even longer." He was at a loss as to what to say next, and just stood there looking at the stretcher with it's terrible secrets.

Then someone else called out, "Well...do you have any missing persons...from back that long ago…that have never turned up?"

"Good question! And all I can say to that is, I really don't know at this time. Since I hadn't anticipated this uh…*discovery*...I uh...I wasn't prepared for it. It will take some time to go back through records...and…uh...well... we'll just have to look into it." John always liked to give the appearance that he was on top of every situation, and he hated the way he felt like he was fumbling this. Just then the coroner came back, and John excused himself to get back to the task of bringing up bones. But, as he was about to jump down into the hole he had a brainstorm, and turned back to the reporters. "You know, I would think…with all the resources that you all have...*you* might dig into this a bit. See if you can come up with any missing persons...say from 1949, when David disappeared, on back a few years.

Now, that would give *you* something to do...while you're waiting around on me."

For a few minutes the crowd just hung about, afraid they'd miss out on something if they left, but before long they had all drifted on back down to the cars to call their editors, and make a few discreet inquiries of their own. And within the next 20 minutes or so, they had all gone back to town. Peeking up out of the cistern, the coroner, a man of few words, grinned at the sheriff and exclaimed, "Brilliant, John, brilliant!"

Before long, John and Sam had all of the second skeleton out of it's resting place, and were carefully sifting through every inch of soil, lest they overlook something pertaining to it, a slow and tedious process. Once satisfied that they had everything, the two men came up for a break. Becca had brought them fresh bottles of water from the car, for which they were very grateful.

"We're fortunate," Sam said, peeling off his latex gloves, "that there isn't any odor left. That would be almost intolerable in this heat." Pouring some water on his handkerchief, he wiped his face and neck.

"Yeah," John agreed, "that would be bad." Then, turning to Fred he said, "You know, Fred, I was just thinking about what you said...about the money. You say he had closed out his checking account?" Fred nodded. "Well," the sheriff continued, "I was just wondering how you knew that?"

"I'm not really sure, John. It was so long ago. I think," Fred began, tentatively, working hard to remember. "I think maybe...he told me...when he came by to ask me ta ship 'im his stuff." The memory was becoming sharper, clearer. "Yeah, that's it! 'Cause...he gave me some money ta ship the stuff fer 'im. And...well, it *seems* like...he told me he'd closed out his checkin' account...but not 'is savin's! That's right! Now I remember. He said...he took everthin' outta checkin'...put some of it inta savin's...an' was keepin' the rest out ta help get resettled...in Texas." Fred took a slow deep breath, as a terrible sadness descended on him. "I...told 'im ta get 'imself some traveler's checks, jest ta be safe. But he jest laughed. Called me an ole' mother hen." Tears welled up in the old man's eyes and, needing to have someplace to go, he turned and walked toward the barn.

Lisa remembered how he always went to do chores when something bothered him, and wished there was something for him to do now. She got up and took Dick by the hand, pulling him along with her, as she called out, "Fred...I have an idea! Let's go down and re-check David's car." The old man turned toward her, and she continued, "Well, we never did finish taking all the hay off, and we...we may have missed something. And...we didn't even look in the trunk!"

Alarmed, the sheriff pulled himself up out of the hole. "Wait! You can't go poking around down there without me being present!" He turned to Sam, asking, "I recon you can handle the rest of this...right?" Sam nodded, motioning him away, as John continued, "I really do need to be there...just in case they find anything else!"

"Go! Go on!" Sam said. "I'm used to doing this by myself. And, besides, Bertha's a great help...siftin' through all this dirt for me." He motioned John away, again. "Go!"

John caught up with the rest just as they got to the barn door. "You know, we're gonna need to get a padlock for this door. Back one, too. I find it hard to believe that *nobody* has pilfered this stuff," he said, making a sweeping gesture of the interior. "But, you can bet, now that people know what's here...stuff'll begin to disappear." Once inside, they all went directly to the vehicle at the back of the barn.

Solemnly Dick took a pitchfork from the wall nearby and proceeded to remove the hay from between the car and the back wall. Then, having done that, he used the gunny sacks to whisk away the remainder from off the back of the vehicle so that they could open the trunk. "It's locked," he said. "Still got those keys with you, Sheriff?"

John unlocked the trunk and opened it. To everyone's surprise, and dismay, there wasn't a thing in it. "Well, that takes care of that," he said, wiping his brow with his handkerchief. "Nothing here! Not even a tire iron!"

"Course not, John," Fred chuckled. "David never kept 'is tools in the trunk. Always kept 'em under the back seat. Used to razz 'im 'bout it, cause the trunk would'a been handier. But he always kept 'em there. Said he was less likely to...lose 'em."

As the sheriff opened the back door of the driver's side, Fred went around and opened the other. "Here, let me help you," he said. As the two men lifted the back bench seat out of the car, Fred grinned, "There! You see. His tools *are here*...jest like I said."

"Yeah, I see," John answered. "And...I see something else. Looks like some kind of wallet. There," he said, pointing. "At the back, Fred. You're closer than me, can you reach it?"

"Well I'll be!" Fred exclaimed, reaching for the flat zippered wallet. "It's travelers checks!" he said, looking inside. "Would you believe? He actually did what I told 'im!" He thumbed through the contents and, dumbfounded, exclaimed, "Why there...must be three, four, thousand here, John!" He handed the wallet over to the sheriff.

"Yeah...at least," John said. "At least that." He carefully counted out five thousand dollars, then shook his head in disbelief. "Well...if the motive was robbery...the perp didn't get what he was looking for!"

"It wasn't robbery..." Lisa mused, softly. "It never was...about robbery."

"What's that?" John asked, turning toward her. "What did you say?"

"I said...it wasn't about robbery." Lisa answered, sadly.

"And just how would you know that?"

"I explained *all that*, Sheriff. Don't you remember? When I told you about all this...back there in your office." She climbed into the front seat of the car and rested her head on her hands on the steering wheel.

"Well, why don't you try explaining it again," John said, not unkindly. "I think...I need to hear it again."

So once more Lisa proceeded to tell how her parents, Joe and Kate Hollander, were involved in that horrible accident that killed five people. And how Joe had tried to say that Kate was driving, when everyone knew that Kate didn't drive, and she, herself, was so severely injured that she couldn't defend herself. And how David had rescued her, Lisa, from that car wreck after everyone else had gone, and had taken care of her until she was well enough to return home. And how, when their mother finally came home from the hospital, David had come to her aid when Joe was cruel to her. And how, when her mother finally decided to leave Joe, David had helped her... helped all of them...escape into Texas. And, finally, how her mother had had something that she was holding over Joe's head, so that he couldn't make good on his threat to kill them all.

The sheriff took his time mulling all that over, then asked, "So...you think your dad killed David...for what? Spite? Because your Mom was holding something over his head...and he couldn't touch any of *you*?"

"Well, he surely knew that Mama was going to marry David...after the divorce was final. Any dummy could have figured that out. I mean, every time he turned around he was bumping into David. David the savior...of **his** family! That must have galled him. And let me tell you, Sheriff, our daddy was not one to take anything he didn't like...off of anybody!" She buried her head in her hands. After a bit she raised her head and looked straight at John.

"Oh, yes, Sheriff. I do believe he killed him out of spite! It surely wasn't for the money. Evidently Daddy didn't even look for it. And, another thing," she glanced at the car, "he didn't even bother to sell the car, or disguise it, or anything. He *saved it*...as a trophy! And he didn't even have to leave it out where others might see it, cause he could come in here anytime he wanted and gloat." She paused for a few moments. "No sir, he couldn't kill us...but he could do the next best thing. Make sure Mama and David could never be together...ever."

"OK. Let's say you're right about all of this," John conceded. "There's still something I don't get. Why...if they were planning to get married as you say...didn't your mama come looking for David, when he didn't show up?"

Fred jumped at that opening, "Well, John...I have the answer to that! We have a letter that Kate sent David. We hadn't never opened it, cause we figured on David comin' back, an' then, after so long, the letter got put away with 'is stuff, an' we jest fergot about it. But, when all this came up...we got to thinkin' about that letter. An' we went an'dug it out...an' opened it. In it Kate was tellin' 'im to carefully think it over, whether he wanted to take on a whole family or not...cause Joe, who she'd come ta believe was crazy, was the daddy o' her kids. She wanted him to *be sure* he could handle that, and be able to be a real daddy to those kids, cause that's what they deserved. An' then she said she would understand if he decided he couldn't do it...and they would just break it off clean...with no hard feelin's. You see, when he didn't write back, she must'a decided he wasn't comin'...so she just let it go."

"And you," John added, "Thought he had gone to be with her. So, *nobody* looked for him, 'cause...*nobody* knew...he was missin'!"

Tears welled up in the old man's eyes. "Right. Who would'a thought he was out here all this time? An' I never would'a suspected anything like murder. I jest figured he didn't want Joe ta find out where they were...so he didn't keep in touch."

"So...tell me," John turned to Lisa, "since Joe held on to this property all that time, did he actually ever live out here? It seems to me that I remember something' about him dying in a hotel room in town?"

"Actually, John, I don't know if he ever lived out here at all. For all that stuff that's in the barn, there's no furniture in the house. Nothing, except an old chest of drawers in the basement," Lisa answered. "But, according to county records, he didn't sell the place until a short time before he died...to a pair of newly-weds...who ended up getting a divorce, and *never did* take possession."

"Yeah," Becca chimed in. "When we did the research in Wray...and found that the bank held the note on it, you can be sure Lisa didn't waste any time getting it back in the family!"

Dick chuckled, "Right...she called me from the bank, telling me to wire the money...that very day! First time I ever bought a piece of property sight unseen."

The sheriff stood there, chin in hand, thinking. Then he asked. "OK, so that takes care of how *David* ended up in the cistern. But...we still have another little problem that needs clearing up. *Who* are the other two skeletons? And..." he looked directly at Lisa, "how is it...that you knew they were there?"

All of the color drained out of Lisa's face. "Well...Sheriff, I was ten," she sighed, "when my father brought me out here with him. When he...uh...dumped them in the cistern. But, Sheriff, I didn't remember any of that, until we had found this old place. Back then...when I was ten...I didn't even know where we were."

"You didn't know *this* place was your Grandfather's homestead?" he asked.

She shook her head. "No. I had no idea who's place it was. I don't know if I had ever been out here before that, but I really don't think so...because I think I would have recognized it...if I had ever been there before. I do remember asking Daddy where we were going. And...he just laughed and said, 'a hunnert miles from nowhere'. He didn't say we were going to his old home, or my grandfather's old place. He said, 'a hunnert miles from nowhere'."

"And...*you* actually saw him...dump those other two into the cistern?"

"Uh...this gets really complicated. What I actually saw was...uh," Lisa struggled to keep her composure, and her head was beginning to pound. She rubbed her temples. "I... uh...saw my daddy...and another man...dump a body into the cistern."

"I thought you said there were *two* more skeletons in there," John prodded.

"I said...p..possibly...two more." She closed her eyes against the sting of fresh tears, praying, silently, "Oh, God, I need you. Help me, please!"

Dick intervened, asking, "Uh...Sheriff...if you don't mind, could we do this later?" He put his arms, protectively, around his wife. "It's really been rough on her...to have to remember all this. How about taking a rest from it? She'll be glad to finish...later."

"Well...I don't see what that could hurt," John said, sympathetically. "It would be awfully hard to have to remember something like this...about your own parent. So, what do you say we go and see if the coroner has actually found another skeleton down there." With that he led the party back to the cistern.

Sam had just climbed out of the hole when they arrived. "Ah, I was just coming to get you, John," he said. "This last one seems to be all wrapped up...in an old Indian blanket. See..." he pointed. "Looks to be Navaho. You can still make out the design on it. Now, I need to preserve as much of the blanket, and it's contents, as possible...so, I'm gonna need you to help me."

"Sure," John said. "What can I do?"

Grabbing a clean sheet, Sam jumped back into the hole, shouting, "Come on down here and let's try to slide this sheet under the whole package."

"OK. That ought'ta work," John said, joining him.

One sight of that Indian blanket and Lisa about lost it. Dick, who was still holding on to her, tightened his grip. She watched in horror as they maneuvered their *package* onto the sheet, carefully lifting it up to Fred and Dick, who finished the work of getting it out..

Then, as Sam and John extricated themselves from the cistern, John looked down one more time. "What's that?" he asked, pointing down. "Have we got *another* body?"

Sam looked down in shock. "What...another one?" He knelt down and brushed the soil off of some fabric. "Nope...it's not a body! It does look like some kind of clothing, though. And pretty well decayed." He looked up at Dick. "We'll need to take these along, Dick, so would you be so kind as to get me a brown paper bag from the back of the hearse? There's a whole box of them." Nodding, Dick ran quickly to get the bag.

"Like I said, we'll have to take all this along," Sam said, carefully gathering up the pieces and dropping them into a bag. "Probably connected, somehow. And, I guess we'll have to finish sifting through all the rest of this dirt, till we actually get down to the cement bottom. Don't wanna take a chance on missin' something important." He stood up and stretched. "But, hey! I'm about famished." He looked at his watch. "And no wonder. It's nearly three...and I've been out here since a little after nine. And you all were here before I was. Whaddya say we take a break? Go get something' to eat. There'll be plenty of daylight left for us to finish after we eat a bite." Not waiting for anyone to actually answer, he climbed out of the hole and started carefully wrapping up each skeleton for transport back to his lab.

John immediately got on his cellphone. "Andy, I need you to come on out here and stand watch while we take a late lunch break. Looks like we got another two or three hours of work to do, and we're all famished. Now, we can't leave till you get out here, so hurry it up, will you?" He started to hang up, then hollered, "Oh, and Andy... are you still there? OK. In the storage room, the middle shelf, just inside the door to the left, is a box of padlocks. You know? OK. Bring a couple...locks and keys. OK, that's all. Now hurry!"

Next he called his wife, Peggy. "Hi Hon. Have you got anything in the house to make sandwiches with? How many? Oh, there are seven of us. We've been at it all day and didn't stop for lunch. And I surely don't want us to have to wade through a bunch of curiosity seekers at the restaurant, so...I thought maybe you wouldn't mind fixin' us a bite of somethin'. Anything'll do, Hon. Just anything you got on hand. You will? All right! Thanks, Peg...you always come through for me, Babe. Thanks!"

When he hung up, the sheriff turned to Dick and Fred. "Now, here's what we're gonna do," he said, pulling a note pad out of his pocket. "I want you folks to go on over to my place, northeast of here," he said, drawing on the pad. "But, I'm gonna send you two different ways," Handing Dick the first map, he continued, "and we're gonna time it... so's you won't arrive together." Tearing off the second map, he shoved the pad back down into his pocket. "And...here's your's, Fred. Just a precaution," he chuckled. "In case anybody's still watchin'." He walked them to their vehicles. "You just tell Peg that we'll be along...soon as Andy gets here."

Dick, Lisa and Becca were the first to leave. At the end of the driveway, they went west for two miles, then north for one, and turned back east for nine miles, after which they turned north again for a mile and a half, finding the house at the end of a long tree lined lane. It was a neat brick ranch style house, surrounded by many outbuildings and full grown trees, providing a very shady yard. Peg was standing in the side yard to keep them from going to the front gate, where they would have been mowed down by two very large but friendly mixed breed dogs. She ushered them in at the back door, sending them on through to the living room with directions on how to find the bathroom to wash up. Then she went back out to wait for Fred and Bertha, who were right behind them. John and Sam arrived about thirty minutes later.

The lunch was a welcome break. Peg had ground up some left over roast beef for the sandwiches, and served it with cantaloupe out of her garden, and iced tea with fresh mint...also from her garden. The meal was both refreshing, and filling. But they didn't linger. John was concerned about leaving Andy alone at the site for long, so they hurried back as quickly as possible.

It's a good thing they did. A couple of reporters had reappeared just as soon as John and Sam left, and Andy was getting a little tired of telling them he didn't know anything, and that they'd have to wait for the sheriff. Fortunately, John had had the foresight to padlock the barn before he left, because he wanted Andy to concentrate his efforts on keeping the cistern site from contamination...and he clearly couldn't be two places at once. The reporters, thinking they could put one over on Andy, hatched a plan whereby one would keep him occupied while the other checked out the barn.

They were more than a little frustrated to find it padlocked. In fact, the one checking out the barn was looking for another way to get in when John and Sam reappeared.

"Now, would you look there, Sam," the sheriff grumbled, screeching to a halt at the barn. "Never ceases to amaze me how some folks just can't read!" He stepped out of his car and hollered at the reporter, who was concentrating on trying to reach a window in the hayloft by climbing onto some old bales of hay stacked against the side of the barn. "Come on back down from there...right now! Before I decide to arrest you for breakin' and enterin', and defiling a crime scene...and whatever else I can think up!" The reporter turned and looked innocently at the sheriff, shrugging his shoulders like he didn't know what was going on. "And don't even bother to tell me you didn't see that yellow tape...that just goes all the way around that barn...telling you to keep out!"

The reporter climbed down, grinning, "Well...sheriff, ya can't blame a guy for tryin'. I'm just doin' my job...tryin' to get a story...you know." He sauntered over to the sheriff's car. "C'mon, Sheriff. You don't haffta be so hard nosed about it. After all, we all haffta work for a livin'. An' *my livin's* gettin' pitchers of crime scenes." He looked coolly at John, flipping his dirty blond hair out of his eyes with a toss of his head. "Pitchers that nobody else has...and...that means I haffta take risks sometimes." He tucked a pinch of tobacco into his cheek and strode off toward his car, calling back over his shoulder, "We're all just tryin' to make a livin', Sheriff."

"Yeah, yeah," John muttered angrily, as he and Sam made their way back to the cistern. "We're all just trying to make a livin'!" he mocked. "It's just that some of us are a wee bit more ethical...in how we go about it... than others!"

They spent what was left of the afternoon digging out and sifting through the dirt that remained in the cistern. Again a slow and tedious job. However, they did find a number of items for their effort, several coins, a small comb, three matching buttons, and a man's leather wallet. It was Sam's guess that all of the items had come from the partially decayed garments that they had found under the last skeleton. He was hoping that the wallet would give him an identification on at least one of the skeletons, but it was all stuck together. He'd have to take it back to his lab and carefully pry it apart. As soon as Sam had everything loaded, he left for town. The others soon followed. *After* Dick and John had gone back into the barn and made sure the hayloft door was shut and bolted from within, and that there were no other openings big enough for any human being to squeeze through.

CHAPTER THIRTY SIX

Fred and Bertha were tired and headed straight for their home, but the others followed the Sheriff back to his office. He had told them it could wait until morning, when they were all fresh, but they just wanted to get it over with. "Suit yourself," he said, unlocking his office. He made some coffee, then, getting a notepad out of his drawer, said, "Ok. So...where do we start?"

"Well, I guess it starts with me," Becca said, telling the sheriff about her dream of being taken to a house in the country when she was three, and how she had come to realize that the dream was actually a memory...after she saw the old house out on Hwy 59. She told how the people snatched her off of Margaret's porch, and how her daddy had come for her...only to get into a fight with a man who had a gun, which went off during a struggle, killing the man. Then she told how her daddy called another man from upstairs to come and help him take the dead man away, leaving her virtually alone in that house.

"And this is where I come in," Lisa said. Then she told of staying home from school and being awakened by a noise coming from the basement, and how, when she had gone down the steps trying to slip unnoticed into the wash room, she had tripped over a dead man lying on the floor, and how her daddy, and somebody called Frank, had taken her with them to dispose of the body...in a place that her daddy said was a hundred miles from nowhere. And how, once they were in that place, how Frank had chased and tackled her, and gotten on the wrong side of their daddy by dumping her in the cistern...on top of the dead guy...causing her daddy to turn on him in rage, smashing in his head with a shovel.

"It was a terrible blow," Lisa said, her voice barely audible. She took a moment to compose herself. "Then he...Daddy...told me to come help him. I assumed he wanted me to help him dump Frank into the cistern...and...I tried. I tried to lift Frank's arm..." she faltered. "But...it was just too heavy. And I was nearly petrified with fear...rendering me practically useless." Tears fell, unchecked, as she continued. "Then...then Daddy got really angry! Angry with *me*! And..." she swallowed hard, eyes filled with pain, "he...he raised the shovel..." She closed her eyes as if to block out the horrible specter. "Oh, it was horrible. He was going to hit *me*...with it! And...then I just screamed...No Daddy! It's me, Lisa...your baby girl, remember? Don't hit me!" Lisa put her hand over her mouth. Then after taking a couple of deep breaths, went on, quietly, "His eyes were crazed...like he didn't know me. Then... after a horribly long minute...he just threw the shovel down...and screamed at me to get out of his sight! His words were, "*Get the hell and gone out of my sight*!" She was crying too hard now to continue, and Dick knelt beside her chair, putting his arms around her.

"It's OK, Lisa...you're all right, Hon," he whispered, gently holding her. "Everything's all right, now. That was a long time ago...but you're here, and...you're safe...with me now."

After a few moments, she looked up at the sheriff. "Well...needless to say...I did. I ran...I ran and hid behind the house, and when he called for me to come back...I didn't come out. I just stayed there and listened. I was afraid of what I'd see if I looked, so I just stayed put. For awhile I could hear him...moving around, digging. Finally, he stopped, and everything was quiet. Too quiet. Then...he just left. He...he just got in the car, and started to drive away! Oh, I was so terrified! He was leaving me out there...with those two dead men!" At that, Becca, who had been valiantly controlling her emotions, could hold it back no longer and dissolved in tears.

Lisa paused for only a brief moment to blow her nose, then continued. "Then, I guess I came to my senses, and I took off running after him, screaming at the top of my lungs, Daddy, don't leave! Don't leave me out here...a hundred miles from nowhere!" Lisa stopped then, rocking back and forth in her chair, as fresh tears made their way down her face, and her husband tried to hold her even closer. When she had once again gained control, she looked up into John's face, and whispered, "Well...that's...about it, Sheriff. That's the story."

No one said or did anything, waiting for John to respond, and he had been so caught up in what Lisa was saying, that it took a few moments for him to do so. He sat tapping his pen on the pad on his desk for a moment, then suddenly aware of the noise it was making, tossed it down. "Well...that's...quite a story," he said, taking out his hanky and blowing his nose. Finally, feeling at a total loss as to what to say or do next, yet knowing the ball was in his court, he said, "And...you think he put the other man...uh, Frank...in the cistern, too?"

Lisa nodded, then grinned wryly, "Well...since we actually found three skeletons...in that cistern...I guess you could say that. Yes, I do believe he dumped Frank into the cistern."

"And...and you don't have any idea who those men were?"

"Well, Sheriff, no...we didn't at first. But, since we have been here, and learned about the car wreck and all...I think we do know the name of the one wrapped up in the Indian blanket." Lisa answered. "Becca and I both recall that Daddy called him Eddie...and we saw a newspaper picture of a man standing beside the car wreck. His name was Edward Bennett. Then...Fred told us that this Edward Bennett ran around with our Dad. In fact...they had a nickname for him...Eddie Bennetti. I'd be willing to bet...that is who is in the blanket." She paused, then said, "And, actually, it makes sense."

The sheriff was distracted, momentarily, turning the Bennett name over in his mind, but then Lisa's last words brought him back. "What do you mean...makes sense?" he asked.

"Well...Daddy took care of the body. Quite unlike what he did with Hank's and David's bodies, he bathed Eddie's, then wrapped it in a blanket for burial...as though he really cared about the man. Even though they just threw him into a cistern...it seemed to me like he was kinda sad. He made a sort of ritual of the burial. That tells me that it was someone he knew well...maybe even cared about."

"It does?" The sheriff looked doubtful.

At that Dick jumped in. "Don't forget, Sheriff, she's a psychologist. Knows a lot about things like that."

"Uh, yeah...that's right. I guess she would," John conceded. Then he turned his attention back to Lisa. "But...you don't have any idea who this Frank might be?"

"Huh uh." Lisa shook her head. "Haven't got a clue. And, I've...we've...been looking, every since we remembered all this. At first Becca thought his name was Hank, but I'm pretty sure it was Frank. Our physical descriptions point to the same guy. And you have to keep in mind, she was only three at the time. A three year old could easily mistake Hank for Frank. But, I was ten. Big difference. We'd usually give more credence to a ten year olds memory over a three year olds...of the same incident. Anyway, I thought...well...maybe you could go back through the Colorado records of missing persons, or something. A person doesn't exist in a vacuum. He had to have been connected to someone. Been someone's son...or husband...or lover."

"Yeah. That's for sure." John said, rubbing his chin, thoughtfully. "Well, I'll do some diggin' around," he said. "See what we come up with." Then he stretched and got to his feet, reaching for his hat. "Well, folks... what do you say we call it a day. See what Sam has for us tomorrow. If I know him...he'll stay up late working on this...maybe all night. Doesn't get real interesting mysteries very often, and I saw that gleam in his eye. Why don't you all go on and get a bite of supper and some rest, and we'll hit it again tomorrow." With that he ushered them out, locking the door behind them.

John hurried right home. "Hey, Peg," he yelled, bailing out of his vehicle, and dashing into the kitchen where she was busy finishing a batch of jelly. "What's the name of that old Bennett Lady in the nursing home?" He planted a kiss on her cheek, then continued. "Mary or Mable...something old fashioned like that...isn't it?"

"Merribelle," Peg answered. "Her name is Merribelle. Why?"

"Well, since you've been volunteering there, I know you've told me about her...dozens of times. I was just trying to remember something you said."

"Humm...something I said. Well, that covers a lot of territory. I've told you a lot of stories about those people...her in particular. But what is it you're trying to remember, and why?" She lavished some fresh grape jelly on a piece of buttered bread and offered it to her husband. "Tell me, why does Ms. Merribelle interest you, John?" She poured him a cup of coffee.

"Umm um," he said relishing the fresh grape jelly. "This is a prize winner!" Then he downed a swig of coffee. "Well...didn't you tell me something about her husband leaving her with two boys to raise...all by herself?"

Peg nodded. "Yeah. Just up and left. Never heard from him again."

"Do you think she'd talk to me?"

"Probably. She loves to have an audience. But, her mind is slipping...and I don't know how much of what she says is real and how much is fantasy." Peg studied her husband. "You want me to take you in to see her?"

He nodded. "They've probably finished supper in there by now haven't they?"

"Oh, yeah. An hour ago...or more. So, evidently...you want to go tonight?"

"Yeah. If you think she would be up to having visitors this late."

"Listen...most of those old folk would take company over a meal! They get pretty lonely...to have someone pay attention to them. And I'll tell you a secret. If you really want to get on her good side, take her a Milky Way. That's her favorite food in all the world."

John grinned. "She can have candy? She's not diabetic...or anything like that?"

"Nope. She's not sick. Just old. And she'll talk your arm off for a candy bar."

Before going over to the nursing home, John stopped at Alco and bought a package of Milky Way bars. When he got back into the car, Peg laughed. "You really do mean business, I see! But, here's another secret, only give her one. If you give her the package she'll eat the whole package tonight...and then *we'll* be in trouble with the staff...because then she really will be sick!"

He grinned, "Oh. OK...you're the expert. I'll take your word for it, and only take her one." He opened the package and took out a bar. Then, closing up the package, he grinned. "Well, who knows. I may have to bribe her again, sometime."

"That very well may be," laughed Peg.

Ms. Merribelle was a spry little old lady, who didn't weigh ninety pounds soaking wet. They found her in the common room, half watching

TV, half dozing. But she sprang to life when it finally dawned on her that these people had actually come to see her. "Well, let's go to *my room* where we can visit without being interrupted every two minutes," she said, making good and sure her fellows heard her. "Too many eyes and ears in this room to suit me," she snipped, leading the way with her trusty walker. "Just follow me." It was slow going, but they admired how determined Merribelle was to remain mobile, and not give in to the pressures to abandon her walker for the ease of a wheel chair.

Once inside the room it didn't take John long to make friends with the feisty old woman. And he won her undying affection when he produced the candy bar. "So...what is it, exactly, that you want to know about my life, Sheriff?" she asked, delicately tearing the wrapper off of her treasure. "There's not much to tell." She sampled a bite of the sweet delicacy. "I've never done much...that would be of interest to anybody."

"Well, Ms. Merribelle, Peg tells me that you raised your family all by yourself. Two...I think she told me you had two boys. Is that right?"

Her mouth was full. "Uh huh," she nodded, taking another bite.

John wished he'd waited to give her the candy. She was never going to tell him anything, until it was all gone. He bided his time, asking to see pictures of her family. She licked her fingers, wiping them on her sweatpants, and going to her dresser got out an album. Then, sitting back down beside John, she took another bite of Milky Way, and opened the album.

"These are my boys," she said, the sweet gooey concoction trickling out the corners of her mouth. Peg jumped up and got her a drink of water, which helped, but not a lot. Merribelle wiped her mouth on a tissue. "This is Pete..." she said, gently stroking the side of his eight year old face with her gnarled finger. "He was my first." She stopped and popped the last bite of candy into her mouth.

John silently thanked God that the candy was finally gone, and waited for her to go on with the pictures.

"And this one is Eddie...my baby. Named for his daddy, Edward." She sat caressing the picture of a wholesome six year old. "Aren't they beautiful?" she asked, then added, "Oh...I know you're not supposed to say boys are pretty or beautiful. Just manly, handsome...and all that. But to me, my boys were beautiful." She smiled at the memory and looked up at the sheriff. "Do you have children?"

"Yes," he answered. "We also have two boys...and a girl. They're grown...and married. We're expecting our first Grandchild, soon."

"Soon?" the old woman repeated. "How soon?"

Peg answered. "In a couple of months. It won't be long now!"

"Well, I should say not. A couple of months goes by awfully fast," the old woman said. "Seems like just yesterday that my boys were little. They grew up too fast." She looked terribly sad. "They grew up...and now they're gone. It went too fast."

John honed in on the word 'gone'. "What do you mean they're gone, Ms. Merribelle?" he asked.

She shrugged. "Gone. Just gone. Dead."

He was surprised. "Dead? Oh, I'm sorry. Has it been long...since they died?"

"A long time...Sheriff. No need to be sorry for this pitiful old lady. They've been gone so long...I sometimes forget how long." She drank the rest of the water Peg had given her, then wiped the remainder of chocolate off of her mouth. "Strange how you get used to it," she added.

"Used to what, Ms. Merribelle?" John asked, kindly.

"Heartache," she said. "Get's to be like a sorry neighbor. He's not a good neighbor, mind you, but he's the only one you got. And you're used to 'im being there. It would be pretty lonesome without 'im. You know what I mean?"

"I think so," John answered. "Yes, I think so." He sat quietly a moment then added. "It sounds like you've had a lot of heartache in your life then."

"Oh, I guess I've had my share." She was quiet a moment then added, wryly, "Sometimes...seems like my share...*plus* another fellas! But I guess the Good Lord knows what we need. At least...I ain't been troubled like that there Job fella. Now, he had his share...plus *several other fella's*!" She slapped her knee with the humor of it, and John decided he really liked this old woman. She was a trooper.

"So, Ms. Merribelle...I'm wondering how you're sons died...were they ill?"

She shook her head. "Nope. They...they both died in car wrecks. Not at the same time, mind you. But they always seemed bent on self destructin'...from the day they were borned!"

"That's too bad," the sheriff said. "Too bad." He gave it a few moments, then added, "I'll bet it was hard on their dad. I don't know if I could stand it if I lost *one* of my kids...much less *two*." He looked up at Merribelle. "How in the world did he stand it?"

Peg smiled, thinking to herself, "Why you old snake charmer!" She was always fascinated at how he could get people to tell him exactly what he wanted to know without usually having to ask direct questions. He had Merribelle Bennett eating out of his hand.

But the old woman looked like she had been slapped in the face. "How did he stand it?" she repeated. Then she became highly agitated. "Well, Sheriff...let me tell you! He wasn't no where around...to stand it, or not! Why, that sorry, no good..." she stopped herself just short of swearing. "Well, anyway, that sorry excuse for a man wasn't around to stand it...or not stand it. He'd already run out on us when the boys was just little tykes. Two and four. Nope! He was no longer in the picture...being a daddy to those boys...when they got themselves killed. He'd written them off...a long time before that! A long time!" She was surprised at the depth of her feelings, *and* at the tears...that she would have sworn were all used up a long time ago. Embarrassed, she accepted the sheriff's clean white hanky, and worked to get herself back under control. "I'm sorry," she whispered.

"It's all right," John said. "I didn't know...and of course you have every right to still feel angry." He paused, then went on. "I can't imagine...what would cause a man to run off...and leave his family."

"I should'a listened to my Pa. He said Eddie was no good...right from the start. But, no...I was in love! What can I say?" She shrugged, attempting a smile. "You know how love is. Makes you so you can't think straight."

"Yeah." He smiled at her. "And...just what was it about Eddie that got you?"

"Oh...he had a way...about him!" She shook her head. "I was a gonner...the first time he told me I was pretty. The first time he told me I was the only woman in the world for him." A wistful smile tugged at her lips. "Yep...I was a gonner! There isn't any other word for it. Just gone. And...he knew it, too!" She blinked back the tears. "And...I guess, I still am. That's why I never even thought about getting me another one. He was...the only man for me."

"If you loved him that much...and I've no doubt you're a good woman...then he couldn't have been all that bad...now, could he?" John asked. "There must have been something...something special...about him. Tell me what it was, Ms. Merribelle."

She blew her nose, and looked up with a spark in her eye. "Oh...he was...so darned charming! And, he believed in magic. Like...he was always looking for the pot at the end of the rainbow. Said it was the Irish in him! And...he had a way of making you believe it too. There was always going to be the 'big score' just around the corner. But, after awhile when nothing happened...I just couldn't believe it anymore." She looked so sad that John reached out and laid a hand on her shoulder. "My Pa said," she continued, "...I was just plain dumb to believe in him in the first place. And even dumber still, to believe that he was *ever* coming back. I guess my Pa was right, I was...dumb. But, I," she blinked back the tears once more. "I...just couldn't believe that he would leave his boys, you know? Me, maybe..." she said with a shrug. "Because...well, because I quit believing in the 'big score'... whatever that was. But *not his boys*!" She buried her face in her hands and sobbed. "Not his boys!"

John tilted her chin up so that she was looking right into his eyes. "How...do you know...he ran off? Maybe something...just happened to him?"

"No...he was up to something! Oh, I didn't know what it was. But, I think he was into something...pretty risky. He told me we were coming into a very large sum of money. Very large...as in *'the big one'*. But he wouldn't tell me what it was. He left that evening really excited. Said he had to go meet a buddy, and that our worries were all a thing of the past. He said...he was talking about 'thousands'! And...and we were going to move to Denver and live the good life! That's what he called it...the good life!" Her face crumpled. "And...that's where I messed up."

"How do you mean 'messed up'?" John asked.

"Well...don't you see...I told him I didn't want to move to Denver. I wanted to stay right here and raise our boys in this little town...where they would grow up around folks that loved 'em. Not in a big city, around a bunch of strangers."

"Well, how did he react to that?"

"He...well, he got angry, that's what! Said I never could leave my Pa...and we'd always have him comin' between us if we stayed here. He just stormed out of the house. Said we'd talk about it later...that he didn't want my pessimistic mood spoilin' everything! Last thing he said to me before he left was, that I'd change my mind when he came back with the money." She lowered her head, and finished sadly, "But...I guess...what he really thought, was, that I wouldn't ever change my mind. So...when he got the money...he just took it and ran." She was drained of energy, and as Peg and John got ready to leave, she saw them to the door of her room. When they said their good-byes she held on to John's hand. "You're a daddy...so tell me, Sheriff...how does a man walk away from his sons? I guess...I'll just never understand that!"

John shook his head sadly, and tenderly kissed her on her forehead. "I don't know, sweet little Mama," he said. "I just don't know."

At that she flashed him a million dollar smile. "*You* are a good daddy...to your children...I can tell." She started to close her door after them, then opened it and called out, "Sheriff?" He turned and looked back at her standing in the doorway. "If you're ever in the neighborhood again, come on in an' visit." John smiled back at her. Then with a mischievous grin she added, "Oh...and don't forget the Milky Way!"

He nodded, touching the brim of his hat in acknowledgement. "You got it, Ms. Merribelle," he said. "You got it!"

CHAPTER THIRTY SEVEN

Sunday morning Becca woke to the sound of rain on her window. She lay there a few minutes just enjoying the sound, thinking it was a good morning to sleep in. But then, when she didn't actually go back to sleep, she got up and went to the door between her room and Lisa and Dick's, listening to see if they were up and about. Hearing nothing, she climbed back into bed with a book, and gradually drifted on back to sleep.

Lisa woke about nine, and thinking it was later than it actually was, jumped up and headed right for the shower. "C'm'on, sleepy head...we gotta get movin' if we're going to make it to Church!" she tossed back over her shoulder to Dick, who wasn't ready to get up yet. Three minutes later she emerged from the shower, towel drying her hair. "Earth calling Dick," she teased. "Come on...or we won't have time for breakfast before Church!" This time she pulled the covers off and flipped him with her wet towel.

"That does it!" he yelled, jumping up and grabbing her, "I've just decided to have breakfast in bed this morning!"

An hour later Becca cautiously knocked on the door between the rooms. "Hey you two! Are you going to go to breakfast with me...or must I go alone?"

"Be ready in a jiff," Lisa giggled. "I'm just finishing my hair! Is it still raining?"

"No...I don't hear it anyway. I'll meet you downstairs," Becca called back. "And please hurry! I'm starved!"

"OK," Dick answered. "We'll be right there."

They had the 'two for two' special, and still made it to Church in time, although the congregation was on it's first hymn when they sneaked into the back pew. It was a good service and they emerged feeling proud of themselves for having made the effort...even a tad bit late. They were joined in the parking lot by the sheriff and his wife.

"Did you enjoy that early rainstorm?" John asked.

"Yes, we did. And it gave us a good excuse to sleep in, I'm afraid. We were a bit late for the service." Becca said, apologetically.

Dick hugged his wife close and grinned, "Yeah, it was hard to get up this morning. We don't get too many mornings to sleep in at home, so have to take advantage of it when we can."

John nodded. "That's what vacations are for." He and Peggy started to move toward their car, then he turned back. "Say, if you folks don't have something better to do, why don't you join us for lunch? We'll toss some burgers down on the grill, and keep it simple."

"Sounds good to me!" Dick answered. "I'm missin' home cookin', and that sounds wonderful."

After lunch as they all sat back enjoying a cool breeze on the patio, John looked at Lisa and said, "I've got someone I want you to meet. Think you're up to it?"

"Why, yes, I guess so," she answered, guardedly. "Who...is it?"

"Her name's Merribelle. Merribelle...Bennett."

Lisa was stunned. "Merribelle *Bennett*?" she repeated. "As in *Eddie Bennetti*, Bennett?"

The sheriff nodded. "His wife. She's quite old. Lives in the nursing home. But she's a great lady, a real trooper. And...I think you'll like her."

"But..." Lisa faltered. "Does she know anything? Did you tell her...what we found?"

"Nope!" John answered, stoking his pipe. I wanted you to know about her first. But...she does have to be told." He busied himself with the pipe, giving her time to digest what he had just said.

"Yes...I know she does." Lisa's face was drained of color. "And, I suppose...well...we really should be the ones to tell her. Or at least be there when *you* do it."

He drew on his pipe. "Yep! That's what I figured."

"Oh, my," Becca sighed. "This is going to be a tough one."

"Yeah..." John drew on his pipe. "But, you ladies are tough. You've handled all of this really well...and I have the utmost confidence in you." He smoked a bit, then added, "She's been through a lot in her life. Had two boys by Bennett. Thought he had run out on her...all this time. She deserves to know what really happened."

Dick was nodding, "Yes...yes, she does."

"Oh, I completely agree," Lisa added. "She has every right to know. I'm...I'm just wondering if I'll have the courage to tell her that our...father...actually killed her husband...all those years ago...and that he managed to get away with it! While all the time she was raising her children alone...without any help…thinking that he had just run out on her! Oh, that must have been really tough!"

"Yeah," Becca said. "What ever happened to her children?"

John took a long draw on his pipe. "Well...actually...they're both dead...killed in separate car accidents. Like I said, she's been through a lot."

"Oh, dear," Lisa said. "The poor dear."

"OK, John," Dick asked. "How's her health?"

"Yeah," Lisa jumped in. "Do you think she could handle such a big shock?"

"Oh, I think she could handle whatever she has to handle. Like I said, she's a trooper...a survivor. People like her handle what they have to handle." He squinted at Lisa. "You should know all about that...being a therapist and all."

"Yes...normally I would know. But remember, I've never met...or even seen...her. I have to depend on your judgment here."

Peggy was pouring a round of fresh coffee. "Well...I've been doing volunteer work at the nursing home for some years, and Meribelle Bennett is one of those rare individuals who always lands on her feet. She always bounces back, it seems...no matter what's thrown at her. I think she'll do just fine."

"Well then," Lisa said, getting to her feet. "What's left to talk about? Let's do it."

"Alright," John agreed, pushing his chair back. "Now, Peggy...what'd we do with those Milky Way bars?" When Peggy went into the house to get them, John grinned at the trio. "The little lady just loves Milky Way. So we'll oblige her...make the bad news a little easier to swallow."

They found Merribelle in the great room as before, dozing in front of the TV. But, she was delighted to have company again, and led them all back to her room. John introduced Merribelle to the newcomers first, then produced her treat from Peggy's bag, and they all just sat and enjoyed watching her enjoy her candy bar.

When she was finished and had wiped her mouth with the tissue that Peg offered her, she turned to John and asked, "Now, who did you say these people are, Sheriff?"

He made the introductions again, then added, "These girls...are the daughters of Kate and Joe Hollander."

"Who?" She scrunched up her face, trying to place the name that was so strange, yet familiar. "Now...I know I should know that name, Hollander," she mused. "But, it's not comin' to me...yet..."

"I'm Lisa. Kate and Joe had five kids...and we're the youngest two, Ms. Merribelle." Lisa, said, trying to help her bridge the gap of years. "Like I said, I'm Lisa, and this is Becca, the youngest one. And I believe...your husband, Eddie, used to be close friends with our daddy,"

"And who was your daddy, again?" the old woman asked, trying hard to make the connection.

"Our daddy was Joe Hollander. Do you remember...a long time ago when your children were little and your husband used to have a friend named Joe?" Lisa struggled to help her.

"Joe," the old woman turned the word over on her tongue as her mind tried to fit it into just the right niche in time. "Oh, yes...that one. Joe. Joe Hollander..." She was becoming agitated. "Joe! That Joe!" She spit the word out like it was poison. "I told Eddie...I told him...not to get mixed up with that one. He wasn't no good...and would only bring us trouble!" She grew quiet, thinking back over the troubles of that time so long ago. Narrowing her eyes, she looked hard at Lisa, as if trying to see the old enemy in his daughter. "So...you're his daughter?"

"Yes...and Becca, here. We're the youngest two. We left Yuma when we were very little. So...we didn't really know much about our dad."

The old woman almost snickered. "Well, Honey...you didn't miss anything!" Then she realized what she had said. "Oh...now, I'm sorry I said such an ugly thing. Forgive me, please!"

Becca reached out and patted the old woman's hand. "It's OK, Ms. Merribelle. Seems like we're the ones who should be apologizing for having such a sorry pa. But, you see...we didn't really have much choice in the matter!"

Merribelle grinned up at Becca and laughed, "You'll do just fine! And you're right about that...none of us has any choice in who we're borned to. Sometimes I think it's a game our Good Lord plays with us...to see just what kind'a stuff we're made of!" She chuckled. "Well...I didn't like your pa...but I think you girls'll prob'ly do just fine!"

"Do your remember our mother?" Lisa asked. "Were you two friends...or was it just the menfolk?"

"Well...seems like your mama and I got along pretty well. But I guess we weren't what you'd call best friends...or anything like that. We had our children to look after. Seems like your mama was a good woman, though. Never had no reason to think otherwise of her." She drifted off into memory for a few moments, then smiled. "I think I was glad when I heard that she'd left 'im. Glad for her I mean. He was a mean one. Used to beat up on her. She'd have the gosh awfulest bruises! An' then she wouldn't want to be seen out in public...so, sometimes I'd go to the store for her...an' do things like that." Merribelle looked sad. "So...yeah, we were friends...but...it was just a bad time in our lives."

"So...it was a bad time for you, too?" Becca prodded. "Was Eddie...abusive, too?"

"Oh, my dear Lord...yes!" she started, then caught herself. "Well...Eddie wasn't as bad. By himself, I mean. But, when he was around your pa...why they was like two peas in a pod. But, I always liked to think that it was all your pa's fault. You know how you like to make excuses for the people you love?" Burying her face in her hands, there was a glint of tears in her eyes, when she looked up. "Well...I stopped believing in fairy tales a long time ago. For a long time after Eddie ran off and left us I blamed your pa. Then...I finally had to just put the blame square in the lap of the one that done it. We had those two boys...and I thought he loved us enough...to keep 'im here! But he just didn't stay. An' that's nobody's fault but his!"

Lisa braced herself for the hard thing she had to do. "Ms. Merribelle...we really have to tell you something, about Eddie...and our pa.

It might be hard for you to understand, so please try to stay with me." She took the old woman's hands in hers to make good contact. "You know, we left Yuma...when Becca and I were very young...and we really had very little memory of our father." Merribelle, nodded. "Well...this summer, Becca and I decided to come back here...to look for our Grandfather Hollander's old homestead, out southwest of town.[' Lisa felt herself flushing, felt the tears start to fall, but she trudged on. "Well...in all of our digging around...we discovered..." She caught her breath, and prayed for strength to continue.

"Go on, child..." Merribelle coaxed, gently. "What...could be causing you such grief? You say it's something to do with my Eddie?"

"Uh, yes...I...I think...we...we may have found him." Lisa stopped to let that soak in.

Merribelle blinked, her mind reeling, not comprehending. "How...could you? I looked for him...all those years, an' never found...not one trace."

"So!" came a voice from the door. "So...he was one of those men in the cistern! Is that what you're saying?" They all turned to face a very angry young man in the doorway.

"Why Robbie...come in here and meet these nice people!" Merribelle said to Rob. "These young ladies...were just telling me..."

"I heard...what she was telling you, Gram." He came into the room and faced Lisa, squarely. "That *was* what you were going to tell her...wasn't it. That my Grandpa...was one of those bodies... skeletons...that you folks dug out of that old cistern out southwest of town?"

Lisa nodded, sadly. "I...I'm afraid so...Rob!"

"Bodies...skeletons? Whatever are you talking about, Robbie?" Merribelle asked.

Rob was too angry to answer his grandmother, but kept his wrath focused on Lisa. "So... how do you know? How could you possibly know...that it was my Grandfather out there? And, why would you come in here and upset my Grandmother like this...without even letting me know... what you were up to? I don't appreciate this...at all!" Then he turned his anger on the sheriff. "And you, Sheriff...you should know better! You could have had the decency to let me know what you were up to...before storming in here like this!" His voice was getting louder by the moment.

"Robbie!" Merribelle called out. "Stop! They weren't doing anything to upset me...and it seems like you're the one being upset! Now...you come over here and sit down by your old Gram...and we'll learn about this news together!" When he didn't budge, she continued. "I said...come over here and sit down by me! I need you...to help me sort this out. And you can't help me...if you're just goin' off half cocked! Now..." she patted the seat next to her, "Now...come over here and sit down...so we can hear what they have to tell us...together. I swear...you're more like your Grandpa every day!" By the time she finished Rob had joined her on her bed. She patted him on the shoulder. "That's my good boy. Now...stop that glowering. These people didn't come in here to hurt me...they have something important to tell me, and...I want to know what it is."

"Well," he started. "The news is all over town...that they found some bodies...skeletons...out southwest of town...in an old cistern. That's what they came here to tell you...and they just should have had the decency to wait... to at least have me with you when they dropped the bombshell...since I'm...your only kin!" He was good and angry, and finding it very difficult to calm himself down.

"You are absolutely right, Rob." Lisa jumped in. "We *should have* included you in this. I apologize. However...I had no idea that you were related. We have only known you by your first name...*Rob*. Had we had any idea...you can be assured that we would have wanted you to be here with your grandmother. And...rest assured that we would never do anything to hurt either of you!"

John put his hand on the young man's shoulder, looking him squarely in the eyes. "Now, Rob...this was my blunder! It never occurred to me to contact you...and that's my error, because I should have. I do apologize. And, please...please forgive my stupidity...and let us get on with what we have to tell you *both*. OK?" Rob nodded, even though he wasn't really sure he wanted to give up and be done with his anger that easily. Now Rob and Merribelle sat together, waiting for Lisa to resume her tale, and she wished desperately that she didn't have to say the words they were waiting to hear.

CHAPTER THIRTY EIGHT

Lisa took a few moments to composed herself, then began. "You see...it's like this. When we came up here from Texas this summer, we had only one thought in mind...to find our grandfather's homestead. And that's all. It's as simple as that. But...practically from the time we got here, things started to happen." She paused to catch her breath.

"What kind of things, child?" Merribelle asked, while Rob sat staring at the baseball cap he was turning in his hands.

"Well...first of all," Becca said. "Right after we got here...I remembered something that happened to me when I was three. Remembered being taken to an old house...out in the country...by people I didn't know." She took a deep breath and trudged on. "It was all very strange. I was sleeping in that house, when I heard a car pull up. When I looked out the window, I could see my daddy coming up the steps. I was excited...because he was coming to get me...but...that's not what happened. When he came through the door...I could tell...he was really angry. And he lit into a man that was there...called him Eddie."

Merrribelle gasped. "My Eddie?"

Becca nodded. "I think so. Well, Daddy...he...was yelling...saying, 'I told you the deals off'! And then... this Eddie...he had a gun in his waistband, and...he pulled it out. Saying something like..."It's already going down... and...and...you can't stop it, now." He pointed the gun at Daddy...but...he just lunged at Eddie...and they struggled on the floor. Then...the gun went off. It...the shot...broke the window...behind my head...and bits of glass fell down on me. It was like they didn't even know I was there. But...somehow...I knew, that whatever it was they were fighting about...it was really about me!" She stopped to wipe a stray tear.

Merribelle was listening very closely, lest she miss anything. "Go on, child," she said. "Tell us what happened next?"

"Well, then, the gun went off...again...and then Daddy was bending over the man called Eddie, calling for someone from upstairs to come and help him. Daddy said...'He's dead...and you have to help me!' The man who came down the stairs...was a big man. I thought his name was something like Hank...or Frank. And...well, he said that he couldn't help Daddy. But Daddy lit into him, and he finally agreed to help. They carried Eddie out and put him in the trunk of a car. It...wasn't Daddy's car...but another one. And then...they just drove off. They just drove off and left me there...like I didn't even exist." Becca faltered then, and let the tears take over. "Like...I didn't even exist!" Lisa hugged her sister to her, wiping the tears. Then she took over.

"The next thing that happened...was...well...I had been ill...and had to stay home from school. I had been sleeping, but was awakened by a noise coming from our basement. Now, we...Becca and I...assume that this was the next morning...after Becca's experience." She stopped, momentarily, to organize her thoughts.

Rob had let his anger go, and was now listening intently to the women. "So...so what happened...then... when you woke up? And how old were you, anyway...if she was just three...you couldn't have been much older...but, you say you were school age?"

Lisa nodded. "I was ten. I'm seven years older than Becca...and our mother had been injured in a bad accident. Since there was no one at home who could care for Becca while Mother was in the hospital in Denver...she was staying with friends...uh, Church people." She took a deep breath, then got back into her narration, "Well... when I went to investigate where the noise was coming from...I...I stumbled over a dead man, lying on our basement floor. Then...since I was already there, Daddy and a man he called Frank...whom I believe was the same man that Becca had seen with Daddy the night before...made me go with them...to...get rid of the body."

"Oh! You poor child!" Merribelle sighed. "What kind of a man would do that to a child?" She shook her head in disbelief. "What kind of a man would do that?"

"Well...whatever kind that is, it seems like...Daddy was...that kind of a man. He didn't seem upset at all by the knowledge that I was there. It was rather like we were going off on some great adventure of his!"

"Oh, my goodness!" Merribelle exclaimed, sitting there shaking her head back and forth. "Oh, my goodness!"

Lisa continued. "We drove out into the country...to a place I didn't recognize. When I asked Daddy where we were going...he just told me it was a 'hunnert miles from nowhere', to put it in his words. But, now, of course, I know that it was our grandfather's homestead." Solemnly Lisa reached over and took Merribelle's hands in hers. "Ms. Merribelle...I...I saw Daddy and Frank...throw Eddie into that cistern." The dam broke, and tears flooded Lisa's face. "I am so sorry to have to tell you this," she paused to wipe her nose. "It's *such an ugly story*! But...you needed to know that...Eddie didn't run out on you. Do you understand what I'm saying? He *didn't leave you*."

Merribelle could scarcely take it in. "What...are you saying? That Eddie...didn't run out...on me and the boys?"

"That's right," Lisa continued. "He didn't run out on you. He just couldn't return...because he was dead."

"And all this time...I thought...I thought he didn't love us..." Merribelle said, her voice barely audible. "But...the truth was...that he didn't run out on us...after all." Then the floodgates opened and she cried. "He really didn't leave us...he just couldn't come back! Oh, my...I don't know what to say."

Rob shook his head. "I...don't get it. How come you never remembered any of this until now? That doesn't make any sense to me. If you saw that happen...why didn't you remember it?"

"Rob...it's called selective amnesia. When a child is overwhelmed by something too awful to remember... the mind deals with it the only way it can...by forgetting that it happened. Then at some later time...when the child is safe...the memory just might come back."

He shrugged, "Does it come back completely? Or what?" He asked, then quickly added, "And you said it comes back when the child is safe. Well...weren't you ever safe...until just this summer?"

Lisa, grinned, "Oh, yes...I've been safe for a long time. But, Rob, there has to be some sort of *trigger*. Or you might say, some reason...to bring the memory back. In our case...it was simply coming back to Yuma...where it all happened. If we hadn't returned...who knows...we might not have ever remembered...any of it."

"But..." he prodded, "Why did you just decide to come here this summer?"

"Why? I believe it was...the prompting of God."

"God? You're saying God made you do it?" He chuckled in disbelief.

"I'm saying...I believe...that God drew us here...at this precise time in our lives...because He wanted your grandmother to know that Eddie didn't run out on her and her boys...while she could still comprehend what that means. None of us knows how long we have to live on this earth...and I pray that she has many, many more years here...but, Rob, I'm sure of this one thing. That...our Great God loves her so much...that He wanted her to have the satisfaction of *knowing* that Eddie loved her too! That *he didn't just run out on her.*"

Merribelle was softly crying as she listened to Lisa try to explain this to Rob. "Oh... Robbie, my boy! You don't know how many times I've cried out to God...to just let me know where he was...that he was OK. And today...I know God answered my prayers. He sent these dear people to tell me...*in answer to my prayer.*" Rob looked like he just couldn't buy it. Then Merribelle added, "Why, just a while back...I think it was at Easter...I asked God, specifically, to send somebody...to let me know, for sure, what happened to Eddie, before I cross over to the other side. I asked Him for this, so that I could tell you what happened. I...I thought it might help to settle you...a bit...to know the whole story. You're so much like your grandpa. And I can't bear to see you throw your life away...like he did."

"Gram! How can you say that? He didn't throw his life away! You just heard them tell you that their Daddy took it from him! How can you sit there and say he threw it away?" Rob was becoming highly agitated. "He *didn't throw...*"

Merribelle interrupted. "He *threw his life away*! Because he was always ready to chase after what he called the 'big score'. He was always up to his eyeballs in any mischief afoot. I *knew* that. I *also knew* that he was up to something with their daddy...that very night. And...I can tell you this, that he was in it of his own free will! You heard Becca say...*he* had the gun...and *he was the one* who pointed it at her daddy. Now...you tell me, Robbie, why, in heaven's name, did he go out there...wherever that was...with a *loaded* gun?"

When Rob didn't answer, she continued. "Robbie...your grandpa was what he was. Always into something no good. And that's just how he was! I loved him...but, I knew he was up to no good. He told me that very night, that we were going to come into a large sum of money. That we would move to Denver, and live the 'good life' with it. He was always after the 'big score'...and it didn't matter that he had a wife and two boys to support. We were the least of his worries!" She looked down at her hands lying limply in her lap. "No, son...he threw his life away...the minute he took up that gun and loaded it. You have to remember that. He did it, himself." She looked sadly at Lisa. "I...I thank you...both of you...for telling me this. And, I'm thankful to know that he didn't run out on us. But, I'm even more thankful that God sent you...to show my dear Robbie...just what his mischief got him into. I do so want to see him settled down...and stable..." she paused, "*before* I'm gone."

"Now, Gram!" Rob protested, nervously. "Don't you be talkin' about being 'gone'...you're gonna be around a long time, yet."

"Well...I might be. Then again...I might not be. Anyway, I still want to see you settled down! You know, you ought to marry that cute little waitress...and settle down and raise a family...*before I'm gone*. I just want to have the satisfaction of seeing you really settled...and happy...with a family of your own! Right now, it's just you and me against the world. And although I enjoy that...I want to know that you'll have somebody when I'm no longer here." Through tear brimmed eyes, she grinned at her grandson and asked, "Now...what's so bad about me wanting to see you...my favorite person in the whole world... happy?"

Rob looked sheepishly at his grandmother, "Not a thing, Gram. Not a thing." He leaned over and kissed her on the cheek. "I'm glad...that you care so much. I really am. It's just that...I've always thought...that I just had the Bennett blood. And would always be a little restless...uh...as you say, *unsettled*. I think about getting married. Then I think...but would I do a girl right? Or would I be like my dad and my grandpa...always chasing after something I can't even define. Messing up everyone's lives, and causing nothing but unhappiness! Dena...deserves better than that!"

"Well, I should say so! She certainly does deserve better than that. But I'm here to tell you, Robbie, that... you have a choice. You don't *have to be* a heartbreaker. They had choices, your dad and grandpa...but they chose *wrong*!" Merribelle, bit her lip. "Nobody's going to hold a gun to your head and make you do wrong, Son. If you go that way...then, that's your choice. But, you *don't have to choose wrong*! Maybe you've forgotten, but...you also have *my blood* in you...and *your Mother's*. And I would say that has got to have diluted the amount of Bennett, in you. So...even if it is in the Bennett genes...and I *doubt* that it is...you also have enough of the rest of us to over power any of those crooked genes left in you!"

Rob grinned, "Well...I never thought about it...like that! You know, when I was little...I just remember Daddy saying that I was just like him...and Grandpa. Why, you even tell me that I'm like them, Gram. So...I never thought about being like anybody else." He flashed her a crooked grin. "Maybe... maybe I just oughta' start actin' more like you! What would you say to that, Gram?" Her face lit up, and everybody laughed.

"Well...you can't go wrong there," John said. "You definitely can't go wrong there!"

Monday morning as Lisa and Dick and Becca loaded their luggage in the car and checked out of the motel, they were glad to be heading home at last. It seemed like they had been gone a year, instead of just a few weeks. When they reached Wray, though, Lisa suddenly said, "Stop, Dick! We have to go back."

"Well, I thought we said all our goodbye's last night...so what's up, Babe?"

"I can't explain...yet!" she said. "There's...there's just something I have to do. Will you trust me on this one? It's very important."

"Well...of course I'll trust you, silly. And if you say we need to go back...then we'll just go back." He swung the car around and headed it back up the road to Yuma. They arrived at the Sheriff's office just as he was about to leave on his morning rounds.

"Wait, John..." Lisa hollered, jumping out of the car as soon as it stopped. "We need just a smidgin more of your time!"

"OK. You got it!" he grinned, turning around and heading back into the office. "So...what's up? I figured you folks would be halfway to the state line by now?"

"I can't explain...but, I need you to get Rob...to meet us at the nursing home. There's something I have to do," Lisa said excitedly. "Oh...and call Dena...and the Johnsons...and Peg, too!"

John looked at Dick and Becca who both shrugged their shoulders. They didn't have the foggiest notion of what she was up to, but Dick could tell from the gleam in her eyes that it was going to be a doozey. After John had called Peg and the Johnsons, and located Rob at the restaurant having breakfast with Dena, and arranged for them to meet at the nursing home, they all headed that way.

Back in their car, Dick asked, "So...don't I...the love of your life...get to be in on this little...little...well, whatever it is that you've got cooked up?"

Grinning, Lisa shook her head. "Please...don't ask! And don't try to make me feel guilty for not telling you. I just have to do this...my way. So...just...try to understand! And, and be patient. Please!"

When they were all once again gathered in Ms. Merribelle's room, Lisa told Rob that she had decided to deed over Grandfather Hollander's property to him...if he still wanted it.

"It's sort of in reparation for all of the wrong that was done...out there!" she said, sadly, giving it a moment to sink in, then adding, "There's not one thing any of us can do...to undo ...any of that. What's done is done. But, Rob, I got the impression last night, that you'd really like to get your life headed in another direction." He nodded in awestruck silence, a single tear making it's way down his lean face. "And, well...maybe this can help." She lowered her eyes, pausing a moment.

"You know...although I was very little...I have *good memories* of Grandpa Hollander. And...I just know that he would not have wanted any of this ugliness to have happened on his place. Though no one could have prevented what happened out there...I just think he'd be happy knowing that his place was once again given over to bless and nourish a family...instead of being a repository for such horror and ugliness. Maybe, in time, the memory of what we did here this summer will fade...in the happy voices of children playing safely under the shade of those grand old trees." She blinked back the tears, and smiled. "And that...would make me very happy."

The End

Lila Conover Bishop

ABOUT THE AUTHOR

Lila Conover Bishop grew up in and around Yuma, Colorado, graduating from Otis High School in 1957. She married Charles Bishop of Indianapolis, Indiana, a Baptist Minister. They have three grown children and seven grand-children. The Bishops have ministered in Texas, and Pennsylvania, as well as their current charge in Chickasha, Oklahoma.

Lila graduated from the University of Science and Arts at Chickasha, and holds an M.Ed. in Counseling from Oklahoma City University. Though she loves Counseling...she says there is no better feeling than empowering others...writing is her passion. She is published in The Song of the Heart: The International Library of Poetry, and THE BEST POEMS & POETS OF 2002.

"100 MILES FROM NOWHERE", a work of fiction, is Lila's first published novel.

Printed in the United States
1159300004B/154-168